Legends from the
End of Time

By the same author

The Tale of the Eternal Champion
New Omnibus Editions, revised and with new introductions by the author.

1 Von Bek
2 The Eternal Champion
3 Hawkmoon
4 Corum
5 Sailing to Utopia
6 A Nomad of the Time Streams
7 The Dancers at the End of Time
8 Elric of Melnibone
9 The New Nature of the Catastrophe
10 The Prince with the Silver Hand
11 Legends from the End of Time
12 Stormbringer*
13 Earl Aubec*
14 Count Brass*

Also: A Warrior of Mars

Science Fiction

The Sundered Worlds
The Shores of Death
The Winds of Limbo
The Rituals of Infinity

Comedy Thrillers

The Chinese Agent
The Wrecks of Time

Karl Glogauer

Behold the Man*
Breakfast in the Ruins*

Cornelius

The Cornelius Quartet*
A Cornelius Calendar*

Colonel Pyat

Byzantium Endures
The Laughter of Carthage
Jerusalem Commands
The Vengeance of Rome ††

Other novels

Gloriana: or, The Unfulfill'd Queen
The Brothel in Rosenstrasse*
Mother London

Short stories and graphic novels

Casablanca
Sojan the Swordsman (juvenile)
My Experiences in the Third World War
Lunching with the Antichrist*
The Swords of Heaven: The Flowers of
    Hell (with Howard Chaykin)
The Crystal and the Amulet
    (with James Cawthorn)
etc.

Non-fiction

The Retreat from Liberty
Letters from Hollywood
    (illus. M. Foreman)
Wizardry and Wild Romance
Death is No Obstacle
    (with Colin Greenland)

Editor

New Worlds
The Traps of Time
The Best of *New Worlds*
Best SF from *New Worlds*
New Worlds: An Anthology
Before Armageddon
England Invaded!
The Inner Landscape

Records

With *The Deep Fix*:
The New Worlds Fair
Dodgem Dude
The Brothel in Rosenstrasse etc.

With *Hawkwind*:
Warriors at the Edge of Time
Choose Your Masques
Zones
Sonic Attack etc.
Also work with *Blue Oyster Cult*,
    Robert Calvert etc.

For further information about Michael Moorcock and his work please send SAE to Nomads of the Time Streams, 18 Laurel Bank, Truss Hill Road, South Ascot, Berks, UK. or PO Box 451048, Atlanta, Georgia, 30345–1048, USA.

* In preparation (Orion Books)   † In preparation (Roc Books)   †† In preparation (Cape)

Michael Moorcock

LEGENDS FROM THE END OF TIME

MILLENNIUM

AN ORION BOOK

LONDON

Pale-Roses, White Stars, Ancient Shadows and
Constant Fire originally appeared in
New Worlds Quarterly © 1976

Elric at the End of Time was originally written for
Rodney Matthews to illustrate
Dragons World © 1981

This edition first published
in Great Britain in 1993 by
Millennium
An imprint of Orion Books Ltd
Orion House, 5 Upper St Martin's Lane
London WC2H 9EA

A CIP catalogue for this book
is available from the British Library

ISBN: (Csd) 1 85798 043 3
(Ppr) 1 85798 044 1

Millennium
Book Twenty Four

Printed and bound in Great Britain by
Richard Clay Ltd
St Ives, plc
Designed by Peter Guy

Dear Reader,

All but the last of these stories were written for the first four issues of *New Worlds Quarterly*, which was what *New Worlds* magazine became after it had been forced to cease monthly publication as a result of problems with its British distributors. British magazine and book distributors have always had to be cautious under our present pernicious libel laws, since they can be prosecuted as thoroughly as the writers and publishers and printers. The fact that our distributors were scarcely literate and had difficulty distinguishing between 'libel' and 'obscenity' and that we were publishing neither, always gave the whole affair a strong element of farce.

Recently *The New Statesman* magazine has suffered a particularly undignified prosecution for libel by John Major (a British prime minister). The magazine was accused of doing the very things it was attacking in its article on 'silent censorship' and sought to stop. As *The New Statesman*'s editor Steve Platt said, while they had no intention of libelling anyone, suing the distributor or the person who puts the magazine through your letterbox is like suing Sony or Ferguson for what a television programme chooses to show. The law was designed as an instrument of censorship and remains one. There are many examples of how the British press is limited and silenced in ways that would be illegal elsewhere. Without a Freedom of Information Act, Britain remains one of the most repressive of the Western Democracies.

Thanks to the untimely nervousness of our distributors, *New Worlds* became a paperback. The paperback contained exactly the same kind of material and received excellent distribution from the same people who had effectively killed the magazine! The farcical aspect of the affair was further emphasized when the same distributors also gave wide distribution to *The Best of New Worlds* and novels serialized in the magazine, all of which had been the source of their nervousness in the first place. We need better laws.

Perhaps because farce seemed to dominate those years so magnificently, I took readily to writing these stories for the first four issues to be published under the aegis of Anthony Cheetham, then director of Sphere Books. Certainly the world of the End of Time seemed no stranger or more bizarre than my own at that point and most of the characters were a lot more attractive.

I took huge pleasure in writing these stories. They are my light-heartd homage to George Meredith, in particular, but also to Dowson, Beardsley, Simons, Swinburne and the Irish wits, to all those contributors to *The Savoy* and *The Yellow Book* who impressed me with their glorious insouciance and cleverness when I was a boy and wanting to have done nothing more than spend an evening at the Café Royal in their company.

Eventually I did get to spend quite a lot of time and money drinking champagne with the late Xyril Bonfiglioli, art-dealer extraordinary, ex-Balliol and the Olympic fencing team and editor of SCIENCE FANTASY magazine, with Brian Aldiss, Diane Lambert, Tom Disch, Dave Britton, Mike Butterworth and a few others in the last of the Grill Room's glory days. Britton and Butterworth went on to found Savoy, that wonderful, eccentric publishing house and record company based in Manchester, and began their own long battle with the authorities through the courts. I would like to dedicate this volume jointly to Britton and Butterworth, for their determination to challenge our repressive press laws, to its current publisher, Anthony Cheetham, who kept us going in our darkest hour, and to that great restaurant, which witnessed more good talk for at least a quarter of a century than any other in England, the Café Royal. All were there when we most needed them.

Yours,
Michael Moorcock

PALE-ROSES

*To the memory of George Meredith,
who taught me, at least,
a technique*

I

In which Werther is Inconsolable

'ou can still *amuse* people, Werther, and that's the main thing,' said Mistress Christia, lifting her skirts to reveal her surprise.

It was rare enough for Werther de Goethe to put on an entertainment (though this one was typical – it was called 'Rain') and rare, too, for the Everlasting Concubine to think in individual terms to please her lover of the day.

'Do you like it?' she asked as he peered into her thighs.

Werther's voice in reply was faintly animated. 'Yes.' His pale fingers traced the tattoos, which were primarily on the theme of Death and the Maiden, but corpses also coupled, skeletons entwined in a variety of extravagant carnal embraces – and at the centre, in bone-white, her pubic hair had been fashioned in the outline of an elegant and somehow quintessentially feminine skull. 'You alone know me, Mistress Christia.'

She had heard the phrase so often, from so many, and it always delighted her. 'Cadaverous Werther!'

He bent to kiss the skull's somewhat elongated lips.

His rain rushed through dark air, each drop a different gloomy shade of green, purple or red. And it was actually wet so that when it fell upon the small audience (the Duke of Queens,

3

Bishop Castle, My Lady Charlotina, and one or two recently arrived, absolutely bemused, time travellers from the remote past) it soaked their clothes and made them shiver as they stood on the shelf of glassy rock overlooking Werther's Romantic Precipice (below, a waterfall foamed through fierce, black rock).

'Nature,' exclaimed Werther. 'The only verity!'

The Duke of Queens sneezed. He looked about him with a delighted smile, but nobody else had noticed. He coughed to draw their attention, tried to sneeze again, but failed. He looked up into the ghastly sky; fresh waves of black cloud boiled in: there was lightning now, and thunder. The rain became hail. My Lady Charlotina, in a globular dress of pink veined in soft blue, giggled as the little stones fell upon her gilded features with an almost inaudible ringing sound.

But Bishop Castle, in his nodding, crenellated *tête* (from which he derived the latter half of his name and which was twice his own height), turned away, saturnine and bored, plainly noting a comparison between all this and his own entertainment of the previous year, which had also involved rain, but with each drop turning into a perfect mannikin as it touched the ground. There was nothing in his temperament to respond to Werther's rather innocent re-creation of a Nature long since departed from a planet which could be wholly re-modelled at the whim of any one of its inhabitants.

Mistress Christia, ever quick to notice such responses, eager for her present lover not to lose prestige, cried: 'But there is more, is there not, Werther? A finale?'

'I had thought to leave it a little longer . . .'

'No! No! Give us your finale now, my dear!'

'Well, Mistress Christia, if it is for you.' He turned one of his power rings, disseminating the sky, the lightning, the thunder, replacing them with pearly clouds, radiated with golden light through which silvery rain still fell.

'And now,' he murmured, 'I give you Tranquillity, and in Tranquillity – Hope . . .'

A further twist of the ring and a rainbow appeared, bridging the chasm, touching the clouds.

Bishop Castle was impressed by what was an example of elegance rather than spectacle, but he could not resist a minor criticism. 'Is black exactly the shade, do you think? I should have supposed it expressed your Idea, well, perhaps not perfectly . . .'

'It is perfect for me,' answered Werther a little gracelessly.

'Of course,' said Bishop Castle, regretting his impulse. He drew his bushy red brows together and made a great show of studying the rainbow. 'It stands out so well against the background.'

Emphatically (causing a brief, ironic glint in the eye of the Duke of Queens) Mistress Christia clapped her hands. 'It is a beautiful rainbow, Werther. I am sure it is much more as they used to look.'

'It takes a particularly original kind of imagination to invent such – simplicity.' The Duke of Queens, well known for a penchant in the direction of vulgarity, fell in with her mood.

'I hope it does more than merely represent.' Satisfied both with his creation and with their responses, Werther could not resist indulging his nature, allowing a tinge of hurt resentment in his tone.

All were tolerant. All responded, even Bishop Castle. There came a chorus of consolation. Mistress Christia reached out and took his thin, white hand, inadvertently touching a power ring.

The rainbow began to topple. It leaned in the sky for a few seconds while Werther watched, his disbelief gradually turning to miserable reconciliation; then, slowly, it fell, shattering against the top of the cliff, showering them with shards of jet.

Mistress Christia's tiny hand fled to the rosebud of her mouth; her round, blue eyes expressed horror already becoming laughter (checked when she noted the look in Werther's dark and tragic orbs). She still gripped his hand; but he slowly withdrew it, kicking moodily at the fragments of the rainbow. The sky was suddenly a clear, soft grey, actually lit, one might have guessed, by the tired rays of the fading star about which the planet continued to circle, and the only clouds were those on Werther's noble brow. He pulled at the peak of his bottle-green cap, he stroked at his long, auburn hair, as if to comfort himself. He sulked.

'Perfect!' praised My Lady Charlotina, refusing to see error.

'You have the knack of making the most of a single symbol, Werther.' The Duke of Queens waved a brocaded arm in the general direction of the now disseminated scene. 'I envy you your talent, my friend.'

'It takes the product of panting lust, of pulsing sperm and eager ovaries, to offer us such brutal originality!' said Bishop Castle, in reference to Werther's birth (he was the product of sexual union, born of a womb, knowing childhood – a rarity, indeed). 'Bravo!'

'Ah,' sighed Werther, 'how cheerfully you refer to my doom: To be such a creature, when all others came into this world as mature, uncomplicated adults!'

'There was also Jherek Carnelian,' said My Lady Charlotina. Her globular dress bounced as she turned to leave.

'At least he was not born malformed,' said Werther.

'It was the work of a moment to re-form you properly, Werther,' the Duke of Queens reminded him. 'The six arms (was it?) removed, two perfectly fine ones replacing them. After all, it was an unusual exercise on the part of your mother. She did very well, considering it was her first attempt.'

'And her last,' said My Lady Charlotina, managing to have her back to Werther by the time the grin escaped. She snapped her fingers for her air car. It floated towards her, a great, yellow rocking horse. Its shadow fell across them all.

'It left a scar,' said Werther, 'nonetheless.'

'It would,' said Mistress Christia, kissing him upon his black velvet shoulder.

'A terrible scar.'

'Indeed!' said the Duke of Queens in vague affirmation, his attention wandering. 'Well, thank you for a lovely afternoon, Werther. Come along, you two!' He signed to the time travellers, who claimed to be from the eighty-third millennium and were dressed in primitive transparent 'exoskin', which was not altogether stable and was inclined to writhe and make it seem that they were covered in hundreds of thin, excited worms. The Duke of Queens had acquired them for his menagerie. Unaware of the difficulties of returning to their own time (temporal travel had, apparently, only just been re-invented in their age), they were inclined to treat the Duke as an eccentric who could be tolerated until it suited them to do otherwise. They smiled condescendingly, winked at each other, and followed him to an air car in the shape of a cube whose sides were golden mirrors decorated with white and purple flowers. It was for the pleasure of enjoying the pleasure they enjoyed, seemingly at his expense, that the Duke of Queens had brought them with him today. Mistress Christia waved at his car as it disappeared rapidly into the sky.

At last they were all gone, save herself and Werther de Goethe. He had seated himself upon a mossy rock, his shoulders hunched, his features downcast, unable to speak to her when she tried to cheer him.

'Oh, Werther,' she cried at last, 'what would make you happy?'

'Happy?' his voice was a hollow echo of her own. 'Happy?' An awkward, dismissive gesture. 'There is no such thing as happiness for such as I!'

'There must be some sort of equivalent, surely?'

'Death, Mistress Christia, is my only consolation!'

'Well, die, my dear! I'll resurrect you in a day or two, and then . . .'

'Though you love me, Mistress Christia – though you know me best – you do not understand. I seek the inevitable, the irreconcilable, the unalterable, the inescapable! Our ancestors knew it. They knew Death *without* Resurrection; they knew what it was to be Slave to the Elements. Incapable of choosing their own destinies, they had no responsibility for their own actions. They were tossed by tides. They were scattered by storms. They were wiped out by wars, decimated by disease, ravaged by radiation, made homeless by holocausts, lashed by lightnings . . .'

'You could have lashed yourself a little today, surely?'

'But it would have been *my decision*. We have lost what is Random, we have banished the Arbitrary, Mistress Christia. With our power rings and our gene banks we can, if we desire, change the courses of the planets, populate them with any kind of creature we wish, make our old sun burst with fresh energy or fade completely from the firmament. We control All. Nothing controls us!'

'There are our whims, our fancies. There are our *characters*, my moody love.'

'Even those can be altered at will.'

'Except that it is a rare nature which would wish to change itself. Would you change yours? I, for one, would be disconsolate if, say, you decided to be more like the Duke of Queens or the Iron Orchid.'

'Nonetheless, it is *possible*. It would merely be a matter of decision. Nothing is impossible, Mistress Christia. Now do you realise why I should feel unfulfilled?'

'Not really, dear Werther. You can be anything you wish, after all. I am not, as you know, intelligent – it is not my choice to be – but I wonder if a love of Nature could be, in essence, a grandiose love of oneself – with Nature identified, as it were, with one's ego?' She offered this without criticism.

For a moment he showed surprise and seemed to be considering her observation. 'I suppose it could be. Still, that has little to do with what we were discussing. It's true that I can be anything – or, indeed, anyone – I wish. That is *why* I feel unfulfilled!'

'Aha,' she said.

'Oh, how I pine for the pain of the past! Life has no meaning without misery!'

'A common view, then, I gather. But what sort of suffering would suit you best, dear Werther? Enslavement by Esquimaux?' She hesitated, her knowledge of the past being patchier than most people's. 'The beatings with thorns? The barbed-wire trews? The pits of fire?'

'No, no – that is primitive. Psychic, it would have to be. Involving – um – morality.'

'Isn't that some sort of wall-painting?'

A large tear welled and fell. 'The world is too tolerant. The world is too kind. They all – you most of all – *approve* of me! There is nothing I can do which would not amuse you – even if it offended your taste – because there is no danger, nothing at stake. There are no *crimes*, inflamer of my lust. Oh, if I could only *sin*!'

Her perfect forehead wrinkled in the prettiest of frowns. She repeated his words to herself. Then she shrugged, embracing him.

'Tell me what sin is,' she said.

2

In which your Auditor Interposes

Our time travellers, once they have visited the future, are only permitted (owing to the properties of Time itself) at best brief returns to their present. They can remain for any amount of time in their future, where presumably they can do no real damage to the course of previous events, but to come back at all is difficult for even the most experienced: to make a prolonged stay has been proved impossible. Half-an-hour with a relative or a loved one, a short account to an auditor, such as myself, of life, say, in the 75th century, a glimpse at an artifact allowed to some interested scientist – these are the best the time traveller can hope for, once he has made his decision to leap into the mysterious future.

As a consequence our knowledge of the future is sketchy, to say the least: we have no idea of how civilizations will grow up or how they will decline; we do not know why the number of planets in the Solar System seems to vary drastically between, say, half-a-dozen to almost a hundred; we cannot explain the popularity in a given age of certain fashions striking us as singularly bizarre or perverse. Are beliefs which we consider fallacious or superstitious based on an understanding of reality beyond our comprehension?

The stories we hear are often partial, hastily recounted, poorly observed, perhaps misunderstood by the traveller. We cannot question him closely, for he is soon whisked away from us (Time insists upon a certain neatness, to protect her own nature, which is essentially of the practical, ordering sort, and should that nature ever be successfully altered, then we might, in turn, successfully alter the terms of the human condition), and it is almost inevitable that we shall never have another chance of meeting him.

Resultantly, the stories brought to us of the Earth's future assume the character of legends rather than history and tend, therefore, to capture the imagination of artists, for serious scientists need permanent, verifiable evidence with which to work, and precious little of that is permitted them (some refuse to believe in the future, save as an abstraction; some believe firmly that returning time travellers' accounts are accounts of dreams and hallucinations and that they have not actually travelled in Time at all!). It is left to the Romancers, childish fellows like myself, to make something of these tales. While I should be delighted to assure you that everything I have set down in this story is based closely on the truth, I am bound to admit that while the outline comes from an account given me by one of our greatest and most famous temporal adventuresses, Mrs Una Persson, the conversations and many of the descriptions are of my own invention, intended hopefully to add a little colour to what would otherwise be a somewhat spare, a rather dry recounting of an incident in the life of Werther de Goethe.

That Werther will exist, only a few entrenched sceptics can doubt. We have heard of him from many sources, usually quite as reliable as the admirable Mrs Persson, as we have heard of other prominent figures of that Age we choose to call 'the End of Time.' If it is this Age which fascinates us more than any other, it is probably because it seems to offer a clue to our race's ultimate destiny.

Moralists make much of this period and show us that on the one hand it describes the pointlessness of human existence or, on the other, the whole point. Romancers are attracted to it for less worthy reasons; they find it colourful, they find its inhabitants glamourous, attractive; their imaginations sparked by the paradoxes, the very ambiguities which exasperate our scientists, by the idea of a people possessing limitless power and using it for nothing but their own amusement, like gods at play. It is pleasure enough for the Romancer to describe a story; to colour it a little, to fill in a few details where they are missing, in the hope that by entertaining himself he entertains others.

Of course, the inhabitants at the End of Time are not the creatures of our past legends, not mere representations of our ancestors' hopes and fears, not mere metaphors, like Siegfried or Zeus or Krishna, and this could be why they fascinate us so much. Those of us who have studied this Age (as best it can be studied) feel on friendly terms with the Iron Orchid, with the

10

Duke of Queens, with Lord Jagged of Canaria and the rest, and even believe that we can guess something of their inner lives.

Werther de Goethe, suffering from the *knowledge* of his, by the standards of his own time, unusual entrance into the world, doubtless felt himself apart from his fellows, though there was no objective reason why he should feel it. In a society where eccentricity is encouraged, where it is celebrated no matter how extreme its realization, Werther felt, we must assume, uncomfortable: wishing for peers who would demand some sort of conformity from him. He could not retreat into a repressive past age; it was well known that it was impossible to remain in the past (the phenomenon had a name at the End of Time: it was called the Morphail Effect), and he had an ordinary awareness of the futility of re-creating such an environment for himself – for *he* would have created it; the responsibility would still ultimately be his own. We can only sympathize with the irreconcilable difficulties of leading the life of a gloomy fatalist when one's fate is wholly, decisively, in one's own hands!

Like Jherek Carnelian, whose adventures I have recounted elsewhere, he was particularly liked by his fellows for his vast and often naïve enthusiasm in whatever he did. Like Jherek, it was possible for Werther to fall completely in love – with Nature, with an Idea, with Woman (or Man, for that matter).

It seemed to the Duke of Queens (from whom we have it on the excellent authority of Mrs Persson herself) that those with such a capacity must love themselves enormously and such love is enviable. The Duke, needless to say, spoke without disapproval when he made this observation: 'To shower such largesse upon the Ego! He kneels before his soul in awe – it is a moody king, in constant need of gifts which must always seem rare!' And what is Sensation, our Moralists might argue, but Seeming Rarity? Last year's gifts re-gilded.

It might be true that young Werther (in years no more than half-a-millennium) loved himself too much and that his tragedy was his inability to differentiate between the self-gratifying sensation of the moment and what we would call a lasting and deeply felt emotion. We have a fragment of poetry, written, we are assured, by Werther for Mistress Christia:

At these times, I love you most when you are sleeping;
Your dreams internal, unrealized to the world at large:
And do I hear you weeping?

Most certainly a reflection of Werther's views, scarcely a description, from all that we know of her, of Mistress Christia's essential being.

Have we any reason to doubt her own view of herself? Rather, we should doubt Werther's view of everyone, including himself. Possibly this lack of insight was what made him so thoroughly attractive in his own time – *le Grand Naïf!*

And, since we have quoted one, it is fair to quote the other, for happily we have another fragment, from the same source, of Mistress Christia's verse:

To have my body moved by other hands;
Not only those of Man,
But Woman, too!
My Liberty in pawn to those who understand:
That Love, alone, is True.

Surely this displays an irony entirely lacking in Werther's fragment. Affectation is also here, of course, but affectation of Mistress Christia's sort so often hides an equivalently sustained degree of self-knowledge. It is sometimes the case in our own age that the greater the extravagant outer show the greater has been the plunge by the showman into the depths of his private conscience: Consequently, the greater the effort to hide the fact, to give the world not what one is, but what it wants. Mistress Christia chose to reflect with consummate artistry the desires of her lover of the day; to fulfil her ambition as subtly as did she reveals a person of exceptional perspicacity.

I intrude upon the flow of my tale with these various bits of explanation and speculation only, I hope, to offer credibility for what is to follow – to give a hint at a natural reason for Mistress Christia's peculiar actions and poor Werther's extravagant response. Some time has passed since we left our lovers. For the moment they have separated. We return to Werther . . .

12

3

In which Werther finds a Soul Mate

Werther de Goethe's pile stood on the pinnacle of a black and mile-high crag about which, in the permanent twilight, black vultures swooped and croaked. The rare visitor to Werther's crag could hear the vultures' voices as he approached. 'Nevermore!' and 'Beware the Ides of March!' and 'Picking a Chicken with You' were three of the least cryptic warnings they had been created to caw.

At the top of the tallest of his thin, dark towers, Werther de Goethe sat in his favourite chair of unpolished quartz, in his favourite posture of miserable introspection, wondering why Mistress Christia had decided to pay a call on My Lady Charlotina at Lake Billy the Kid.

'Why should she wish to stay here, after all?' He cast a suffering eye upon the sighing sea below. 'She is a creature of light – she seeks colour, laughter, warmth, no doubt to try to forget some secret sorrow – she needs all the things I cannot give her. Oh, I am a monster of selfishness!' He allowed himself a small sob. But neither the sob nor the preceding outburst produced the usual satisfaction; self-pity eluded him. He felt adrift, lost, like an explorer without chart or compass in an unfamiliar land. Manfully, he tried again:

'Mistress Christia! Mistress Christia! Why do you desert me? Without you I am desolate! My pulsatile nerves will sing at your touch only! And yet it must be my doom forever to be destroyed by the very things to which I give my fullest loyalty. Ah, it is hard! It is hard!'

He felt a little better and rose from his chair of unpolished quartz, turning his power ring a fraction so that the wind blew harder through the unglazed windows of the tower and whipped at his hair, blew his cloak about, stung his pale, long face. He raised one jackbooted foot to place it on the low sill and stared through the rain and the wind at the sky like a

13

dreadful, spreading bruise overhead, at the turbulent, howling sea below.

He pursed his lips, turning his power ring to darken the scene a little more, to bring up the wind's wail and the ocean's roar. He was turning back to his previous preoccupation when he perceived that something alien tossed upon the distant waves; an artifact not of his own design, it intruded upon his careful conception. He peered hard at the object, but it was too far away for him to identify it. Another might have shrugged it aside, but he was painstaking, even prissy, in his need for artistic perfection. Was this some vulgar addition to his scene made, perhaps, by the Duke of Queens in a misguided effort to please him?

He took his parachute (chosen as the only means by which he could leave his tower) from the wall and strapped it on, stepping through the window and tugging at the rip cord as he fell into space. Down he plummetted and the scarlet balloon soon filled with gas, the nacelle opening up beneath him, so that by the time he was hovering some feet above the sombre waves, he was lying comfortably on his chest, staring over the rim of his parachute at the trespassing image he had seen from his tower. What he saw was something resembling a great shell, a shallow boat of mother-of-pearl, floating on that dark and heaving sea.

In astonishment he now realized that the boat was occupied by a slight figure, clad in filmy white, whose face was pale and terrified. It could only be one of his friends, altering his appearance for some whimsical adventure. But which? Then he caught, through the rain, a better glimpse and he heard himself saying:

'A child? A child? Are you a child?'

She could not hear him; perhaps she could not even see him, having eyes only for the watery walls which threatened to engulf her little boat and carry her down to the land of Davy Jones. How could it be a child? He rubbed his eyes. He must be projecting his hopes – but there, that movement, that whimper! It *was* a child! Without doubt!

He watched, open-mouthed, as she was flung this way and that by the elements – *his* elements. She was powerless: actually powerless! He relished her terror; he envied her her fear. Where had she come from? Save for himself and Jherek Carnelian there had not been a child on the planet for thousands upon

14

thousands of years.

He leaned further out, studying her smooth skin, her lovely rounded limbs. Her eyes were tight shut now as the waves crashed upon her fragile craft; her delicate fingers, unstrong, courageous, clung hard to the side; her white dress was wet, outlining her new-formed breasts; water poured from her long, auburn hair. She panted in delicious impotence.

'It *is* a child!' Werther exclaimed. 'A sweet, frightened child!'

And in his excitement he toppled from his parachute with an astonished yell, and landed with a crash, which winded him, in the sea-shell boat beside the girl. She opened her eyes as he turned his head to apologize. Plainly she had not been aware of his presence overhead. For a moment he could not speak, though his lips moved. But she screamed.

'My dear . . .' The words were thin and high and they faded into the wind. He struggled to raise himself on his elbows. 'I apologize . . .'

She screamed again. She crept as far away from him as possible. Still she clung to her flimsy boat's side as the waves played with it: a thoughtless giant with too delicate a toy; inevitably, it must shatter. He waved his hand to indicate his parachute, but it had already been borne away. His cloak was caught by the wind and wrapped itself around his arm; he struggled to free himself and became further entangled; he heard a new scream and then some demoralized whimpering.

'I will save you!' he shouted, by way of reassurance, but his voice was muffled even in his own ears. It was answered by a further pathetic shriek. As the cloak was saturated it became increasingly difficult for him to escape its folds. He lost his temper and was deeper enmeshed. He tore at the thing. He freed his head.

'I am not your enemy, tender one, but your saviour,' he said. It was obvious that she could not hear him. With an impatient gesture he flung off his cloak at last and twisted a power ring. The volume of noise was immediately reduced. Another twist and the waves became calmer. She stared at him in wonder.

'Did you do that?' she asked.

'Of course. It is my scene, you see. But how you came to enter it, I do not know!'

'You are a wizard, then?' she said.

15

'Not at all. I have no interest in sport.' He clapped his hands and his parachute re-appeared, perhaps a trifle reluctantly as if it had enjoyed its brief independence, and drifted down until it was level with the boat. Werther lightened the sky. He could not bring himself, however, to dismiss the rain, but he let a little sun shine through it.

'There,' he said. 'The storm has passed, eh? Did you like your experience?'

'It was horrifying! I was so afraid. I thought I would drown.'

'Yes? And did you like it?'

She was puzzled, unable to answer as he helped her aboard the nacelle and ordered the parachute home.

'You *are* a wizard!' she said. She did not seem disappointed. He did not quiz her as to her meaning. For the moment, if not for always, he was prepared to let her identify him however she wished.

'You are actually a child?' he asked hesitantly. 'I do not mean to be insulting. A time traveller, perhaps? Or from another planet?'

'Oh, no. I am an orphan. My father and mother are now dead. I was born on Earth some fourteen years ago.' She looked in faint dismay over the side of the craft as they were whisked swiftly upward. '*They* were time travellers. We made our home in a forgotten menagerie – underground, but it was pleasant. My parents feared recapture, you see. Food still grew in the menagerie. There were books, too, and they taught me to read – and there were other records through which they were able to present me with a reasonable education. I am not illiterate. I know the world. I was taught to fear wizards.'

'Ah,' he crooned, 'the world! But you are not a part of it, just as I am not a part.'

The parachute reached the window and, at his indication, she stepped gingerly from it to the tower. The parachute folded itself and placed itself upon the wall. Werther said: 'You will want food, then? I will create whatever you wish!'

'Fairy food will not fill mortal stomachs, sir,' she told him.

'You are beautiful,' he said. 'Regard me as your mentor, as your new father. I will teach you what this world is really like. Will you oblige me, at least, by trying the food?'

'I will.' She looked about her with a mixture of curiosity and

16

suspicion. 'You lead a Spartan life.' She noticed a cabinet. 'Books? You read, then?'

'In transcription,' he admitted. 'I listen. My enthusiasm is for Ivan Turgiditi, who created the Novel of Discomfort and remained its greatest practitioner. In, I believe, the 900th (though they could be spurious, invented, I have heard) . . .'

'Oh, no, no! I have read Turgiditi.' She blushed. 'In the original. *Wet Socks* – four hours of discomfort, every second brought to life and in less than a thousand pages!'

'My favourite,' he told her, his expression softening still more into besotted wonderment. 'I can scarcely believe – in this Age – one such as you! Innocent of device. Uncorrupted! Pure!'

She frowned. 'My parents taught me well, sir. I am not . . .'

'You cannot know! And dead, you say? Dead! If only I could have witnessed – but no, I am insensitive. Forgive me. I mentioned food.'

'I am not really hungry.'

'Later, then. That I should have so recently mourned such things as lacking in this world. I was blind. I did not look. Tell me everything. Whose was the menagerie?'

'It belonged to one of the lords of this planet. My mother was from a period she called the October Century, but recently recovered from a series of interplanetary wars and fresh and optimistic in its rediscoveries of ancestral technologies. She was chosen to be the first into the future. She was captured upon her arrival and imprisoned by a wizard like yourself.'

'The word means little. But continue.'

'She said that she used the word because it had meaning for her and she had no other short description. My father came from a time known as the Preliminary Structure, where human kind was rare and machines proliferated. He never mentioned the nature of the transgression he made from the social code of his day, but as a result of it he was banished to this world. He, too, was captured for the same menagerie and there he met my mother. They lived originally, of course, in separate cages, where their normal environments were re-created for them. But the owner of the menagerie became bored, I think, and abandoned interest in his collection . . .'

'I have often remarked that people who cannot look after their collections have no business keeping them,' said Werther.

17

'Please continue, my dear child.' He reached out and patted her hand.

'One day he went away and they never saw him again. It took them some time to realize that he was not returning. Slowly the more delicate creatures, whose environments required special attention, died.'

'No one came to resurrect them?'

'No one. Eventually my mother and father were the only ones left. They made what they could of their existence, too wary to enter the outer world in case they should be recaptured, and, to their astonishment, conceived me. They had heard that people from different historical periods could not produce children.'

'I have heard the same.'

'Well, then, I was a fluke. They were determined to give me as good an upbringing as they could and to prepare me for the dangers of your world.'

'Oh, they were right! For one so innocent, there are many dangers. I will protect you, never fear.'

'You are kind.' She hesitated. 'I was not told by my parents that such as you existed.'

'I am the only one.'

'I see. My parents died in the course of this past year, first my father, then my mother (of a broken heart, I believe). I buried my mother and at first made an attempt to live the life we had always led, but I felt the lack of company and decided to explore the world, for it seemed to me I, too, could grow old and die before I had experienced anything!'

'Grow old,' mouthed Werther rhapsodically, 'and die!'

'I set out a month or so ago and was disappointed to discover the absence of ogres, of malevolent creatures of any sort – and the wonders I witnessed, while a trifle bewildering, did not compare with those I had imagined I would find. I had fully expected to be snatched up for a menagerie by now, but nobody has shown interest, even when they have seen me.'

'Few follow the menagerie fad at present.' He nodded. 'They would not have known you for what you were. Only I could recognize you. Oh, how lucky I am. And how lucky *you* are, my dear, to have met me when you did. You see, I, too, am a child of the womb. I, too, made my own hard way through the uterine gloom to breathe the air, and find the light of this faded, this senile globe. Of all those you could have met, you have met the only one who understands you, who is likely to share your passion, to relish your education. We are soul mates, child!'

He stood up and put a tender arm about her young shoulders.

'You have a new mother, a new father now! His name is Werther!'

4

In which Werther finds Sin at Last

Her name was Catherine Lilly Marguerite Natasha Dolores Beatrice Machineshop-Seven Flambeau Gratitude (the last two names but one being her father's and her mother's respectively).

Werther de Goethe continued to talk to her for some hours. Indeed, he became quite carried away as he described all the exciting things they would do, how they would live lives of the purest poetry and simplicity from now on, the quiet and tranquil places they would visit, the manner in which her education would be supplemented, and he was glad to note, he thought, her wariness dissipating, her attitude warming to him.

'I will devote myself entirely to your happiness,' he informed her, and then, noticing that she was fast asleep, he smiled tenderly: 'Poor child. I am a worm of thoughtlessness. She is exhausted.'

He rose from his chair of unpolished quartz and strode to where she lay curled upon the iguana-skin rug; stooping, he placed his hands under her warm-smelling, her yielding body, and somewhat awkwardly lifted her. In her sleep she uttered a tiny moan, her cherry lips parted and her newly budded breasts rose and fell rapidly against his chest once or twice until she sank back into a deeper slumber.

He staggered, panting with the effort, to another part of the tower, and then he lowered her with a sigh to the floor. He realized that he had not prepared a proper bedroom for her.

Fingering his chin, he inspected the dank stones, the cold obsidian which had suited his mood so well for so long and now seemed singularly offensive. Then he smiled.

'She must have beauty,' he said, 'and it must be subtle. It must be calm.'

An inspiration, a movement of a power ring, and the walls were covered with thick carpets embroidered with scenes from his own old book of fairy tales. He remembered how he had listened to the book over and over again – his only consolation in the lonely days of his extreme youth.

Here, Man Shelley, a famous harmonican, ventured into Odeon (a version of Hell) in order to be re-united with his favourite three-headed dog, Omnibus. The picture showed him with his harmonica (or 'harp') playing 'Blues for a Nightingale' – a famous lost piece. There, Casablanca Bogard, with his single eye in the middle of his forehead, wielded his magic spade, Sam, in his epic fight with that ferocious bird, the Malted Falcon, to save his love, the Acrilan Queen, from the power of Big Sleepy (a dwarf who had turned himself into a giant) and Mutinous Caine, who had been cast out of Hollywood (or paradise) for the killing of his sister, the Blue Angel.

Such scenes were surely the very stuff to stir the romantic, delicate imagination of this lovely child, just as his had been stirred when – he felt the *frisson* – he had been her age. He glowed. His substance was suffused with delicious compassion for them both as he recalled, also, the torments of his own adolescence.

That she should be suffering as he had suffered filled him with the pleasure all must feel when a fellow spirit is recognized, and at the same time he was touched by her plight, determined that she should not know the anguish of his earliest years. Once, long ago, Werther had courted Jherek Carnelian, admiring him for his fortitude, knowing that locked in Jherek's head were the memories of bewilderment, misery and despair which would echo his own. But Jherek, pampered progeny of that most artificial of all creatures, the Iron Orchid, had been unable to recount any suitable experiences at all, had, whilst cheerfully eager to please Werther, recalled nothing but pleasurable times, had reluctantly admitted, at last, to the possession of the happiest of childhoods. That was when Werther had concluded that Jherek Carnelian had no soul worth speaking of, and he had never altered his opinion (now he secretly doubted Jherek's origins and sometimes believed that Jherek merely pretended to have been a child – merely one more of his boring and superficial affectations).

Next, a bed – a soft, downy bed, spread with sheets of silver silk, with posts of ivory and hangings of precious Perspex, antique and yellowed, and on the floor the finely tanned skins of albino hamsters and marmalade cats.

Werther added gorgeous lavs of intricately patterned red and blue ceramic, their bowls filled with living flowers: with whispering toadflax, dragonsnaps, goldilocks and shanghai lilies, with blooming scarlet margravines (his adopted daughter's name-flower, as he knew to his pride), with soda-purple poppies and tea-green roses, with iodine and cerise and crimson hanging johnny, with golden cynthia and skyblue truelips, calomine and creeping larrikin, until the room was saturated with their intoxicating scents.

Placing a few bunches of hitler's balls in the corners near the ceiling, a toy fish-tank (capable of firing real fish), which he remembered owning as a boy, under the window, a trunk (it could be opened by pressing the navel) filled with clothes near the bed, a full set of bricks and two bats against the wall close to the doorway, he was able, at last, to view the room with some satisfaction.

Obviously, he told himself, she would make certain changes according to her own tastes. That was why he had shown such restraint. He imagined her naïve delight when she wakened in the morning. And he must be sure to produce days and nights of regular duration, because at her age routine was the main thing a child needed. There was nothing like the certainty of a consistently glorious sunrise! This reminded him to make an alteration to a power ring on his left hand, to spread upon the black cushion of the sky crescent moons and stars and starlets in profusion. Bending carefully, he picked up the vibrant youth of her body and lowered her to the bed, drawing the silver sheets up to her vestal chin. Chastely he touched lips to her forehead and crept from the room, fashioning a leafy door behind him, hesitating for a moment, unable to define the mood in which he found himself. A rare smile illumined features set so long in lines of gloom. Returning to his own quarters, he murmured:

'I believe it is Contentment!'

A month swooned by. Werther lavished every moment of his time upon his new charge. He thought of nothing but her youthful satisfactions. He encouraged her in joy, in idealism, in a love of Nature. Gone were his blizzards, his rocky spires, his bleak wastes and his moody forests, to be replaced with gentle landscapes of green hills and merry, tinkling rivers, sunny glades in copses of poplars, rhododendrons, redwoods, laburnum, banyans and good old amiable oaks. When they went on a picnic, large-eyed cows and playful gorillas would come and nibble scraps of food from Catherine Gratitude's palm. And when it was day, the sun always shone and the sky was always blue, and if there were clouds, they were high, hesitant puffs of whiteness and soon gone.

He found her books so that she might read. There was Turgiditi and Uto, Pett Ridge and Zakka, Pyat Sink – all the ancients. Sometimes he asked her to read to him, for the luxury of dispensing with his usual translators. She had been fascinated by a picture of a typewriter she had seen in a record, so he fashioned an air car in the likeness of one, and they travelled the world in it, looking at scenes created by Werther's peers.

'Oh, Werther,' she said one day, 'you are so good to me. Now that I realize the misery which might have been mine (as well as the life I was missing underground), I love you more and more.'

'And I love you more and more,' he replied, his head a-swim. And for a moment he felt a pang of guilt at having forgotten Mistress Christia so easily. He had not seen her since Catherine had come to him, and he guessed that she was sulking somewhere. He prayed that she would not decide to take vengeance on him.

They went to see Jherek Carnelian's famous 'London, 1896', and Werther manfully hid his displeasure at her admiration for his rival's buildings of white marble, gold and sparkling quartz. He showed her his own abandoned tomb, which he privately considered in better taste, but it was plain that it did not give her the same satisfaction.

They saw the Duke of Queens' latest, 'Ladies and Swans', but not for long, for Werther considered it unsuitable. Later they paid a visit to Lord Jagged of Canaria's somewhat abstract 'War and Peace in Two Dimensions,' and Werther thought it too stark to please the girl, judging the experiment 'successful.' But Catherine laughed with glee as she touched the living figures, and found that somehow it was true. Lord Jagged had given them length and breadth but not a scrap of width – when they turned aside, they disappeared.

*

23

It was on one of these expeditions, to Bishop Castle's 'A Million Angry Wrens' (an attempt in the recently revised art of Aesthetic Loudness), that they encountered Lord Mongrove, a particular confidant of Werther's until they had quarrelled over the method of suicide adopted by the natives of Uranus during the period of the Great Sodium Breather. By now, if Werther had not found a new obsession, they would have patched up their differences, and Werther felt a pang of guilt for having forgotten the one person on this planet with whom he had, after all, shared something in common.

In his familiar dark green robes, with his leonine head hunched between his massive shoulders, the giant, apparently disdaining an air carriage, was riding home upon the back of a monstrous snail.

The first thing they saw, from above, was its shining trail over the azure rocks of some abandoned, half-created scene of Argonheart Po's (who believed that nothing was worth making unless it tasted delicious and could be eaten and digested). It was Catherine who saw the snail itself first and exclaimed at the size of the man who occupied the swaying howdah on its back.

'He must be ten feet tall, Werther!'

And Werther, knowing whom she meant, made their typewriter descend, crying:

'Mongrove! My old friend!'

Mongrove, however, was sulking. He had chosen not to forget whatever insult it had been which Werther had levelled at him when they had last met. 'What? Is it Werther? Bringing freshly sharpened dirks for the flesh between my shoulder blades? It is that Cold Betrayer himself, whom I befriended when a bare boy, pretending carelessness, feigning insouciance, as if he cannot remember, with relish, the exact degree of bitterness of the poisoned wine he fed me when we parted. Faster, steed! Bear me away from Treachery! Let me fly from further insult! No more shall I suffer at the hands of Calumny!' And, with his long, jewelled stick he beat upon the shell of his molluscoid mount. The beast's horns waved agitatedly for a moment, but it did not really seem capable of any greater speed. In good-humoured puzzlement, it turned its slimy head towards its master.

'Forgive me, Mongrove! I take back all I said,' announced

24

Werther, unable to recall a single sour syllable of the exchange. 'Tell me why you are abroad. It is rare for you to leave your doomy dome.'

'I am making my way to the Ball,' said Lord Mongrove, 'which is shortly to be held by My Lady Charlotina. Doubtless I have been invited to act as a butt for their malice and their gossip, but I go in good faith.'

'A Ball? I know nothing of it.'

Mongrove's countenance brightened a trifle. 'You have not been invited? Ah!'

'I wonder . . . But, no – My Lady Charlotina shows unsuspected sensitivity. She knows that I now have responsibilities – to my little Ward here. To Catherine – to my Kate.'

'The child?'

'Yes, to my child. I am privileged to be her protector. Fate favours me as her new father. This is she. Is she not lovely? Is she not innocent?'

Lord Mongrove raised his great head and looked at the slender girl beside Werther. He shook his huge head as if in pity for her.

'Be careful, my dear,' he said. 'To be befriended by de Goethe is to be embraced by a viper!'

She did not understand Mongrove; questioningly she looked up at Werther. 'What does he mean?'

Werther was shocked. He clapped his hands to her pretty ears.

'Listen no more! I regret the overture. The movement, Lord Mongrove, shall remain unresolved. Farewell, spurner of good-intent. I had never guessed before the level of your cynicism. Such an accusation! Goodbye, for ever, most malevolent of mortals, despiser of altruism, hater of love! You shall know me no longer!'

'You have known yourself not at all,' snapped Mongrove spitefully, but it was unlikely that Werther, already speeding skyward, heard the remark.

And thus it was with particular and unusual graciousness that Werther greeted My Lady Charlotina when, a little later, they came upon her.

She was wearing the russet ears and eyes of a fox, riding her yellow rocking horse through the patch of orange sky left over from her own turbulent 'Death of Neptune.' She waved to them. 'Cock-a-doodle-do!'

'My dear Lady Charlotina. What a pleasure it is to see you. Your beauty continues to rival Nature's mightiest miracles.'

It is with such unwonted effusion that we will greet a person, who has not hitherto aroused our feelings, when we are in a position to compare him against another, closer, acquaintance who has momentarily earned our contempt or anger.

She seemed taken aback, but received the compliment equably enough.

'Dear Werther! And is this that rarity, the girl-child I have heard so much about and whom, in your goodness, you have taken under your wing? I could not believe it! A child! And how lucky she is to find a father in yourself – of all our number the one best suited to look after her.'

It might almost be said that Werther preened himself beneath the golden shower of her benediction, and if he detected no irony in her tone, perhaps it was because he still smarted from Mongrove's dash of vitriol.

'I have been chosen, it seems,' he said modestly, 'to lead this waif through the traps and illusions of our weary world. The burden I shoulder is not light . . .'

'Valiant Werther!'

'. . . but it is shouldered willingly. I am devoting my life to her upbringing, to her peace of mind.' He placed a bloodless hand upon her auburn locks, and, winsomely, she took his other one.

'You are tranquil, my dear?' asked My Lady Charlotina kindly, arranging her blue skirts over the saddle of her rocking horse. 'You have no doubts?'

'At first I had,' admitted the sweet child, 'but gradually I learned to trust my new father. Now I would trust him in anything!'

'Ah,' sighed My Lady Charlotina, 'trust!'

'Trust,' said Werther. 'It grows in me, too. You encourage me, charming Charlotina, for a short time ago I believed myself doubted by all.'

'Is it possible? When you are evidently so reconciled – so – happy!'

'And I am happy, also, now that I have Werther,' carolled the commendable Catherine.

'Exquisite!' breathed My Lady Charlotina. 'And you will, of course, both come to my Ball.'

'I am not sure . . .' began Werther, 'perhaps Catherine is too young . . .'

But she raised her tawny hands. 'It is your duty to come. To show us all that simple hearts are the happiest.'

'Possibly . . .'

'You must. The world must have examples, Werther, if it is to follow your Way.'

Werther lowered his eyes shyly. 'I am honoured,' he said. 'We accept.'

'Splendid! Then come soon. Come now, if you like. A few arrangements, and the Ball begins.'

'Thank you,' said Werther, 'but I think it best if we return to my castle for a little while.' He caressed his ward's fine, long tresses. 'For it will be Catherine's first Ball, and she must choose her gown.'

And he beamed down upon his radiant protégée as she clapped her hands in joy.

My Lady Charlotina's Ball must have been at least a mile in circumference, set against the soft tones of a summer twilight, red-gold and transparent so that, as one approached, the guests who had already arrived could be seen standing upon the inner wall, clad in creations extravagant even at the End of Time.

The Ball itself was inclined to roll a little, but those inside it were undisturbed; their footing was firm, thanks to My Lady Charlotina's artistry. The Ball was entered by means of a number of sphincterish openings, placed more or less at random in its outer wall. At the very centre of the Ball, on a floating platform, sat an orchestra comprised of the choicest musicians, out of a myriad of ages and planets, from My Lady's great menagerie (she specialized, currently, in artists).

When Werther de Goethe, a green-gowned Catherine Gratitude upon his blue velvet arm, arrived, the orchestra was playing some primitive figure of My Lady Charlotina's own composition. It was called, she claimed as she welcomed them, 'On the Theme of Childhood', but doubtless she thought to please them, for Werther believed he had heard it before under a different title.

Many of the guests had already arrived and were standing in small groups chatting to each other. Werther greeted an old friend, Li Pao, of the 27th century, and such a kill-joy that he had never been wanted for a menagerie. While he was forever criticizing their behaviour, he never missed a party. Next to him stood the Iron Orchid, mother of Jherek Carnelian, who was not present. In contrast to Li Pao's faded blue overalls, she wore rags of red, yellow and mauve, thousands of sparkling bracelets, anklets and necklaces, a head-dress of woven peacock's wings, slippers which were moles and whose beady eyes looked up from the floor.

'What do you mean – waste?' she was saying to Li Pao. 'What else could we do with the energy of the universe? If our sun burns out, we create another. Doesn't that make us conservatives? Or is it preservatives?'

'Good evening, Werther,' said Li Pao in some relief. He bowed politely to the girl. 'Good evening, miss.'

'Miss?' said the Iron Orchid. 'What?'

'Gratitude.'

'For whom?'

'This is Catherine Gratitude, my Ward,' said Werther, and the Iron Orchid let forth a peal of luscious laughter.

'The girl-bride, eh?'

'Not at all,' said Werther. 'How is Jherek?'

'Lost, I fear, in Time. We have seen nothing of him recently. He still pursues his paramour. Some say you copy him, Werther.'

He knew her bantering tone of old and took the remark in good part. 'His is a mere affectation,' he said. 'Mine is Reality.'

'You were always one to make that distinction, Werther,' she said. 'And I will never understand the difference!'

'I find your concern for Miss Gratitude's upbringing most worthy,' said Li Pao somewhat unctuously. 'If there is any way I can help. My knowledge of twenties' politics, for instance, is considered unmatched – particularly, of course, where the 26th and 27th centuries are concerned . . .'

'You are kind,' said Werther, unsure how to take an offer which seemed to him overeager and not entirely selfless.

Gaf the Horse in Tears, whose clothes were real flame, flickered towards them, the light from his burnng, unstable face

28

almost blinding Werther. Catherine Gratitude shrank from him as he reached out a hand to touch her, but her expression changed as she realized that he was not at all hot – rather, there was something almost chilly about the sensation on her shoulder. Werther did his best to smile. 'Good evening, Gaf.'

'She is a dream!' said Gaf. 'I know it, because only I have such a wonderful imagination. Did I create her, Werther?'

'You jest.'

'Ho, ho! Serious old Werther.' Gaf kissed him, bowed to the child, and moved away, his body erupting in all directions as he laughed the more. 'Literal, literal Werther!'

'He is a boor,' Werther told his charge. 'Ignore him.'

'I thought him sweet,' she said.

'You have much to learn, my dear.'

The music filled the Ball and some of the guests left the floor to dance, hanging in the air around the orchestra, darting streamers of coloured energy in order to weave complex patterns as they moved.

'They are very beautiful,' said Catherine Gratitude. 'May we dance soon, Werther?'

'If you wish. I am not much given to such pastimes as a rule.'

'But tonight?'

He smiled. 'I can refuse you nothing, child.'

She hugged his arm and her girlish laughter filled his heart with warmth.

'Perhaps you should have made yourself a child before, Werther?' suggested the Duke of Queens, drifting away from the dance and leaving a trail of green fire behind him. He was clad all in soft metal which reflected the colours in the Ball and created other colours in turn. 'You are a perfect father. Your métier.'

'It would not have been the same, Duke of Queens.'

'As you say.' His darkly handsome face bore its usual expression of benign amusement. 'I am the Duke of Queens, child. It is an honour.' He bowed, his metal booming.

'Your friends are wonderful,' said Catherine Gratitude. 'Not at all what I expected.'

'Be wary of them,' murmured Werther. 'They have no conscience.'

'Conscience? What is that?'

Wether touched a ring and led her up into the air of the Ball. 'I am your conscience, for the moment, Catherine. You shall learn in time.'

Lord Jagged of Canaria, his face almost hidden by one of his high, quilted collars, floated in their direction.

'Werther, my boy! This must be your daughter. Oh! Sweeter than honey! Softer than petals! I have heard so much – but the praise was not enough! You must have poetry written about you. Music composed for you. Tales must be spun with you as the heroine.' And Lord Jagged made a deep, an elaborate bow, his long sleeves sweeping the air below his feet. Next, he addressed Werther:

'Tell me, Werther, have you seen Mistress Christia? Everyone else is here, but not she.'

'I have looked for the Everlasting Concubine without success,' Werther told him.

'She should arrive soon. In a moment My Lady Charlotina announces the beginning of the masquerade – and Mistress Christia loves the masquerade.'

'I suspect she pines,' said Werther.

'Why so?'

'She loved me, you know.'

'Aha! Perhaps you are right. But I interrupt your dance. Forgive me.'

And Lord Jagged of Canaria floated, stately and beautiful, towards the floor.

'Mistress Christia?' said Catherine. 'Is she your Lost Love?'

'A wonderful woman,' said Werther. 'But my first duty is to you. Regretfully I could not pursue her, as I think she wanted me to do.'

'Have I come between you?'

'Of course not. Of course not. That was infatuation – this is sacred duty.'

And Werther showed her how to dance – how to notice a gap in a pattern which might be filled by the movements from her body. Because it was a special occasion he had given her her very own power ring – only a small one, but she was proud of it, and she gasped so prettily at the colours her train made that Werther's anxieties (that his gift might corrupt her precious innocence) melted entirely away. It was then that he realized

30

with a shock how deeply he had fallen in love with her.

At the realization, he made an excuse, leaving her to dance with, first, Sweet Orb Mace, feminine tonight, with a latticed face, and then with O'Kala Incarnadine who, with his usual preference for the bodies of beasts, was currently a bear. Although he felt a pang as he watched her stroke O'Kala's ruddy fur, he could not bring himself just then to interfere. His immediate desire was to leave the Ball, but to do that would be to disappoint his ward, to raise questions he would not wish to answer. After a while he began to feel a certain satisfaction from his suffering and remained, miserably, on the floor while Catherine danced on and on.

And then My Lady Charlotina had stopped the orchestra and stood on the platform calling for their attention.

'It is time for the masquerade. You all know the theme, I hope.' She paused, smiling. 'All, save Werther and Catherine. When the music begins again, please reveal your creations of the evening.'

Werther frowned, wondering her reasons for not revealing the theme of the masquerade to him. She was still smiling at him as she drifted towards him and settled beside him on the floor.

'You seem sad, Werther. Why so? I thought you at one with yourself at last. Wait. My surprise will flatter you, I'm sure!'

The music began again. The Ball was filled with laughter – and there was the theme of the masquerade!

Werther cried out in anguish. He dashed upward through the gleeful throng, seeing each face as a mockery, trying to reach the side of his girl-child before she should realize the dreadful truth.

'Catherine! Catherine!'

He flew to her. She was bewildered as he folded her in his arms.

'Oh, they are monsters of insincerity! Oh, they are grotesque in their apings of all that is simple, all that is pure!' he cried.

He glared about him at the other guests. My Lady Charlotina had chosen 'Childhood' as her general theme. Sweet Orb Mace had changed himself into a gigantic single sperm, his own face still visible at the glistening tail; the Iron Orchid had become a monstrous newborn baby with a red and bawling face which

31

still owed more to Paint than to Nature; the Duke of Queens, true to character, was three-year-old Siamese twins (both the faces were his own, softened); even Lord Mongrove had deigned to become an egg.

'What ith it, Werther?' lisped My Lady Charlotina at his feet, her brown curls bobbing as she waved her lollipop in the general direction of the other guests. 'Doeth it not pleathe you?'

'Ugh! This is agony! A parody of everything I hold most perfect!'

'But, Werther . . .'

'What is wrong, dear Werther?' begged Catherine. 'It is only a masquerade.'

'Can you not see? It is you – what you and I mean – that they mock. No – it is best that you do not see. Come, Catherine. They are insane; they revile all that is sacred!' And he bore her bodily towards the wall, rushing through the nearest doorway and out into the darkened sky.

He left his typewriter behind, so great was his haste to be gone from that terrible scene. He fled with her willy-nilly through the air, through daylight, through pitchy night. He fled until he came to his own tower, flanked now by green lawns and rolling turf, surrounded by songbirds, swamped in sunshine. And he hated it: landscape, larks and light – all were hateful.

He flew through the window and found his room full of comforts – of cushions and carpets and heady perfume – and with a gesture he removed them. Their particles hung gleaming in the sun's beams for a moment. But the sun, too, was hateful. He blacked it out and night swam into that bare chamber. And all the while, in amazement, Catherine Gratitude looked on, her lips forming the question, but never uttering it. At length, tentatively, she touched his arm.

'Werther?'

His hands flew to his head. He roared in his mindless pain.

'Oh, Werther!'

'Ah! They destroy me! They destroy my ideals!'

He was weeping when he turned to bury his face in her hair.

'Werther!' She kissed his cold cheek. She stroked his shaking back. And she led him from the ruins of his room and down the passage to her own apartment.

32

'Why should I strive to set up standards,' he sobbed, 'when all about me they seek to pull them down. It would be better to be a villain!'

But he was quiescent; he allowed himself to be seated upon her bed; he felt suddenly drained. He sighed. 'They hate innocence. They would see it gone forever from this globe.'

She gripped his hand. She stroked it. 'No, Werther. They meant no harm. I saw no harm.'

'They would corrupt you. I must keep you safe.'

Her lips touched his and his body came alive again. Her fingers touched his skin. He gasped.

'I must keep you safe.'

In a dream, he took her in his arms. Her lips parted, their tongues met. Her young breasts pressed against him – and for perhaps the first time in his life Werther understood the meaning of physical joy. His blood began to dance to the rhythm of a sprightlier heart. And why should he not take what they would take in his position? He placed a hand upon a pulsing thigh. If cynicism called the tune, then he would show them he could pace as pretty a measure as any. His kisses became passionate, and passionately were they returned.

'Catherine!'

A motion of a power ring and their clothes were gone, the bed hangings drawn.

And your auditor, not being of that modern school which salaciously seeks to share the secrets of others' passions (secrets familiar, one might add, to the great majority of us), retires from this scene.

But when he woke the next morning and turned on the sun, Werther looked down at the lovely child beside him, her auburn hair spread across the pillows, her little breasts rising and falling in tranquil sleep, and he realized that he had used his reaction to the masquerade to betray his trust. A madness had filled him; he had raised an evil wind and his responsibility had been borne off by it, taking Innocence and Purity, never to return. His lust had lost him everything.

Tears reared in his tormented eyes and ran cold upon his heated cheeks. 'Mongrove was perceptive indeed,' he murmured. 'To be befriended by Werther is to be embraced by a viper. She can never trust me – anyone – again. I have lost my

33

right to offer her protection. I have stolen her childhood.'

And he got up from the bed, from the scene of that most profound of crimes, and he ran from the room and went to sit in his old chair of unpolished quartz, staring listlessly through the window at the paradise he had created outside. It accused him; it reminded him of his high ideals. He was astonished by the consequences of his actions: he had turned his paradise to hell.

A great groan reverberated in his chest. 'Oh, now I know what sin is!' he said. 'And what terrible tribute it exacts from the one who tastes it!'

And he sank almost luxuriously into the deepest gloom he had ever known.

5

In which Werther finds Redemption of Sorts

He avoided Catherine Gratitude all that day, even when he heard her calling his name, for if the landscape could fill him with such agony, what would he feel under the startled inquisition of her gaze? He erected himself a heavy dungeon door so that she could not get in, and, as he sat contemplating his poisoned paradise, he saw her once, walking on a hill he had made for her. She seemed unchanged, of course, but he knew in his heart how she must be shivering with the chill of lost innocence. That it should have been himself, of all men, who had introduced her so young to the tainted joys of carnal love! Another deep sigh and he buried his fists savagely in his eyes.

'Catherine! Catherine! I am a thief, an assassin, a despoiler of souls. The name of Werther de Goethe becomes a synonym for Treachery!'

It was not until the next morning that he thought himself able to admit her to his room, to submit himself to a judgement which he knew would be worse for not being spoken. Even when she did enter, his shifty eye would not focus on her for long. He looked for some outward sign of her experience, somewhat surprised that he could detect none.

He glared at the floor, knowing his words to be inadequate. 'I am sorry,' he said.

'For leaving the Ball, darling Werther! The epilogue was infinitely sweeter.'

'Don't!' He put his hands to his ears. 'I cannot undo what I have done, my child, but I can try to make amends. Evidently you must not stay here with me. You need suffer nothing further on that score. For myself, I must contemplate an eternity of loneliness. It is the least of the prices I must pay. But Mongrove would be kind to you, I am sure.' He looked at her. It seemed that she had grown older. Her bloom was fading now that it had been touched by the icy fingers of that most sinister, most insinuating of libertines, called Death. 'Oh,' he sobbed, 'how haughty was I in my pride! How I congratulated myself on my high-mindedness. Now I am proved the lowliest of all my kind!'

'I really cannot follow you, Werther dear,' she said. 'Your behaviour is rather odd today, you know. Your words mean very little to me.'

'Of course they mean little,' he said. 'You are unworldly, child. How can you anticipate . . . ah, ah . . .' and he hid his face in his hands.

'Werther, please cheer up. I have heard of *le petit mal*, but this seems to be going on for a somewhat longer time. I am still puzzled . . .'

'I cannot, as yet,' he said, speaking with some difficulty through his palms, 'bring myself to describe in cold words the enormity of the crime I have committed against your spirit – against your childhood. I had known that you would – eventually – wish to experience the joys of true love – but I had hoped to prepare your soul for what was to come – so that when it happened it would be beautiful.'

'But it *was* beautiful, Werther.'

He found himself experiencing a highly inappropriate impatience with her failure to understand her doom.

'It was not the right *kind* of beauty,' he explained.

'There are certain correct kinds for certain times?' she asked. 'You are sad because we have offended some social code?'

'There is no such thing in this world, Catherine – but you, child, could have known a code. Something I never had when I was your age – something I wanted for you. One day you will realize what I mean.' He leaned forward, his voice thrilling, his eye hot and hard, 'And if you do not hate me now, Catherine, oh, you will hate me then. Yes! You will hate me then.'

Her answering laughter was unaffected, unstrained. 'This is silly, Werther. I have rarely had a nicer experience.'

He turned aside, raising his hands as if to ward off blows. 'Your words are darts – each one draws blood in my conscience.' He sank back into his chair.

Still laughing, she began to stroke his limp hand. He drew it away from her. 'Ah, see! I have made you lascivious. I have

36

introduced you to the drug called lust!'

'Well, perhaps to an aspect of it!'

Some change in her tone began to impinge on Werther, though he was still stuck deep in the glue of his guilt. He raised his head, his expression bemused, refusing to believe the import of her words.

'A wonderful aspect,' she said. And she licked his ear.

He shuddered. He frowned. He tried to frame words to ask her a certain question, but he failed.

She licked his cheek and she twined her fingers in his lacklustre hair. 'And one I should love to experience again, most passionate of anachronisms. It was as it must have been in those ancient days – when poets ranged the world, stealing what they needed, taking any fair maiden who pleased them, setting fire to the towns of their publishers, laying waste the books of their rivals: ambushing their readers. I am sure you were just as delighted, Werther. Say that you were!'

'Leave me!' he gasped. 'I can bear no more.'

'If it is what you want.'

'It is.'

With a wave of her little hand, she tripped from the room.

And Werther brooded upon her shocking words, deciding that he could only have misheard her. In her innocence she had seemed to admit an understanding of certain inconceivable things. What he had half-interpreted as a familiarity with the carnal world was doubtless merely a child's romantic conceit. How could she have had previous experience of a night such as that which they had shared?

She had been a virgin. Certainly she had been that.

He wished that he did not then feel an ignoble pang of pique at the possibility of another having also known her. Consequently this was immediately followed by a further wave of guilt for entertaining such thoughts and subsequent emotions. A score of conflicting glooms warred in his mind, sent tremors through his body.

'Why,' he cried to the sky, 'was I born! I am unworthy of the gift of life. I accused My Lady Charlotina, Lord Jagged and the Duke of Queens of base emotions, cynical motives, yet none are baser or more cynical than mine! Would I turn my anger against my victim, blame her for my misery, attack a little child because she tempted me? That is what my diseased mind would do. Thus do I seek to excuse myself my crimes. Ah, I am vile! I am vile!'

He considered going to visit Mongrove, for he dearly wished to abase himself before his old friend, to tell Mongrove that the giant's contempt had been only too well founded; but he had lost the will to move; a terrible lassitude had fallen upon him. Hating himself, he knew that all must hate him, and while he knew that he had earned every scrap of their hatred, he could not bear to go abroad and run the risk of suffering it.

What would one of his heroes of Romance have done? How would Casablanca Bogard or Eric of Marylebone have exonerated themselves, even supposing they could have committed such an unbelievable deed in the first place?

He knew the answer.

It drummed louder and louder in his ears. It was implacable and grim. But still he hesitated to follow it. Perhaps some other, more original act of retribution would occur to him? He racked his writhing brain. Nothing presented itself as an alternative.

At length he rose from his chair of unpolished quartz. Slowly, his pace measured, he walked towards the window, stripping off his power rings so that they clattered to the flagstones.

He stepped upon the ledge and stood looking down at the rocks a mile below at the base of the tower. Some jolting of a power ring as it fell had caused a wind to spring up and to blow coldly against his naked body. 'The Wind of Justice,' he thought.

He ignored his parachute. With one final cry of 'Catherine! Forgive me!' and an unvoiced hope that he would be found long after it proved impossible to resurrect him, he flung himself, unsupported, into space.

Down he fell and death leapt to meet him. The breath fled from his lungs, his head began to pound, his sight grew dim, but the spikes of black rock grew larger until he knew that he had struck them, for his body was a-flame, broken in a hundred places, and his sad, muddled, doom-clouded brain was chaff upon the wailing breeze. Its last coherent thought was: *Let none say Werther did not pay the price in full*. And thus did he end his life with a proud negative.

'Oh, Werther, what an adventure!'

It was Catherine Gratitude looking down on him as he opened his eyes. She clapped her hands. Her blue eyes were full of joy.

Lord Jagged stood back with a smile. 'Re-born, magnificent Werther, to sorrow afresh!' he said.

He lay upon a bench of marble in his own tower. Surrounding the bench were My Lady Charlotina, the Duke of Queens, Gaf the Horse in Tears, the Iron Orchid, Li Pao, O'Kala Incarnadine and many others. They all applauded.

'A splendid drama!' said the Duke of Queens.

'Amongst the best I have witnessed,' agreed the Iron Orchid (a fine compliment from her).

Werther found himself warming to them as they poured their praise upon him; but then he remembered Catherine Gratitude and what he had meant himself to be to her, what he had actually become, and although he felt much better for having paid his price, he stretched out his hand to her, saying again, 'Forgive me.'

'Silly Werther! Forgive such a perfect rôle? No, no! If anyone needs forgiving, then it is I.' And Catherine Gratitude touched one of the many power rings now festooning her fingers and returned herself to her original appearance.

'It is you!' He could make no other response as he looked upon the Everlasting Concubine. 'Mistress Christia?'

'Surely you suspected towards the end?' she said. 'Was it not everything you told me you wanted? Was it not a fine "sin", Werther?'

'I suffered . . .' he began.

'Oh, yes! *How* you suffered! It was unparalleled. It was equal, I am sure, to anything in History. And, Werther, did you not find the "guilt" particularly exquisite?'

'You did it for me?' He was overwhelmed. 'Because it was what I said I wanted most of all?'

'He is still a little dull,' explained Mistress Christia, turning to their friends. 'I believe that is often the case after a resurrection.'

'Often,' intoned Lord Jagged, darting a sympathetic glance at Werther. 'But it will pass, I hope.'

'The ending, though it could be anticipated,' said the Iron Orchid, 'was absolutely right.'

Mistress Christia put her arms around him and kissed him. 'They are saying that your performance rivals Jherek Carnelian's,' she whispered. He squeezed her hand. What a wonderful woman she was, to be sure, to have added to his experience and to have increased his prestige at the same time.

He sat up. He smiled a trifle bashfully. Again they applauded.

'I can see that this was where "Rain" was leading,' said Bishop Castle. 'It gives the whole thing point, I think.'

'The exaggerations were just enough to bring out the essential mood without being too prolonged,' said O'Kala Incarnadine, waving an elegant hoof (he had come as a goat).

'Well, I had not . . .' began Werther, but Mistress Christia put a hand to his lips.

'You will need a little time to recover,' she said.

Tactfully, one by one, still expressing their most fulsome congratulations, they departed, until only Werther de Goethe and the Everlasting Concubine were left.

'I hope you did not mind the deception, Werther,' she said. 'I had to make amends for ruining your rainbow and I had been wondering for ages how to please you. My Lady Charlotina helped a little, of course, and Lord Jagged – though neither knew too much of what was going on.'

'The real performance was yours,' he said. 'I was merely your foil.'

'Nonsense. I gave you the rough material with which to work. And none could have anticipated the wonderful, consummate use to which you put it!'

Gently, he took her hand. 'It was everything I have ever dreamed of,' he said. 'It is true, Mistress Christia, that you alone know me.'

'You are kind. And now I must leave.'

'Of course.' He looked out through his window. The comforting storm raged again. Familiar lightnings flickered; friendly thunder threatened; from below there came the sound of his old consoler the furious sea flinging itself, as always, at the rock's black fangs. His sigh was contented. He knew that their liaison was ended; neither had the bad taste to prolong it and thus produce what would be, inevitably, an anti-climax, and yet he felt regret, as evidently did she.

'If death were only permanent,' he said wistfully, 'but it cannot be. I thank you again, granter of my deepest desires.'

'If death,' she said, pausing at the window, 'were permanent, how would we judge our successes and our failures? Sometimes, Werther, I think you ask too much of the world.' She smiled. 'But you are satisfied for the moment, my love?'

'Of course.'

It would have been boorish, he thought, to have claimed anything else.

WHITE STARS

Rose of all Roses, Rose of all the World!
You, too, have come where the dim tides are hurled
Upon the wharves of sorrow, and heard ring
The bell that calls us on; the sweet far thing.
Beauty grown sad with its eternity
Made you of us, and of the dim grey sea.
Our long ships loose thought-woven sails and wait,
For God has bid them share an equal fate;
And when at last, defeated in His wars,
They have gone down under the same white stars,
We shall no longer hear the little cry
Of our sad hearts, that may not live nor die.

W. B. Yeats
'The Rose of Battle'

I

A Brief Word from our Auditor

f these fragments of tales from the End of Time appear to have certain themes in common, then it is the auditor and his informants who must be held responsible for the selection they have made from available information. A fashion for philosophical and sociological rediscovery certainly prevailed during this period but there must have been other incidents which did not reflect the fashion as strongly, and we promise the reader that if we should hear of some such story we shall not hesitate to present it. Yet legends – whether they come to us from past or future – have a habit of appealing to certain ages in certain interpretations, and that factor, too, must be considered, we suppose.

This story, said to involve among others the Iron Orchid, Bishop Castle and Lord Shark, is amended, interpreted, embellished by your auditor, but in its essentials is the same as

45

he heard it from his most familiar source, the temporal excursionist, Mrs Una Persson.

2

A Stroll across the Dark Continent

'We were all puzzled by him,' agreed the Duke of Queens as he stepped carefully over an elephant, 'but we put it down to an idiosyncratic sense of humour.' He removed his feathered hat and wiped his brow. The redder plumes clashed horribly with his cerise skin.

'Some of his jokes,' said the Iron Orchid with a glance of distaste at the crocodile clinging by its teeth to her left foot, 'were rather difficult to see. However, he seems at one with himself now. Wouldn't you say?' She shook the reptile loose.

'Oh, yes! But then I'm notorious for my lack of insight.' They strolled away from Southern Africa into the delicate knee-high forests of the Congo. The Iron Orchid smiled with delight at the brightly coloured little birds which flitted about her legs, sometimes clinging to the hem of her parchment skirt before flashing away again. Of all the expressions of the duke's obsession with the ancient nation called by him 'Afrique', this seemed to her to be the sweetest.

They were discussing Lord Jagged of Canaria (who had vanished at about the same time as the Iron Orchid's son, Jherek). Offering no explanation as to how his friends might have found themselves, albeit for a very short while, in 19th-century London, together with himself, Jherek, some cyclopean aliens and an assortment of natives of the period, Jagged had returned, only to hide himself away underground.

'Well,' said the duke, dismissing the matter, 'it was rewarding, even if it does suggest, as Brannart Morphail somewhat emphatically pointed out, that Time itself is becoming unstable. It must be because of all these other disruptions in the universe we are hearing about.'

'It is very confusing,' said the Iron Orchid with disapproval. 'I do hope the end of the world, when it comes, will be a little better organized.' She turned. 'Duke?' He had disappeared.

With a smile of apology he clambered back to land. 'Lake Tanganyika,' he explained. 'I knew I'd misplaced it.' He used one of his power rings to dissipate the water in his clothing.

'It is the trees,' she said. 'They are too tall.' She was having difficulty in pressing on through the waist-high palms. 'I do believe I've squashed one of your villages, Duke.'

'Please don't concern yourself, lovely Iron Orchid. I've crowded too much in. You know how I respond to a challenge!' He looked vaguely about him, seeking a way through the jungle. 'It is uncomfortably hot.'

'Is not your sun rather close?' she suggested.

'That must be it.' He made an adjustment to a ruby power ring and the miniature sun rose, then moved to the left, sinking again behind a hillock he had called Kilimanjaro, offering them a pleasant twilight.

'That's much better.'

He took her hand and led her towards Kenya, where the trees were sparser. A cloud of tiny flamingoes fluttered around her, like midges, for a moment and then were gone on their way back to their nesting places.

'I do love this part of the evening, don't you?' he said. 'I would have it all the time, were I not afraid it would begin to pall.'

'One must orchestrate,' she murmured, glad that his taste seemed, at long last, to be improving.

'One must moderate.'

'Indeed.' He helped her across the bridge over the Indian Ocean. He looked back on Afrique, his stance melancholy and romantic. 'Farewell Cape City,' he proclaimed, 'farewell Byzantium, Dodge and Limoges; farewell the verdant plains of Chad and the hot springs of Egypt. Farewell!'

The Duke of Queens and the Iron Orchid climbed into his monoplane, parked nearby. Overhead now a bronze and distant sun brightened a hazy, yellow sky; on the horizon were old, worn mountains which, judging by their peculiar brown colouring, might have been an original part of the Earth's topography, for hardly anyone visited this area.

As the duke pondered the controls, the Iron Orchid put her head to one side, thinking she had heard something. 'Do you detect,' she asked, 'a sort of clashing sound?'

'I have not yet got the engine started.'

'Over there, I mean.' She pointed. 'Are those people?'

He peered in the direction she indicated. 'Some dust rising, certainly. And, yes, perhaps two figures. Who could it be?'

'Shall we see?'

'If you wish, we can –' He had depressed a button and the rest of his remark was drowned by the noise of his engine. The propellor began to spin and whine and then fell from the nose, bouncing over the barren ground and into the Indian Ocean. He pressed the button again and the engine stopped. 'We can walk there,' he concluded. They descended from the monoplane.

The ground they crossed was parched and cracked like old leather which had not been properly cared for.

'This needs a thorough restoration,' said the Iron Orchid somewhat primly. 'Who usually occupies this territory?'

'You see him,' murmured the Duke of Queens, for now it was possible to recognize one of the figures.

'Aha!' She was not surprised. It had been two or three centuries since she had last seen the man who, with a bright strip of metal clutched in one gauntleted hand, capered back and forth in the dust, while a second individual, also clasping an identical strip, performed similar steps. From time to time they would bring their strips forcefully together, resulting in the clashing sound the Iron Orchid had heard originally.

'Lord Shark the Unknown,' said the Duke of Queens. He called out, 'Greetings to you, my mysterious Lord Shark!'

The man half-turned. The other figure leapt forward and touched his body with his metal strip. Lord Shark gasped and fell to one knee. Through the fishy mask he always wore, his red eyes glared at them.

They came up to him. He did not rise. Instead he presented his gauntleted palm. 'Look!' Crimson liquid glistened.

The Iron Orchid inspected it. 'Is it unusual?'

'It is blood, madam!' Lord Shark rose painfully to his feet. 'My blood.'

'Then you must repair yourself at once.'

'It is against my principles.'

Lord Shark's companion stood some distance away, wiping Lord Shark's blood from his weapon.

'That, I take it, is a sword,' said the Iron Orchid. 'I had

49

always imagined them larger, and more ornate.'

'I know such swords.' Lord Shark the Unknown loosened the long white scarf he wore around his dark grey neck and applied it to the wound in his shoulder. 'They are decadent. These,' he held up his own, 'are finely tempered, perfectly balanced épées. We were duelling,' he explained, 'my automaton and I.'

Looking across at the machine, the Iron Orchid saw that it was a reproduction of Lord Shark himself, complete with fierce shark-mask.

'It could kill you, could it not?' she asked. 'Is it programmed to resurrect you, Lord Shark?'

He dismissed her question with a wave of his blood-stained scarf.

'And strange, that you should be killed, as it were, by yourself,' she added.

'When we fight, is it not always with ourselves, madam?'

'I really don't know, sir, for I have never fought and I know no one who does.'

'That is why I must make automata. You know my name, madam, but I fear you have the advantage of me.'

'It has been so long. I looked quite different when we last met. At Mongrove's Black Ball, you'll recall. I am the Iron Orchid.'

'Ah, yes.' He bowed.

'And I am the Duke of Queens,' said the duke kindly.

'I know you, Duke of Queens. But you had another name then, did you not?'

'Liam Ty Pam Caesar Lloyd George Zatopek Finsbury Ronnie Michelangelo Yurio Iopu 4578 Rew United,' supplied the duke. 'Would that be it?'

'As I remember, yes.' A sigh escaped the gash which was the shark's mouth. 'So there have been some few small changes in the outside world, in society. But I suppose you still while away your days with pretty conceits?'

'Oh, yes!' said the Iron Orchid enthusiastically. 'They have been at their best this season. Have you seen the duke's "Afrique"? All in miniature. Over there.'

'Is that what it is called? I wondered. I had been growing lichen, but no matter.'

'I spoiled a project of yours?' The duke was mortified.

50

Lord Shark shrugged.

'But, my lonely lord, I must make amends.'

The eyes behind the mask became interested for a moment. 'You would fight with me. A duel? Is that what you mean?'

'Well . . .' the Duke of Queens fingered his chin, 'if that would placate you, certainly. Though I've had no practice at it.'

The light in the eyes dimmed. 'True. It would be no fight at all.'

'But,' said the duke, 'lend me one of your machines to teach me, and I will return at an agreed hour. What say you?'

'No, no, sir. I took no umbrage. I should not have suggested it. Let us part, for I weary very swiftly of human company.' Lord Shark sheathed his sword and snapped his fingers at his automaton, which copied the gesture. 'Good day to you, Iron Orchid. And to you, Duke of Queens.' He bowed again.

Ignoring the Iron Orchid's restraining hand upon his sleeve, the duke stepped forward as Lord Shark turned away. 'I insist upon it, sir.'

His dark grey, leathery cloak rustling, the masked recluse faced them again. 'It would certainly fulfill an ambition. But it would have to be done properly, and only when you had thoroughly learned the art. And there would have to be an understanding as to the rules.'

'Anything.' The duke made an elaborate bow. 'Send me, at your convenience, an instructor.'

'Very well.' Lord Shark the Unknown signed to his automaton and together they began to walk across the plain, towards the brown mountains. 'You will hear from me soon, sir.'

'I thank you, sir.'

They strolled in the direction of the useless monoplane. The duke seemed very pleased. 'What a wonderful new fashion,' he remarked, 'duelling. And this time, with the exception of Lord Shark, of course, I *shall* be the first.'

The Iron Orchid was amused. 'Shall we all, soon, be drawing one another's blood with those thin sticks of steel, extravagant duke?'

He laughed and kissed her cheek. 'Why not? I tire of "Cities", and even "Continents" pall. How long is it since we have had a primitive sport?'

'Nothing since the ballhead craze,' she confirmed.

'I shall learn all I can, and then I can teach others. When Jherek returns, we shall have something fresh for him to enjoy.'

'It will, at least, be in keeping with his current obsessions, as I understand them.'

Privately the Iron Orchid wondered if the duke would, at last, be responsible for an entirely new fashion. She hoped, for his sake, that he would, but it was hard, at the moment, to see the creative possibilities of the medium. She was afraid that it would not catch on.

Something of the History of Lord Shark the Unknown

If gloomy Mongrove, now touring what was left of the galaxy with the alien Yusharisp, had affected aloofness, then Lord Shark was, without question, genuinely reclusive. Absorbed in his duel, he had not noticed the approach of the Iron Orchid and the Duke of Queens, for if he had he would have made good his escape well before they could have hailed him. In all his life he had found pleasure in the company of only one human being: a short-lived time traveller who had refused immortality and died many centuries since.

Lord Shark was not merely contemptuous of the society which presently occupied the planet, he was contemptuous of the very planet, the universe, of the whole of existence. Compared with him, Werther de Goethe was an optimist (as, indeed, secretly he was). Werther had once made overtures to Lord Shark, considering him a fellow spirit, but Lord Shark would have none of him, judging him to be as silly and as affected as all the others. Lord Shark was the last true cynic to come into being at the End of Time and found no pleasure in any pursuit save the pursuit of death, and in this he must be thought the unluckiest man in the world, for everything conspired to thwart him. Wounded, he refused to treat the wounds, and they healed. Injured, his injuries were never critical. He considered suicide, as such, to be unworthy of him, feeble, but dangers which would have brought certain death to others only seemed to bring Lord Shark at best some passing inconvenience.

As he returned home, Lord Shark could feel the pain in his shoulder already subsiding and he knew that it would not be long before there would only be a small scar to show where the sword blade had entered. He was regretting his bargain with the Duke of Queens. He was sure that the duke would never attain the skill necessary to beat him, and, if he were not beaten, and killed, he would in his opinion have wasted his time. His pride now refused to let him go back on the bargain, for to do so would be to show him as feckless a fellow as any other and would threaten his confidence in his own superiority, his only consolation. It was the pride of the profoundly unimaginative man, for it was Lord Shark's lot to be without creative talent of any kind in a world where all were artists – good or bad, but artists, still. Even his mask was not of his own invention and had been made for him by his time-travelling friend shortly before that man's death (his name had come from the same source). He had taken both mask and name without humour, on good faith. It is perhaps unkind to speculate as to whether even this stalwart friend had been unable to resist playing one good joke upon poor Lord Shark, for it is a truism that those without humour find themselves the butts of all who possess even a spark of it themselves.

Whoever had created Lord Shark (and he had never been able to discover who his parents might be, perhaps because they were too embarrassed to claim him) might well have set out to create a perfect misanthrope, a person as unsuited to this particular society as was possible. If so, they had achieved their ambition absolutely. He had appeared in public only twice in the thousand or so years of his life, and the last time had been three hundred years ago at Mongrove's celebrated Black Ball. Lord Shark had stayed little more than half-an-hour at this, having rapidly reached the conclusion that it was as pointless as all the other social activities on the planet. He had considered time travel, as an escape, but every age he had studied seemed equally frivolous and he had soon ceased to entertain that scheme. He contented himself with his voluntary exile, his contempt, his conviction in the pointlessness of everything, and he continued to seek ways of dying suggested to him by his studies of history. His automata were created in his own image not from perversity, not from egocentricity, but because no other image presented itself to his mind.

Lord Shark trudged on, his grey-booted feet making the dust of his arid domain dance, giving the landscape a semblance of life, and came in a while to his rectangular domicile at the foot of those time-ground ridges, the ragged remains of the Rockies. Two guards, identical in appearance to each other and to Lord Shark, were positioned on either side of his single small door, and they remained rigid, only their eyes following him as he let himself in and marched up the long, straight, sparsely lit passage which passed through the centre of the internal grid (the house was divided into exactly equal sections, with rooms of exactly equal proportions) to the central chamber of the building, in which he spent the greater part of his days. There he sat himself down upon a chair of grey metal and began to brood.

Regretfully, he must pursue his agreement with the Duke of Queens, but he felt no demand to hurry the business through; the longer it took, the better.

4

In which Unwilling Travellers Arrive at the End of Time

Walking slowly across the ceiling of his new palace, the Duke of
Queens looked up to see that Bishop Castle had already arrived
and was peering with some pleasure through a window. 'Shall
we join him?' asked the duke of the Iron Orchid and, at her nod
of assent, turned a jewel on one of his rings. Elegantly they
performed half a somersault so that they, too, were upside
down and, from this new perspective, descending towards the
floor. Bishop Castle hailed them. 'Such a simple idea, duke, but
beautiful.' He waved a white-gloved hand at the view. The sky
now lay like a sea, spread out below, while inverted trees and
gardens and lawns were overhead.

'It is refreshing,' confirmed the duke, pleased. 'But I can take
no credit. The idea was the Iron Orchid's.'

'Nonsense, most dashing of dukes. Actually,' she murmured
to Bishop Castle, 'I borrowed it from Sweet Orb Mace. How is
she, by the by?'

'Recovered completely, though the resurrection was a little
late. I believe the snow helped preserve her, for all its heat.'

'We have just seen Lord Shark the Unknown,' she announced.
'And he challenged the Duke of Queens to, my lord bishop, a
duel!'

'It was not exactly a challenge, luscious blossom. Merely an
agreement to fight at some future date.'

'To fight?' Bishop Castle's large eyebrows rose, almost touching the rim of his tall crown. 'Would that involve "violence"?'

'A degree of it, I believe,' said the duke demurely. 'Yes, blood
will be spilled, if today's experience is typical. These little
sticks . . .' He turned with a questioning frown to the Iron
Orchid.

'Swords,' she said.

'Yes, swords – with points, you know, to pierce the flesh.
You will have seen them in the old pictures and possibly won-

56

dered at their function. We have used them for decoration, of course, in the past – many believing them to be some sort of ancient totem, some symbol of rank – but it emerges that they were meant to kill.'

Bishop Castle was apologetic. 'The conceptions involved are a little difficult to grasp, as with so many of these ancient pastimes, though of course I have witnessed, in visitors to our age, the phenomena. Does it not involve "anger", however?'

'Not necessarily, from what little I know.'

The conversation turned to other subjects; they discussed their recent adventures and speculated upon the whereabouts of the Iron Orchid's son, Jherek Carnelian, of Mrs Underwood, whom he loved, of Lord Jagged of Canaria, and the uncouth alien musicians who had called themselves the Lat.

'Brannart Morphail, querulous as ever, refuses to discuss any part he might have played in the affair,' Bishop Castle told his friends. 'He merely hints at the dangers of "meddling with the fabric of Time", but I cannot believe he is entirely objective, for he has always affected a somewhat proprietorial attitude towards Time.'

'Nonetheless, it *is* puzzling,' said the Iron Orchid. 'And I regret the disappearance of so many entertaining people. Those space travellers, the Lat, were they, do you think, "violent"?'

'That would explain the difficulties we had in communicating with them, certainly. But we can talk further when we see My Lady Charlotina.' Bishop Castle was evidently tiring of the discussion. 'Shall we go?'

As they drifted, still upside down, from the house, Bishop Castle complimented the Iron Orchid on her costume. It was dark blue and derived from the clothing of some of those she had encountered at the Café Royal, in the 19th century. The helmet suited her particularly, but Bishop Castle was not sure he liked the moustache.

Righting themselves, they all climbed into Bishop Castle's air carriage, a reproduction of a space vehicle of the 300th Icecream Empire, all red-gold curlicues and silver body work, and set off for Lake Billy the Kid, where My Lady Charlotina's reception (to celebrate, as she put it, their safe return) had already started.

They had gone no more than a few hundred miles when they

encountered Werther de Goethe, magnificently pale in black, voluminous satin robes, riding upon his monstrous tombstone, a slab of purple marble, and evidently recovered from his recent affair with Mistress Christia, the Everlasting Concubine, in such good spirits that he deigned to acknowledge their presence as they put their heads through the portholes and waved to him. The slab swung gracefully over the tops of some tall pine trees and came to rest, hovering near them.

'Do you go to My Lady Charlotina's, moody Werther?' asked the Iron Orchid.

'Doubtless to be insulted again by her, but, yes, I go,' he confirmed. 'I suppose you have seen the newcomers already?'

'Newcomers?' The light breeze curled the duke's feathers around his face. 'From space?'

'Who knows? They are humanoid. My Lady Charlotina has endomed them, near Lake Billy the Kid. Her whole party has gone to watch. I will see you there, then?'

'You shall, sorrowing son of Nature,' promised the Iron Orchid.

Werther was pleased with the appellation. He swept on. The spaceship turned to follow him.

Soon they saw the stretch of blue water which was My Lady Charlotina's home, the presence of her vast subaqueous palace marked only by a slight disturbance of the surface of the water in the middle of the lake where the energy-tube made its exit. They rose higher into the air, over the surrounding mountains, and at length saw the shimmering, green-tinted air indicating a force-dome. Descending, they saw that the dome, all but invisible, was surrounded by a large throng of people. They landed in the vicinity of a number of other air carriages of assorted designs and disembarked.

My Lady Charlotina, naked, with her skin coloured in alternate bands of black and white, saw them. She already had her arm through Werther's. 'Come and see what I have netted for my menagerie,' she called. 'Time travellers. I have never seen so many at once.' She laughed. 'Brannart, of course, takes a very gloomy view, but I'm delighted! There isn't another set like it!'

Brannart Morphail, still in the traditional humpback and club-foot of the scientist, limped towards them. He shook a bony finger at the Iron Orchid. 'This is all your son's fault. And where is Lord Jagged to explain himself?'

'We have not seen him since our return,' she said. 'You fret so, Brannart. Think how entertaining life has become of late!'

'Not for long, delicate metal, fragile flower. Not for long.' Grumbling to himself, he hobbled past them. 'I must get my instruments.'

They made their way through the gathering until they reached the wall of the force-dome. The Iron Orchid put her hand to her lips in astonishment. 'Are they intelligent?'

'Oh, yes. Primitive, naturally, but otherwise . . .' My Lady Charlotina smiled. 'They growl and rave so! We have not yet had a proper talk with them.'

Orange fire splashed against the inner wall and spread across it, obscuring the scene within.

'They keep doing that,' explained My Lady Charlotina. 'I am not sure if they mean to burn us or the wall. A translator is in operation, though they are still a trifle incoherent. Their voices can be very loud.'

As the fire dissipated, the Iron Orchid stared curiously at the twenty or thirty men inside the dome. Their faces were bruised, bleeding and smudged with oil; they wore identical costumes of mottled green and brown; there were metal helmets on their heads, and what she supposed to be some sort of breathing apparatus (unused) on their backs. In their hands were artifacts consisting basically of a metal tube to which was fixed a handle, probably of plastic. It was from these tubes that the flames occasionally gouted.

'They look tired,' she said sympathetically. 'Their journey must have been difficult. Where are they from?'

'They were not clear. We put the dome up because they seemed ill at ease in the open; they kept burning things. Four of my guests had to be taken away for resurrection. I think they must calm down eventually, don't you, Duke of Queens?'

'They invariably do,' he agreed. 'They'll exhaust themselves, I suppose.'

'So many!' murmured Bishop Castle. He fingered the lobe of his ear.

'That is what makes them such a catch,' said the Duke of Queens. 'Well, Werther, you are an expert – what period would you say they were from?'

'Very early. The twentieth century?'

'A little later?' suggested Bishop Castle.

'The twenty-fifth, then.'

Bishop Castle nodded. 'That seems right. Are any of your guests, My Lady Charlotina, from that age?'

'Not really. You know how few we get from those Dawn Age periods. Doctor Volospion might have one, but . . .'

Mistress Christia approached, her eyes wide, her lips wet. 'What *brutes*!' she gasped. 'Oh, I envy you, My Lady Charlotina. When did you find them?'

'Not long ago. But I've no idea how much time they've been here.'

More fire spread itself over the wall, but it seemed fainter. One of the time travellers flung down his tube, growling and glaring. Some of the audience applauded.

'If only Jherek were here,' said the Iron Orchid. 'He understands these people so well! Where is their machine?'

'That's the odd thing. Brannart has been unable to find a trace of one. He insists that one exists. He thinks that it might have returned to its period of origin – that sometimes happens, I gather. But he says that no machine registered on his detectors, and it has caused him to become even more bad-tempered than usual.' My Lady Charlotina withdrew her arm from Werther's. 'Ah, Gaf the Horse in Tears, have you seen my new time travellers yet?'

Gaf lifted his skirts. 'Have you seen my new *wheels*, My Lady Charlotina?'

They wandered away together.

Bishop Castle was trying to address one of the nearest of the time travellers. 'How do you do?' he began politely. 'Welcome to the End of Time!'

The time travellers said something to him which defeated the normally subtle translator.

'Where are you from?' asked the Iron Orchid of one.

Another of the time travellers shouted to the man addressed. 'Remember, trooper. Name, rank and serial number. It's all you have to tell 'em.'

'Sarge, they must know we're from Earth.'

'Okay,' assented the other, 'you can tell 'em that, too.'

'Kevin O'Dwyer,' said the man, 'Trooper First Class, 000885–9376.' He added, 'From Earth.'

'What year?' asked the Duke of Queens.

Trooper First Class Kevin O'Dwyer looked pleadingly at his sergeant. 'You're the ranking officer, sir. I shouldn't have to do this.'

'Let them do the talking,' snapped the sergeant. 'We'll do the fighting.'

'Fighting?' The Duke of Queens grinned with pleasure. 'Ah, you'll be able to help me. Are you soldiers, then?'

Again the translation was muddy.

'Soldiers?' asked Bishop Castle, in case they had not heard properly.

The sergeant sighed. 'What do you think, buddy?'

'This is splendid!' said the Duke of Queens.

5

In which the Duke of Queens seeks Instruction

As soon as it was evident that the soldiers had used up all their fire, My Lady Charlotina released the one called 'sergeant', whose full name, on further enquiry, turned out to be Sergeant Henry Martinez, 0008832942. After listening in silence to their questions for a while he said:

'Look, I don't know what planet this is, or if you think you're fooling me with your disguise, but you're wasting your time. We're hip to every trick in the Alpha Centauran book.'

'Who are the Alpha Centaurans?' asked My Lady Charlotina, turning to Werther de Goethe.

'They existed even before the Dawn Age,' he explained. 'They were intelligent horses of some kind.'

'Very funny,' said Sergeant Martinez flatly. 'You know damn well who you are.'

'He thinks we're horses? Perhaps some optical disturbance, coupled with . . .' Bishop Castle creased his brow.

'Stow it, will you?' asked the sergeant firmly. 'We're prisoners of war. Now I know you guys don't pay too much attention to things like the Geneva Convention in Alpha Centauri, for all you –'

'It's a star system!' said Werther. 'I remember. I think it was used for something a long while ago. It doesn't exist any more, but there was a war between Earth and this other system in the 24th century – you are 24th century, I take it, sir? – which went on for many years. These are typical warriors of the period. The Alpha Centaurans were, I thought, bird-like creatures . . .'

'The Vultures,' supplied Sergeant Martinez. 'That's what we call you.'

'I assure you, we're as human as you are, sergeant,' said My Lady Charlotina. 'You are an ancestor of ours. Don't you recognize the planet? And we have some of your near-contemporaries with us. Li Pao? Where's Li Pao? He's from the 27th.'
But the puritanical Chinaman had not yet arrived.

'If I'm not mistaken,' said Martinez patiently, 'you're trying to convince me that the blast which got us out there beyond Mercury sent us into the future. Well, it's a good try – we'd heard your interrogation methods were pretty subtle and pretty damn elaborate – but it's too fancy to work. Save your time. Put us in the camp, knock us off, or do whatever you normally do with prisoners. We're Troopers and we're too tough and too tired to play this kind of fool game. Besides, I can tell you for nothing, we don't *know* nothing – we get sent on missions. We do what we're told. We either succeed, or we die or, sometimes, we get captured. We got captured. That's what *we* know. There's nothing else we can tell you.'

Fascinated, the Iron Orchid and her friends listened attentively and were regretful when he stopped. He sighed. 'Bad Sugar!' he exclaimed. 'You're like kids, ain't you? Can you understand what I'm saying?'

'Not entirely,' Bishop Castle told him, 'but it's very interesting for us. To study you, you know.'

Muttering, Sergeant Martinez sat down on the ground.

'Aren't you going to say any more?' Mistress Christia was extremely disappointed. 'Would you like to make love to me, Sergeant Martinez?'

He offered her an expression of cynical contempt. 'We're up to that one, too,' he said.

She brightened, holding out her hand. 'Wonderful! You don't mind, do you, My Lady Charlotina?'

'Of course not.'

When Sergeant Martinez did not accept her hand, Mistress Christia sat down beside him and stroked his cropped head.

Firmly, he replaced the helmet he had been holding in his hands. Then he folded his arms across his broad chest and stared into the middle-distance. His colour seemed to have changed. Mistress Christia stroked his arm. He jerked it away.

'I must have misunderstood you,' she said.

'I can take it or leave it alone,' he told her. 'You got it? Okay, I'll take it. When I want it. But if you expect to get any information from me that way, that's where you're wrong.'

'Perhaps you'd rather do it in private?'

A mirthless grin appeared on his battered features. 'Well, I sure ain't gonna do it out here, in front of all your friends am I?'

'Oh, I see,' she said, confused. 'You must forgive me if I seem tactless, but it's so long since I entertained a time traveller. We'll leave it for a bit, then.'

The Iron Orchid saw that some of the men inside the force-dome had stretched out on the ground and had shut their eyes. 'They probably need to rest,' she suggested, 'and to eat something. Shouldn't we feed them, My Lady Charlotina?'

'I'll transfer them to my menagerie,' agreed her hostess. 'They'll probably be more at ease there. Meanwhile, we can continue with the party.'

Some time went by; the world continued in pretty much its normal fashion, with parties, experiments, games and inventions. Eventually, so the Iron Orchid heard when she emerged from a particularly dull and enjoyable affair with Bishop Castle, the soldiers from the 24th century had become convinced that they had travelled into the future, but were not much reconciled. Some, it seemed, were claiming that they would rather have been captured by their enemies. No news came from Lord Shark, and the two or three messages the Duke of Queens had sent him had not been answered. Jherek Carnelian did not come back, and Lord Jagged of Canaria refused all visitors. Brannart Morphail bewailed the inconsistencies which he claimed had appeared in the fabric of Time. Korghon of Soth created a sentient kind of mould which he trained to do tricks; Mistress Christia, having listened to an old tape, became obsessed with learning the language of the flowers and spent hour after hour listening to them, speaking to them in simple words; O'Kala Incarnadine became a sea-lion and thereafter could not be found. The craze for 'Cities' and 'Continents' died and nothing replaced it. Visiting the Duke of Queens, the Iron Orchid mentioned this, and he revealed his growing impatience with Lord Shark. 'He promised he would send me an instructor. I have had to fall back on Trooper O'Dwyer, who knows a little about knives, but nothing at all about swords. This is the perfect moment for a new fashion. Lord Shark has let me down.'

Trooper O'Dwyer, ensconced in luxury at the duke's palace, had agreed to assist the duke, his sergeant having succumbed at last to the irresistible charms of Mistress Christia, but the duke

confided to the Iron Orchid that he was not at all sure if bay-
onet drill were the same as fencing.

'However,' he told her, 'I am getting the first principles. You
decide, to start, that you are superior to someone else – that is
that you have more of these primitive attributes than the other
person or persons – love, hate, greed, generosity and so on . . .'

'Are not some of these opposites?' Her conversations with her
son had told her that much.

'They are . . .'

'And you claim you have all of them?'

'*More* of them than someone else.'

'I see. Go on.'

'Patriotism is difficult. With that you identify yourself with a
whole country. The trick is to see that country as yourself so
that any attack on the country is an attack on you.'

'A bit like Werther's Nature?'

'Exactly. Patriotism, in Trooper O'Dwyer's case, can extend
to the entire planet.'

'Something of a feat!'

'He accomplishes it easily. So do his companions. Well,
armed with all these emotions and conceptions you begin a
conflict – either by convincing yourself that you have been insulted by someone (who often has something you desire to own)
or by goading him to believe that he has been insulted by you
(there are subtle variations, but I do not thoroughly understand
them as yet). You then try to kill that person – or that nation –
or that planet – or as many members as possible. That is what
Trooper O'Dwyer and the rest are currently attempting with
Alpha Centauri.'

'They will succeed, according to Werther. But I understand
that the rules do not allow resurrection.'

'They are *unable* to accomplish the trick, most delectable of
blossoms, most marvellous of metals.'

'So the deaths are permanent?'

'Quite.'

'How odd.'

'They had much higher populations in those days.'

'I suppose that must explain it.'

'Yet, it appears, every time one of their members was killed,
they grieved – a most unpleasant sensation, I gather. To rid

themselves of this sense of grief, they killed more of the opposing forces, creating grief in them so that they would wish to kill more – and so on, and so on.'

'It all seems rather – well – unaesthetic.'

'I agree. But we must not dismiss their arts out of hand. One does not always come immediately to terms with the principles involved.'

'Is it even Art?'

'They describe it as such. They use the very word.'

One eyebrow expressed her astonishment. She turned as Trooper O'Dwyer shuffled into the room. He was eating a piece of brightly coloured fruit and he had an oddly shaped girl on his arm (created, whispered the duke, to the trooper's exact specifications). He nodded at them. 'Duke,' he said. 'Lady.' His stomach had grown so that it hung over his belt. He wore the same clothes he had arrived in, but his wounds had healed and he no longer had the respiratory gear on his back.

'Shall we go to the – um – "gym", Trooper O'Dwyer?' asked the duke in what was, in the Iron Orchid's opinion, a rather unnecessarily agreeable tone.

'Sure.'

'You must come and see this,' he told her.

The 'gym' was a large, bare room, designed by Trooper O'Dwyer, hung with various ropes, furnished with pieces of equipment whose function was, to her, unfathomable. For a while she watched as, enthusiastically, the Duke of Queens leapt wildly about, swinging from ropes, attacking large, stuffed objects with sharp sticks, yelling at the top of his voice, while, seated in the comfortable chair with the girl beside him, Trooper O'Dwyer called out guttural words in an alien tongue. The Iron Orchid did her best to be amused, to encourage the duke, but she found it difficult. She was glad when she saw someone enter the hall by the far door. She went to greet the newcomer. 'Dear Lord Shark,' she said, 'the duke has been so looking forward to your visit.'

The figure in the shark-mask stopped dead, pausing for a moment or two before replying.

'I am not Lord Shark. I am his fencing automaton, programmed to teach the Duke of Queens the secrets of the duel.'

'I am very pleased you have come,' she said in genuine relief.

6

Old-Fashioned Amusements

Sergeant Martinez and his twenty-five troopers relaxed in the comparative luxury of a perfect reproduction of a partially ruined Martian bunker, created for them by My Lady Charlotina. It was better than they had expected, so they had not complained, particularly since few of them had spent much of their time in the menagerie.

'The point is,' Sergeant Martinez was saying, as he took a long toke on the large black Herodian cigar, 'that we're all going soft and we're forgetting our duty.'

'The war's over, Sarge,' Trooper Gan Hok reminded him. He grinned. 'By a couple million years or so. Alpha Centauri's beaten.'

'That's what they're telling us,' said the sergeant darkly. 'And maybe they're right. But what if this *was* all a mirage we're in? An illusion created by the Vultures to make us *think* the war's over, so we make no attempt to escape.'

'You don't really believe that, do you, Sarge?' enquired squat Trooper Pleckhanov. 'Nobody could make an illusion this good. Could they?'

'Probably not, trooper, but it's our duty to *assume* they could and get back to our own time.'

'That girl of yours dropped you, Sarge?' enquired Trooper Denereaz, with the perspicacity for which he was loathed throughout the squad. Some of the others began to laugh, but stopped themselves as they noted the expression on the sergeant's face.

'Have you got a plan, Sarge?' asked Trooper George diplomatically. 'Wouldn't we need a time machine?'

'They exist. You've all talked with that Morphail guy.'

'Right. But would he give us one?'

'He refused,' Sergeant Martinez told them. 'What does that suggest to you, Trooper Denereaz?'

'That they want us to remain here?' suggested Denereaz dutifully.

'Right.'

'Then how are we going to get hold of one, Sarge?' asked Trooper Gan Hok.

'We got to use our brains,' he said sluggishly, staring hard at his cigar. 'We got one chance of a successful bust-out. We're gonna need some hardware, hostages maybe.' He yawned and slowly began to describe his scheme in broad outline while his men listened with different degrees of attention. Some of them were not at all happy with the sergeant's reminder of their duty.

Trooper O'Dwyer had not been present at the conference, but remained at the palace of the Duke of Queens, where he had become very comfortable. Occasionally he would stroll into the gym to see how the duke's fencing lessons were progressing. He was fascinated by the robot instructing the duke; it was programmed to respond to certain key commands, but within those terms could respond with rapid and subtle reflexes, while at the same time giving a commentary on the duke's proficiency, which currently afforded Trooper O'Dwyer some easy amusement.

The words Lord Shark used in his programming were in the ancient language of Fransai, authentic and romantic (though the romance had certainly escaped Lord Shark). To begin a duel the Duke of Queens would cry:

'En tou rage!'

– and if struck (the robot was currently set not to wound) he would retort gracefully:

'Tou jours gai, mon coeur!'

Trooper O'Dwyer thought that he had noted an improvement in the duke's skill over the past week or so (not that weeks, as such, existed in this world, and he was having a hard time keeping track of days, let alone anything else) thanks, thought the trooper, to the original basic training. A good part of the duke's time was spent with the robot, and he had lost interest in all other activities, all relationships, including that with Trooper O'Dwyer, who was content to remain at the palace, for he was given everything his heart desired.

A month or two passed (by Trooper O'Dwyer's reckoning) and the Duke of Queens grew increasingly skillful. Now he cried 'En tou rage!' more often than 'Tou jours gai!' and he confided, pantingly, one morning to the trooper that he felt he was almost ready to meet Lord Shark.

'You reckon you're as good as this other guy?' asked O'Dwyer.

'The automaton has taught me all it can. Soon I shall pay a visit to Lord Shark and display what I have learned.'

'I wouldn't mind getting a gander at Lord Shark myself,' said Trooper O'Dwyer, casually enough.

'Accompany me, by all means.'

'Okay, duke.' Trooper O'Dwyer winked and nudged the duke in the ribs. 'It'll break the monotony. Get me?'

The Duke of Queens, removing his fencing mask (fashioned in gold filigree to resemble a fanciful fox), blinked but made no answer. O'Dwyer could be interestingly cryptic sometimes, he thought. He noticed that the automaton was still poised in the ready position and he commanded it to come to attention. It did, its sword pointing upwards and almost touching its fishy snout.

The duke drew O'Dwyer's attention to his new muscles. 'I had nothing to do with their appearance,' he said in delight. 'They came – quite naturally. It was most surprising!'

The trooper nodded and bit into a fruit, reflecting that the duke now seemed to be in better shape than he was.

The Iron Orchid and My Lady Charlotina lay back upon the cushions of their slowly moving air carriage, which had been designed in the likeness of the long-extinct gryphon, and wondered where they might be. They had been making languid love. Eventually, My Lady Charlotina put her golden head over the edge of the gryphon's back and saw, not far off, the Duke of Queens' inverted palace. She suggested to her friend that they might visit the duke; the Iron Orchid agreed. They adjusted their gravity rings and flew towards the top-most (or the lowest) door, leaving the gryphon behind.

'You seem unenthusiastic, my dear,' murmured My Lady Charlotina, 'about the duke's current activities.'

'I suppose I am,' assented the Iron Orchid, brightening her silver skin a touch. 'He has such hopes of beginning a fashion.'

'And you think he will fail? I am quite looking forward to the

'– what is it – the fight?'

'The duel,' she said.

'And many others I know await it eagerly.' They floated down a long, curling passage whose walls were inset at regular intervals with cages containing pretty song-children. 'When is it to take place, do you know?'

'We must ask the duke. I gather he practises wholeheartedly with the automaton Lord Shark sent him.'

'Lord Shark is so mysterious, is he not,' whispered My Lady Charlotina with relish. 'I suspect that the interest in the duel comes, as much as anything, from people's wish to inspect one so rarely seen in society. Is duelling his *only* pastime?'

'I know nothing at all of Lord Shark the Unknown, save that he affects a surly manner and that he is pleased to assume the role of a recluse. Ah, there is the "gym". Probably we shall find the Duke of Queens therein.'

They came upon the duke as he divested himself of the last of his duelling costume.

'How handsome your body is, manly master of Queens,' purred My Lady Charlotina. 'Have you altered it recently?'

He kissed her hand. 'It changed itself – a result of all my recent exercise.' He inspected it with pleasure. 'It is how they used to change their bodies, in the old days.'

'We wondered when your duel with Lord Shark the Unknown was to take place,' she said, 'and came to ask. Everyone is anxious to watch.'

He was flattered. 'I go today to visit Lord Shark. It is for him to name the time and the location.' The duke indicated Trooper O'Dwyer, who lay half-hidden upon an ermine couch. 'Trooper O'Dwyer accompanies me. Would you care to come, too?'

'It is my understanding that Lord Shark does not encourage visitors,' said the Iron Orchid.

'You think you would not be welcome, then?'

'It is best to assume that.'

'Thank you, Iron Orchid, for saving me once again from a lapse of manners. I was ever tactless.' He smiled. 'It was that which led to this situation, really.'

'Trooper O'Dwyer!' My Lady Charlotina drifted towards the reclining warrior. 'Have you seen anything of your compatriots of late?'

70

'Nope. Have they gone missing?' He showed no great interest in his one-time messmates.

'They appear to have vanished, taking with them some power rings and a large air carriage I had given them for their own use. They have deserted my menagerie.'

'I guess they'll come back when they feel like it.'

'I do hope so. If they were not happy with their habitat they had only to tell me. Well,' turning with a smile to the duke, 'we shall not keep you. I hope your encounter with Lord Shark is satisfactory today. And you must tell us, at once, if you agree place and time, so that we can tell everyone to make plans to be there.'

He bowed. 'You will be the first, My Lady Charlotina, Iron Orchid.'

'Is that your "sword"?'

'It is.'

She stroked the slender blade. 'I must get one for myself,' she said, 'and then you can teach me, too.'

As they returned to their gryphon, the Iron Orchid touched her friend's arm. 'You could not have said a more pleasing thing to him.'

My Lady Charlotina laughed. 'Oh, we live to indulge such honest souls as he. Do we not, Iron Orchid?'

'Do I detect a slightly archaic note in your choice of phrase?'

'You do, my dear. I have been studying, too, you see!'

7

The Terms of the Duel

Lord Shark's warning devices apprised him of the approach of an air car, and his screens revealed the nature of that car, a large kite-like contraption from which hung a gondola – in the gondola, two figures.

'Two,' murmured Lord Shark the Unknown to himself. Beneath his mask he frowned. The car drifted closer and was seen to contain the Duke of Queens and a plump individual in poorly fitting overalls of some description.

He instructed his automata, his servants, to admit the couple when they reached the building, then he sat back to wait.

Lord Shark's grey mind considered the information on the screens, but dismissed the questions raised until the Duke of Queens could supply answers. He hoped that the duke had come to admit himself incapable of learning the skills of the duel and that he need not, therefore, be further bothered by the business which threatened to interrupt the routines of all the dull centuries of his existence. The only person on his planet who had not heard the news that the universe was coming to an end, he was the only one who would have been consoled by the knowledge or, indeed, even interested, for nobody else had paid it too much attention, save perhaps Lord Jagged of Canaria. Yet, even had Lord Shark known, he would still have preferred to await the end by following his conventional pursuits, being too much of a cynic to believe news until it had been confirmed by the event itself.

He heard footfalls in the passage. He counted thirty-four before they reached his door. He touched a stud. The door opened and there stood the Duke of Queens, in feathered finery, and lace, and gold, bowing with elaborate and meaningless courtesy.

'Lord Shark, I am here to receive your instructions!' He straightened, stroking his large black beard and looking about the room with a curiosity Lord Shark found offensive.

'This other? Is he your second?'

'Trooper O'Dwyer.'

'Of the 46th Star Squadron,' said Trooper O'Dwyer by way of embellishment. 'Nice to know you, Lord Shark.'

Lord Shark's small sigh was not heard by his visitors as he rose from behind his consoles. 'We shall talk in the gunroom,' he said. 'This way.'

He led them along a perfectly straight corridor into a perfectly square room which was lined with all the weapons his long-dead companion had collected in his lifetime.

'Phew!' said Trooper O'Dwyer. 'What an armoury!' He reached out and took down a heavy energy-rifle. 'I've seen these. We were hoping for an allocation.' He operated the moving parts, he sighted down the barrel. 'Is it charged?'

Lord Shark said tonelessly, 'I believe that they are all in working condition.' While Trooper O'Dwyer whistled and enthused, Lord Shark drew the Duke of Queens to the far end of the room where stood a rack of swords. 'If you feel that you wish to withdraw from our agreement, my lord duke, I should like you to know that I would also be perfectly happy to forget –'

'No, no! May I?' The Duke of Queens wrapped his heavy cloak over his arm and selected an ancient sabre from the rack, flexing it and testing it for balance. 'Excellent!' He smiled. 'You see, Lord Shark, that I know my blades now! I am ready to meet you at any time, anywhere you decide. Your automaton proved an excellent instructor and can best me no longer. I am ready. Besides,' he added, 'it would not do to call off the duel. So many of my friends intend to watch. They would be disappointed.'

'Friends? Come to watch?' Lord Shark was in despair. The Duke of Queens was renowned for his vulgarity, but Lord Shark had not for a moment considered that he would turn such an event into a sideshow.

'So if you will name when and where . . .' the Duke of Queens replaced the sword in the rack.

'Very well. It might as easily be where we first met, on the plain, as anywhere.'

'Good. Good.'

'As to time – say a week from today?'

'A *week*? I know the expression. Let me think . . .'

'Seven days – seven rotations of the planet around the sun.'

'Ah, yes . . .' The duke still seemed vague, so Lord Shark said impatiently:

'I will make you the loan of one of my chronometers. I will set it to indicate when you should leave to arrive at the appropriate time.'

'You are generous, Lord Shark.'

Lord Shark turned away. 'I will be glad when this is over,' he said. He glared at Trooper O'Dwyer, but the trooper was oblivious to his displeasure. He was now inspecting another weapon.

'I'd sure love the chance of trying one of these babies out,' he hinted.

Lord Shark ignored him.

'We shall fight, Duke of Queens, until one of us is killed. Does that suit you?'

'Certainly. It is what I expected.'

'You are not reluctant to die. I assumed . . .'

'I've died more than once, you know,' said the duke airily. 'The resurrection is sometimes a little disorientating, but it doesn't take long to –'

'I shall not expect to be resurrected,' Lord Shark told him firmly. 'I intend to make that one of the terms of this duel. If killed – then it is final.'

'You are serious, sir?' The Duke of Queens was surprised.

'It is my nature to be ever serious, Duke of Queens.'

The Duke of Queens considered for a moment, stroking his beard. 'You would be annoyed with me if I did see to it that you were resurrected?'

'I would consider it extremely bad-mannered, sir.'

The duke was conscious of his reputation for vulgarity. 'Then, of course, I must agree.'

'You may still withdraw.'

'No. I stand by your terms, Lord Shark. Absolutely.'

'You will accept the same terms for yourself, if I kill you?'

'Oh!'

'You will accept the same terms, sir?'

'To remain dead?'

Lord Shark was silent.

Then the Duke of Queens laughed. 'Why not? Think of the

entertainment it will provide for our friends!'

'Your friends,' said Lord Shark the Unknown pointedly.

'Yes. It will give the duel an authentic flavour. And there would be no question that I would not have created a genuine stir, eh? Though, of course, I would not be in a position to enjoy my success.'

'I gather, then,' said Lord Shark in a peculiar voice, 'that you are willing to die for the sake of this frivolity?'

'I am, sir. Though "frivolity" is hardly the word. It is, at very least, an enjoyable jest – at best an act of original artistry. And that, I confide to you, Lord Shark, is what it has always been my ambition to achieve.'

'Then we are agreed. There is no more to say. Would you choose a sword?'

'I'll leave that to you, sir, for I respect your judgement better than my own. If I might continue to borrow your automaton until the appointed time . . .?'

'Of course.'

'Until then.' The Duke of Queens bowed. 'O'Dwyer?'

The trooper looked up from a gun he had partially dismantled. 'Duke?'

'We can leave now.'

Reluctantly, but with expert swiftness, Trooper O'Dwyer re-assembled the weapon, cheerfully saluted Lord Shark and, as he left, said, 'I'd like to come back and have another look at these sometime.'

Lord Shark ignored him. Trooper O'Dwyer shrugged and followed the Duke of Queens from the room.

A little later, watching the great kite float into the distance, Lord Shark tried to debate with himself the mysteries of the temperament the Duke of Queens had revealed, but an answer was beyond him; he merely found himself confirmed in his opinion of the stupidity of the whole cosmos. It would do no great harm, he thought, to extinguish one small manifestation of that stupidity: the Duke of Queens certainly embodied everything Lord Shark most loathed about his world. And, if he himself, instead, were slain, then that would be an even greater consolation – though he believed the likelihood was remote.

8

Matters of Honour

Not long after the exchange between the Duke of Queens and Lord Shark, Trooper Kevin O'Dwyer, becoming conscious of his own lack of exercise, waddled out for a stroll in the sweet-smelling forest which lay to the west of the duke's palace.

Trooper O'Dwyer was concerned for the duke's safety. It had only just dawned on him what the stakes were to be. He took a kindly and patronizing interest in the well-being of the Duke of Queens, regarding his host with the affection one might feel towards a large, stupid Labrador, an amiable Labrador. This was perhaps a naïve view of the duke's character, but it suited the good-natured O'Dwyer to maintain it. Thus, he mulled the problem over as he sat down under a gigantic daffodil and rested a pair of legs which had become unused to walking.

The scent of the monstrous flowers was very heady and it made the already weary Trooper O'Dwyer rather drowsy, so that he had not accomplished very much thinking before he began to nod off, and would have fallen into a deep sleep had he not been tapped smartly on the shoulder. He opened his eyes with a grunt and looked into the gaunt features of his old comrade Trooper Gan Hok. With a gesture, Trooper Gan Hok cautioned O'Dwyer to silence, whispering, 'Is anyone else with you?'

'Only you.' Trooper O'Dwyer was pleased with his wit. He grinned.

'This is serious,' said Trooper Gan Hok, wriggling the rest of his thin body from the undergrowth. 'We've been trying to contact you for days. We're busting off. Sergeant Martinez sent me to find you. Didn't you know we'd escaped?'

'I heard you'd disappeared, but I didn't think much of it. Has something come up?'

'Nothing special, only we decided it was our duty to try to get back. Sergeant Martinez reckons that we're as good as deserters.'

'I thought we were as good as POWs?' said O'Dwyer reasonably. 'We can't get back. Only experienced time travellers can even *attempt* it. We've been told.'

'Sergeant Martinez doesn't believe 'em.'

'Well,' said O'Dwyer, 'I do. Don't you?'

'That's not the point, trooper,' said Gan Hok primly. 'Anyway, it's time to rejoin your squad. I've come to take you back to our HQ. We've got a foxhole on the other side of this jungle, but time's running out, and so are our supplies. We can't work the power rings. We need food and we need weapons before we can put the rest of the sergeant's plan into operation.'

Through one of the gaps in his shirt Trooper O'Dwyer scratched his stomach. 'It sounds crazy. What's your opinion? Is Martinez in his right mind?'

'He's in command. That's all we have to know.'

Before he had become a guest of the Duke of Queens, Trooper O'Dwyer would have accepted this logic, but now he was not sure he found it palatable. 'Tell the sergeant I've decided to stay. Okay?'

'That *is* desertion. Look at you – you've been corrupted by the enemy!'

'They're not the enemy, they're our descendants.'

'And they wouldn't exist today if we hadn't done our duty and wiped out the Vultures – that's assuming what they say is true.' Gan Hok's voice took on the hysterical tones of the very hungry. 'If you don't come, you'll be treated as a deserter.' Meaningly, Trooper Gan Hok fingered the knife at his belt.

O'Dwyer considered his position and then replied. 'Okay, I'll come with you. There isn't any chance of this plan working anyhow.'

'The sergeant's got it figured, O'Dwyer. There's a good chance.'

With a sigh, Trooper O'Dwyer climbed to his feet and lumbered after Trooper Gan Hok as he moved with nervous stealth back into the forest.

'But dearest of dukes, you cannot take such terms seriously!' The Iron Orchid's skin flickered through an entire spectrum of colour as, in agitation, she paced the floor of the 'gym'.

Embarrassed, he fingered the cloak of the dormant duelling automaton. 'I have agreed,' he said quietly. 'I thought you would find it amusing – you, in particular, my petalled pride.'

'I believe,' she replied, 'that I feel sad.'

'You must tell Werther. He will be curious. It is the emotion he most yearns to experience.'

'I would miss your company so much if Lord Shark kills you. And kill you he will, I am sure.'

'Nonsense. I am the match for his automaton, am I not?'

'Who knows how Lord Shark programmed the beast? He could be deceiving you.'

'Why should he? Like you, he tried to dissuade me from the duel.'

'It might be a trick.'

'Lord Shark is incapable of trickery. It is not in his nature to be devious.'

'What do you know of his nature? What do any of us know?'

'True. But I have my instincts.'

The Iron Orchid had a low opinion of those.

'If you wait,' he said consolingly, 'you will observe my skill. The automaton is programmed to respond to certain verbal commands. I intend, now, to allow it to try to wound me.' He turned, presented his sword at the ready and said to the automaton, 'We fight to wound.' Immediately the mechanical duellist prepared itself, balancing on the balls of its feet in readiness for the duke's attack.

'Forgive me,' said the Iron Orchid coldly, 'if I do not watch. Farewell, Duke of Queens.'

He was baffled by her manner. 'Goodbye, lovely Iron Orchid.' His sword touched the automaton's; the automaton feinted; the duke parried. The Iron Orchid fled from the hall.

Righting herself at the exit, she entered her little air car, the bird of paradise, and instructed it to carry her as rapidly as possible to the house of Lord Shark the Unknown. The car obeyed, flying over many partially built and partially destroyed scenes, several of them the duke's own, of mountains, luscious sunrises, cities, landscapes of all descriptions, until the barren plain came in sight and beyond it the brown mountains, under the shadow of which lay Lord Shark's featureless dwelling.

The bird of paradise descended completely to the ground, its scintillating feathers brushing the dust; out of it climbed the Iron Orchid, walking determinedly to the door and knocking upon it.

A masked figure opened it immediately.

'Lord Shark, I have come to beg –'

'I am not Lord Shark,' said the figure in Lord Shark's voice. 'I am his servant. My master is in his duelling room. Is your business important?'

'It is.'

'Then I shall inform him of your presence.' The machine closed the door.

Impatient and astonished, for she had had no real experience of such behaviour, the Iron Orchid waited until, in a while, the door was opened again.

'Lord Shark will receive you, the automaton told her. 'Follow me.'

She followed, remarking to herself on the unaesthetic symmetry of the interior. She was shown into a room furnished with a chair, a bench and a variety of ugly devices which she took to be crude machines. On one side of her stood Lord Shark the Unknown, a sword still in his gloved hand.

'You are the Iron Orchid?'

'You remember that we met when you challenged my friend the Duke of Queens?'

'I remember. But I did not challenge him. He asked how he might make amends for destroying the lichen I had been growing. He built his continent upon it.'

'His Afrique.'

'I do not know what he called it. I suggested a duel, because I wished to test my abilities against those of another mortal. I regretted this suggestion when I understood the light in which the duke accepted it.'

'Then you would rather not continue with it?'

'It does not please me, madam, to be a clown, to be put to use for the entertainment of those foolish and capricious individuals you call your friends!'

'I do not understand you.'

'Doubtless you do not.'

'I regret, however, that you are displeased.'

'Why should you regret that?' He seemed genuinely puzzled. 'I regret only that my privacy has been disturbed. You are the *third* to visit me.'

'You have only to refuse to fight and you are saved from enduring that which disturbs you.'

The shark-mask looked away from her. 'I must kill your Duke of Queens, as an example to the rest of you — as an example of the futility of all existence, particularly yours. If he should kill me, then I am satisfied, also. There is a question of honour involved.'

'Honour? What is that?'

'Your ignorance confirms my point.'

'So you intend to pursue this silly adventure to the bitter end?'

'Call it what you like.'

'The duke's motives are not yours.'

'His motives do not interest me.'

'The duke loves life. You hate it.'

'Then he can withdraw.'

'But you will not?'

'You have presented no arguments to convince me that I should.'

'But he seeks only to please his fellows. He agreed to the duel because he hoped it would please you.'

'Then he deserves death.'

'You are unkind, Lord Shark.'

'I am a man of intellect, madam, whose misfortune it is to find himself alone in an irrational universe. I do you all the credit of having the ability to see what I see, but I despise you for your unwillingness to accept the truth.'

'You see only one form of truth.'

'There *is* only one form of truth.' His grey shoulders shrugged. 'I see, too, that your reasons for visiting me were whimsical, after all. I would be grateful if you would leave.'

As she turned to go, something mechanical screamed from the desk. She paused. With a murmur of displeasure, Lord Shark the Unknown hurried to his consoles.

'This is intolerable!' He stared into a screen. 'A horde has arrived! When you leave, please ask them to go away.'

She craned her neck to look at the screen. 'Why!' she exclaimed. 'It is My Lady Charlotina's missing time travellers. What could their reason be, Lord Shark, for visiting you?'

9

Questions of Power

Brannart Morphail was not in a good temper. The scientist gesticulated at My Lady Charlotina, who had come to see him in his laboratories, which were attached to her own apartments at Below the Lake. 'Another time machine? Why should I waste one? I have so few left!'

'Surely you have one which you like less than the others?' she begged.

'Big enough to take twenty-five men? It is impossible!'

'But they are so destructive!'

'What serious harm can they do if their demands are simply ignored?'

'The Iron Orchid and Lord Shark are their prisoners. They have all those weapons of Lord Shark's. They have already destroyed the mountains in a most dramatic way.'

'I enjoyed the spectacle.'

'So did I, dear Brannart.'

'And if they destroy the Iron Orchid and Lord Shark, we can easily resurrect them again.'

'They intend to subject them to *pain*, Brannart, and I gather that pain is enjoyable only up to a point. Please agree.'

'The responsibility for those creatures was yours, My Lady Charlotina. You should not have let them wander about willy-nilly. Now look what has happened. They have invaded Lord Shark's home, captured both Lord Shark and the Iron Orchid (what on earth was she doing there?), seized those silly guns, and are now demanding a time machine in which to return to their own age. I have spoken to them already about the Morphail Effect, but they choose not to believe me.' He limped away from her. 'They shall not have a time machine.'

'Besides,' said My Lady Charlotina, 'Lord Shark is due, very shortly, to fight his duel with the Duke of Queens. We have all been looking forward to it so much. Think of the disappointment. I know you wanted to watch.'

His hump twitched. 'That's a better reason, I'd agree.' He frowned. 'There might be a solution.'

'Tell me what it is, most sagacious of scientists!'

Sergeant Martinez glared at Lord Shark and the Iron Orchid who, bound firmly, lay propped in a corner of the room. He and his men were armed with the pick of the weapons and they looked much more confident than when they had pushed past the Iron Orchid as she opened the door of Lord Shark's house.

'We don't like to do this,' said Sergeant Martinez, 'but we're running out of patience. Your friend Lady Charlotina is going to get your ear if someone doesn't deliver that time ship soon.'

'Why should she need it?' The Iron Orchid was enjoying herself. Her sense of boredom had lifted completely and she felt that if they continued to be prisoners for a little longer, the duel would have to be forgotten about. She wished, however, that Sergeant Martinez had not taken *all* her power rings from her fingers.

'Tell your robot to get us some more grub,' ordered the sergeant, digging Lord Shark in the ribs with the toe of his boot. Lord Shark complied. He seemed unmoved by what was happening; it rather confirmed his general view of an unreasonable and hostile universe. He felt vindicated.

A screen came to life. Trooper O'Dwyer, looking miserable, tuned the image with the manual control he had been playing with. 'It's the old crippled guy,' he informed his sergeant.

Sergeant Martinez said importantly, 'I'll take over, trooper. Hi,' he addressed Brannart Morphail. 'Have you agreed to give us a ship?'

'One is on its way to you.'

Sergeant Martinez looked pleased with himself. 'Okay. We get the ship and you get the hostages back.'

The Iron Orchid's heart sank. 'Do not give in to them, Brannart!' she cried. 'Let them do their worst!'

'I must warn you,' said Brannart Morphail, 'that it will do you little good. Time refuses paradox. You will not be able to return to your own age – or, at least, not for long. You would do better to forget this whole ridiculous venture . . .'

Sergeant Martinez switched him off.

'See?' he said to Trooper O'Dwyer. 'I told you it would work. Like a dream.'

'They must be treating it as a game,' said O'Dwyer. 'They've got nothing to fear. By using those power rings they could wipe us out in a second.'

Sergeant Martinez looked at the rings he had managed to get onto his little finger. 'I can't figure out why they don't work for me.'

'They are, in essence, biological,' said the Iron Orchid. 'They work only for the individual who owns them, translating his desires much as a hand does — without conscious thought.'

'Well, we'll see about that. What about the robots, will they obey anybody?'

'If so programmed,' said Lord Shark.

'Okay' (of the automaton which had re-entered with a tray of food), 'tell that one to obey me.'

Lord Shark instructed the robot accordingly. 'You will obey the soldiers,' he said.

'There's some kind of vehicle arrived outside.' O'Dwyer looked up from the screen. He addressed Lord Shark. 'How come this equipment looks like it's out of a museum?'

'My companion,' explained Lord Shark, 'he built it.'

'Funny-looking thing. More like a space ship than a time ship.' Trooper Denereaz stared at the image: a long, tubular construction, tapering at both ends, hovering just above the ground.

'It's going to be good to get back amongst the cold, clean stars,' said Sergeant Martinez sentimentally, 'where the only things a man's got to trust is himself and a few buddies, and he knows he's fighting for something important. Maybe you people don't understand that. Maybe there's no need for you *to* understand. But it's because there are men like us, prepared to go out there and get their guts shot out of them in order to keep the universe a safe place to live in, that the rest of you sleep well in your beds at night, dreaming your nice, comfortable dreams . . .'

'Hadn't we better get going, Sergeant?' asked Trooper O'Dwyer. 'If we're going.'

'It could be a trap,' said Sergeant Martinez grimly, 'so we'd better go out in groups of five. First five occupies the ship,

84

checks for occupants, booby traps and so on, then signals to the next five, until we're all out. Trooper O'Dwyer, keep a watch on that screen until you see we're all aboard and nobody's shooting at us, then follow – oh, and bring that robot with you. We can use him.'

'Yes, sir.'

'And if there's any smell of a set-up, kill the hostages.'

'Yes, sir,' said Trooper O'Dwyer sceptically.

A bell began to ring.

'What does that mean?' demanded Sergeant Martinez.

'It means that I shall be able to keep my appointment with the Duke of Queens,' Lord Shark told him.

10

The Duel

The remains of the Rocky Mountains were still smouldering in the background as, from a safe distance, the crowd watched the ship containing the troopers rise into the air. Behind the crowd, feeling a little upset by the lack of attention, the Duke of Queens stood, sword in hand, awaiting his antagonist. The Duke was early. He had no interest in these other events, which he regarded as an unwelcome interruption, threatening to diffuse the drama of his duel with Lord Shark the Unknown; he thought that Sergeant Martinez and his men had behaved rather badly. Certainly, at any other time, he would have been as diverted by their actions as anyone, but, as it was, they had confused the presentation and robbed it of some of its tension.

At last the duke noticed that heads were beginning to turn in his direction, and he heard someone call:

'The Iron Orchid – Lord Shark – they emerge! They are saved!'

There came a chorus of self-conscious exultation.

The ranks parted; now the Iron Orchid, her slender fingers bare of rings, walked with a self-satisfied air beside Lord Shark the Unknown, stiff, sworded and stern.

They confronted each other over a narrow fissure in the earth. The Duke of Queens bowed. Lord Shark the Unknown, after a second's hestitation, bowed.

The Iron Orchid seemed reconciled. She took a step back. 'May the best man win!' she said.

'My lord.' The duke presented his sword. 'To the death!'

Silently, Lord Shark the Unknown replied to the courtesy.

'En tou rage, mon coeur!' The Duke of Queens adopted the traditional stance, balancing on the balls of his feet, his body poised, one hand upon his hip, ready for the lunge. Lord Shark's body fell into the same position as precisely as that of one of his own automata.

The crowd moved forward, but kept its distance.

Lord Shark lunged. The Duke of Queens parried, at the same time leaning back to avoid the point of the blade. Lord Shark continued his forward movement, crossing the fissure, lunged again, was parried again. This time the Duke of Queens lunged and was parried. For a short while it was possible for the spectators to follow the stylized movements of the duellists, but gradually, as the combatants familiarized themselves with each other's method of fighting, the speed increased, until it was often impossible to see the thin blades, save for a gleaming blur as they met, parted, and met again.

Back and forth across the dry, dancing dust of that plain the two men moved, the duke's handsome, heavy features registering every escape, every minor victory, while the immobile mask of Lord Shark the Unknown gave no indication of how that strange, bleak recluse felt when his shoulder was grazed by the duke's blade, or when he came within a fraction of an inch of skewering his opponent's rapidly beating heart.

At first some of the crowd would applaud a near-miss or gasp as one of the duellists turned his body aside from a lunge which seemed unerring; soon, however, they fell silent, realizing that they must feel some of the tension the ancients had felt when they attended such games.

The duke, refusing in homage to those same ancestors to allow himself any energy boosts, understood that he was tiring much more than he had tired during his tuition, but he understood, also, that Lord Shark the Unknown had patterned his automata entirely after himself, for Lord Shark fought in exactly the same manner as had his mechanical servant, and this made the Duke of Queens more hopeful. Dimly he became aware of the implications of his bargain with Lord Shark: to die and never to be resurrected, to forego the rich enjoyment of life, to become unconscious forever. His attention wavered as these thoughts crept into his mind, he parried a lunge a little too late. He felt the sharp steel slide into his body. He knew pain. He gasped. Lord Shark the Unknown stepped back as the Duke of Queens staggered.

Lord Shark was expectant, and the duke realized that he had forgotten to acknowledge the wound.

'Tou jours gai, mon coeur!' He wondered if he were dying,

but no, the pain faded and became an unpleasant ache. He was still able to continue. He drew himself upright, conscious of the Iron Orchid's high-pitched voice in the background.

'En tou rage!' he warned, and lunged before he had properly regained his balance, falling sideways against Lord Shark's sword, but able to step back in time, recall his training and position himself properly so that when Lord Shark lunged again, he parried the stroke, returned it, parried again and returned again.

The Duke of Queens wondered at the temperature changes in his body. He had felt uncomfortably warm and now he felt a chill throughout, from head to toe, with only his wound glowing hot, but no longer very painful.

And Lord Shark the Unknown pushed past the duke's defence and the point of his sword gouged flesh from the duke's left arm, just below the shoulder.

'Oh!' cried the duke, and then, 'Tou jours gai!'

In grim silence, Lord Shark the Unknown gave him a few moments in which to recover.

The Duke of Queens was surprised at his own reaction now, for he quickly resumed his stance, coolly gave his warning, and found that a new emotion directed him. He believed that the emotion must be 'fear'.

And his lunges became more precise, his parries swifter, firmer, so that Lord Shark the Unknown lost balance time after time and was hard-pressed to regain it. It seemed to some of those who watched that Lord Shark was nonplussed by this new, cold attack. He began to lose ground, backing further and further away under the momentum of the duke's new-found energy.

And then the Duke of Queens, unthinking, merely a duellist, thrust once and struck Lord Shark the Unknown in the heart.

Although he must have been quite dead, Lord Shark stood erect for a little while, gradually lowering his sword and then falling, as stiff in death as he had been in life, onto the hard earth; his blood flooded from him, giving nourishment to the dust.

The Duke of Queens was astonished by what he had accomplished. Even as the Iron Orchid and his other friends came slowly towards him, he found that he was shaking.

The duke dropped his blade. His natural reaction, at this time, would have made immediate arrangements for Lord Shark's resurrection, but Lord Shark had been firm, remorseless in his affirmation that if death came to him he must remain dead through the rest of Time. The duke wondered at the thoughts and feelings, all unfamiliar, which filled him.

He could not understand why the Iron Orchid smiled and kissed him and congratulated him, why My Lady Charlotina babbled of the excitement he had provided, why Bishop Castle and his old acquaintance Captain Oliphaunt clapped him on the back and reminded him of his wounds.

'You are a Hero, darling duke!' cried the Everlasting Concubine. 'You must let me nurse you back to health!'

'A fine display, glamorous Lord of Queens!' heartily praised the captain. 'Not since "Cannibals" has there been such entertainment!'

'Indeed, the fashion begins already! Look!' Bishop Castle displayed a long and jewelled blade.

The Duke of Queens groaned and fell to his knees. 'I have killed Lord Shark,' he said. A tear appeared on his cheek.

In the reproduction of what had been either a space or air ship, part of the collection long since abandoned by the Duke of Queens, Sergeant Martinez and his men peered through portholes at the distant ground. The ship had ceased to rise but now was borne by the currents of the wind. No response came from the engines; propellors did not turn, rockets did not fire – even the little sails rigged along the upper hull would not unfurl when Sergeant Martinez sent a reluctant Denereaz out to climb the ladder which clung to the surface of what was either a gas bag or a fuel tank.

'We have been suckered,' announced Sergeant Martinez, after some thought. 'This is not a time machine.'

'Not so far,' agreed Trooper Gan Hok, helping himself to exotic food paste from a cabinet. The ship was well stocked with provisions, with alcohol and dope.

'We could be up here forever,' said Sergeant Martinez.

'Well, for a good while,' agreed Trooper Smith. 'After all, Sarge, what goes up must, eventually, come down – if we're still in this planet's gravity field, that is. Which we are.'

Only Trooper Keven O'Dwyer appeared to have accepted the situation with equanimity. He lay on a divan of golden plush while the stolen automaton brought him the finest food from the cabinets.

'And what I'd like to know, O'Dwyer, is why that damn robot'll only respond to your commands,' said Sergeant Martinez darkly.

'Maybe it respects me, Sarge?'

Without much conviction, Sergeant Martinez said: 'You ought to be disciplined for insubordination, O'Dwyer. You seem to be enjoying all this.'

'We ought to make the best of it, that's all,' said O'Dwyer. 'Do you think there's any way of getting in touch with the surface? We could ask them to send up some girls.'

'Be careful, O'Dwyer.' Sergeant Martinez lay back on his own couch and closed his eyes, taking a strong pull on his cigar. 'That sounds like fraternization to me. Don't forget that those people have to be regarded as alien belligerents.'

'Sorry, Sarge. Robot, bring me another drink of that green stuff, will you?'

The automaton seemed to hesitate.

'Hurry it up,' said O'Dwyer.

Returning with the drink, the automaton handed it to O'Dwyer and then hissed through its mask. 'What purpose is there any longer to this deception, O'Dwyer?'

O'Dwyer rose and took the robot by the arm, leading it from the main passenger lounge into the control chamber, now unoccupied. 'You must realize, Lord Shark, that if they realize I made a mistake and brought you up here instead of the robot, they'll use you as a bargaining counter.'

'Should I care?'

'That's for you to decide.'

'Your logic in substituting one of my automata for me and sending it out with the Iron Orchid to fight the Duke of Queens is still a mystery to me.'

'Well, it's pretty simple to explain, Sharko. The duke was used to fighting robots – so I gave him a sporting chance. Also, when it's discovered it's a robot, and he's dead, they'll be able to bring him back to life – 'cause the rules will have been broken. Get it? If the robot's been put out of action, so what?

90

Yeah?'

'Why should you have bothered to interfere?'

'I like the guy. I didn't want to see him killed. Besides, it was a favour to the Iron Orchid, too – and she looks like a lady who likes to return a favour. We worked it out between us.'

'I heard you. Releasing me from my bonds when it was too late for me to return, then suggesting to your comrades that I was an automaton. Well, I shall tell them that you have deceived them.'

'Go ahead. I'll deny it.'

Lord Shark the Unknown walked to the porthole, studying the peculiar purple clouds which someone had created in this part of the sky.

'All my life I have been unable to see the point of human activity,' he said. 'I have found every experience further proof of the foolishness of my fellows, of the absolute uselessness of existence. I thought that no expression of that stupidity could bewilder me again. Now I must admit that my assumptions, my opinions, my most profound beliefs seem to dissipate and leave me as confused as I was when I first came into this tired and decadent universe. You are an alien here yourself. Why should you help the Duke of Queens?'

'I told you. I like him. He doesn't know when to come in out of the rain. I fixed things so nobody lost. Is that bad?'

'You did all that, including risking the disapproval of your fellows, out of an emotion of – what – affection? – for that buffoon?'

'Call it enlightened self-interest. The fact is that the whole thing's de-fused. I didn't think we'd get off this planet, or out of this age, and I'm glad we haven't. I like it here. But Sergeant Martinez had to make the attempt, and I had to go along with him, to keep him happy. Don't worry, we'll soon be on-planet again.'

He gave Lord Shark the Unknown a friendly slap on the back. 'All honour satisfied, eh?'

And Lord Shark laughed.

ANCIENT SHADOWS

> *In ancient shadows and twilights*
> *Where childhood had stray'd,*
> *The world's great sorrows were born*
> *And its heroes were made.*
> *In the lost boyhood of Judas*
> *Christ was betray'd.*
>
> G. W. Russell ('Æ')
> 'Germinal'

I

A Stranger to the End of Time

Upon the shore of a glowing chemical lake, peering through a visor of clouded Perspex, a stranger stood, her dark features showing profound awe and some disapproval, while behind her there rustled and gibbered a city, half-organic in its decadence, palpitating with obscure colours, poisonous and powerful. And overhead, in the sallow sky, a small old sun spread withered light, parsimonious heat, across the planet's dissolute topography.

'Thus it ends,' murmured the stranger. She added, a little self-consciously, 'What pathetic monuments to mankind's Senility!'

As if for reassurance, she pressed a gloved hand to the surface of her time machine, which was unadorned and box-like, smooth and spare, according to the fashions of her own age. Lifting apparently of its own volition, a lid at the top opened and a little freckled head emerged. With a frown she gestured her companion back, but then, changing her mind, she helped the child, which was clad in a small suit and helmet matching her own, from the hatch.

'Witness this shabby finale, my son. Could I begrudge it you?'

Guilelessly the child said, 'It is awfully pretty, mama.'

95

It was not her way to contradict a child's judgement. She shrugged. 'I am fulfilled, I suppose, and unsurprised, though I had hoped, well, for Hope.' From the confusion of her private feelings she fled back to practicality. 'Your father will be anxious. If we return now we can at least report to the committee tonight. And report success!' A proud glove fell upon her son's shoulder. 'We have travelled the limit of the machine's capacity! Here, Time has ceased to exist. The instruments say so, and their accuracy is unquestionable.' Her eye was caught by a shift of colour as the outline of one building appeared to merge with another, separate, and re-form. 'I had imagined it bleaker, true.'

The city coughed, like giant in slumber, and was silent for a while.

The boy made to remove his helmet. She stopped him. 'The atmosphere! Noxious, Snuffles, without doubt. One breath could kill.'

It seemed for a moment that he would argue with her opinion. Eye met grey-blue eye; jaws set; he sighed, lowering his head and offering the side of the machine a petulant kick. From the festering city, a chuckle, causing the boy to whirl, defensive and astonished. A self-deprecating grin, the lips gleaming at the touch of the dampening tongue; a small gauntlet reaching for the large one. An indrawn breath.

'You are probably correct, mama, in your assessment.'

She helped him back into their vessel, glanced once, broodingly, at the shimmering city, at the pulsing lake, then followed her son through the hatch until she stood again at her controls in the machine's green-lit and dim interior.

As she worked the dials and levers, she was studied by her son. Her curly brown hair was cut short at the nape, her up-curving lips gave an impression of amiability denied by the sobriety and intensity of her large, almond-shaped brown eyes. Her hands were small, well-formed, and, to a person from the 20th century, her body would have seemed slight, in proportion with those hands (though she was thought tall and shapely by her own folk). Moving efficiently, but with little instinctive feel for her many instruments, considering each action rapidly and intelligently and carrying it through in the manner of one who has learned a lesson thoroughly but unenthusiastically, she adjusted settings and figures. Her son seated himself in his padded chair, tucked beneath the main console at which his mother stood, and used his own small computer to make the simpler calculations required by her for the re-programming of the machine so that it could return to the exact place and almost the exact time of its departure.

When she had finished, she withdrew a pace or two from the controls, appraised them and was satisfied. 'We are ready, Snuffles, to begin the journey home. Strap in, please.'

He was already safely buckled. She crossed to the chair facing him, arranged her own harness, spread gloved fingers across the seven buttons set into the arm of the chair, and pressed four of them in sequence. The green light danced across her visor and through it to her face as she smiled encouragement to her son. She betrayed no nervousness; her body and her features were mastered absolutely. It was left to her child to display some anxiety, the upper teeth caressing the lower lip, the eyes darting from mother to those dials visible to him, one hand tugging a trifle at a section of the webbing holding his body to the chair. The machine quivered and, barely audible, it hissed. The sound was unfamiliar. The boy's brows drew closer together. The green light became a faint pink. The machine signalled its perplexity. It had not moved a moment or a centimetre. There was no reason for this; all functions were in perfect operation.

Permitting herself no sign of a reaction, she re-set the buttons. The green light returned. She repeated the preliminary code, whereupon the light grew a deeper pink and two blue lamps began to blink. She returned all functions to standby, pulled the harness from her body, rose to her feet and began to make her calculations from the beginning. Her original accuracy was confirmed. She went back to her seat, fastened her webbing, pressed the four buttons in sequence. And for the third time the machine stated its inability to carry out the basic return procedure.

'Is the time machine broken, mama?'

'Impossible.'

'Then someone is preventing us from leaving.'

'The least welcome but the likeliest suggestion. We were unwise not to bring protection.'

'The baboons do not travel well.'

'It is our misfortune. But we had not expected any life at all at the End of Time.' She fingered her ear. 'We shall have to rule out metaphysical interference.'

'Of course.' He had been brought up by the highest standards. There were some things which were not mentioned, nor, better yet, considered, by the polite society of his day. And Snuffles was an aristocrat of boys.

She consulted the chronometer. 'We shall remain inside the machine and make regular attempts to return at every hour out of twenty hours. If by then we have failed, we shall consider another plan.'

'You are not frightened, mama?'

'Mystified, merely.'

Patiently, they settled down to let the first hour pass.

2

An Exploratory Expedition

Hand in hand and cautiously they set their feet upon a pathway neither liquid nor adamantine, but apparently of a dense, purple gas which yielded only slightly as they stepped along it, passing between forms which could have been the remains either of buildings or of beasts.

'Oh, mama!' The eyes of the boy were bright with unusual excitement. 'Shall we find monsters?'

'I doubt if it is life, in any true sense, that we witness here, Snuffles. There is only a moral. A lesson for you – and for myself.'

Streamers of pale red wound themselves around the whispering towers, like pennants about their poles. Gasping, he pointed, but she refused the sight more than a brief glance. 'Sensation, only,' she said. 'The appeal to the infantile imagination is obvious – the part of every adult that should properly be suppressed and which should not be encouraged too much in children.'

Blue winds blew and the buildings bent before them, crouching and changing shape, grumbling as they passed. Clusters of fragments, bloody marble, yellow-veined granite, lilac-coloured slate, frosted limestone, gathered like insects in the air; fires blazed and growled, and then where the pathway forked they saw human figures and stopped, watching.

It was an arrangement of gallants, all extravagant cloaks and jutted scabbards. It stuck legs and elbows at brave angles so the world should know its excellence and its self-contained beauty, so that the collective bow, upon the passing of a lady's carriage, should be accomplished with the precision of effect, swords raised, like so many tails, behind, heads bent low enough for doffed plumes to trail, and be soiled, upon the pavings.

Calling, she approached the group, but it had vanished, background, carriages and all, before she had taken three paces, to be replaced by exotic palms which forever linked and twisted their leaves and leaned one towards the other, as if in a love dance. She hesitated, thinking that she saw beyond the trees a plaza where stood a familiar old man, her father, but it was a statue, and then it was a pillar, then a fountain, and through the rainbow waters she saw three or four faces which she recognized, fellow children, known before her election to adult status, smiling at her, memories of an innocence she sometimes caught herself yearning for; a voice spoke, seemingly into her ear (she felt the breath, surely!): 'The Armatuce shall be Renowned through you, Dafnish . . .' Turning, clutching her son's hand, she discovered only four stately birds walking on broad, careful feet into a shaft of light which absorbed them. Elsewhere, voices sang in strange, delicate languages, of sadness, love, joy and death. A cry of pain. The tinkling of bells and lightly brushed harp strings. A groan and deep-throated laughter.

'Dreams,' said the boy. 'Like dreams, mama. It is so wonderful.'

'Treachery,' she murmured. 'We are misled.' But she would not panic.

Once or twice more, in the next few moments, buildings shaped themselves into well-known scenes from her recent past. In the shifting light and the gas it was as if all that had ever existed existed again for a brief while.

She thought: 'If Time has ceased to be, then Space, too, becomes extinct − is all this simply illusion − a memory of a world? Do we walk a void, in reality? We must consider that a likelihood.'

She said to Snuffles: 'We had best return to our ship.'

A choir gave voice in the surrounding air, and the city swayed to the rhythm. A young man sang in a language she knew:

> Ten times thou saw'st the fleet fly by:
> The skies illum'd in shining jet
> And gold, and lapis lazuli.
> How clear above the engines' cry
> Thy voice of sweet bewilderment!
> (Remember, Nalorna, remember the Night).

Then, wistfully, the voice of an older woman:

> *'Could I but know such ecstasy again,*
> *When all those many heroes of the air*
> *Knel't down as one and call'd me fair,*
> *Then I would judge Nalorna more than bless'd!*
> *Immortal Lords immortal, too, made me!*
> *(I am Nalorna, whom the flying godlings loved).'*

And she paused to listen, against the nagging foreboding at the back of her brain, while an old man sang:

> *'Ah, Nalorna, so many that are dead loved thee!*
> *Slain like wingèd game that falls beneath the hunter's shot.*
> *First they rose up, and then with limbs outspread, they*
>   *drop'd;*
> *Through fiery Day they plung'd, their bodies bright;*
> *Stain'd bloody scarlet in the sun's sweet mourning light.*
> *(But Remember, Nalorna, remember only the Night).'*

A little fainter, the young man's voice came again:

> *Ten times, Nalorna, did the fleet sweep by!*
> *Ten hands saluted thee, ten mouths*
> *Ten garlands kiss't; ten silent sighs*
> *Sailed down to thee. And then, in pride,*
> *Thou rais'd soft arms and pointed South.*
> *(Oh, Remember, Nalorna, only the Night).*

Telling herself that her interest was analytical, she bent her head to hear more, but though the singing continued, very faintly, the language had changed and was no longer in a tongue she could comprehend.

'Oh, mama!' Snuffles glanced about him, as if seeking the source of the singing. 'They tell of a great air battle. Is it that which destroyed the folk of this city?'

'. . . *without which the third level is next to useless* . . .' said an entirely different voice in a matter-of-fact tone.

Rapidly, she shook her head, to clear it of the foolishness intimidating her habitual self-control. 'I doubt it, Snuffles. If you would seek a conqueror, then Self-Indulgence is the villain who held those last inhabitants in sway. Every sight we see confirms that fact. Oh, and Queen Sentimentality ruled here, too. The song is her testament – there were doubtless thousands

101

of similar examples – books, plays, tapes – entertainments of every sort. The city reeks of uncontrolled emotionalism. What used to be called Art.'

'But we have Art, mama, at home.'

'Purified – made functional. We have our machine-makers, our builders, our landscapers, our planners, our phrasemakers. Sophisticated and specific, our Art. This – all this – is coarse. Random fancies have been indulged, potential has been wasted . . .'

'You do not find it in any way attractive?'

'Of course not! My sensibility has long since been mastered. The intellects which left this city as their memorial were corrupt, diseased. Death is implicit in every image you see. As a festering wound will sometimes grow fluorescent, foreshadowing the end, so this city shines. I cannot find putrescence pleasing. By its existence this place denies the point of every effort, every self-sacrifice, every martyrdom of the noble Armatuce in the thousand years of its existence!'

'It is wrong of me, therefore, to like it, eh, mama?'

'Such things attract the immature mind. Children once made up the only audience a senile old man could expect for his silly ravings, so I've heard. The parallel is obvious, but your response is forgivable. The child who would attain adult status among the Armatuce must learn to cultivate the mature view, however. In all you see today, my son, you will discover a multitude of examples of the aberrations which led mankind so close, so many times, to destruction.'

'They were evil, then, those people?'

'Unquestionably. Self-Indulgence is the enemy of Self-Interest. Do not the School Slogans say so?'

'And "Sentimentality Threatens Survival",' quoted the pious lad, who could recall perfectly every one of the Thousand Standard Maxims and several score of the Six Hundred Essential Slogans for Existence (which every child should know before he could even consider becoming an adult).

'Exactly.' Her pride in her son helped dispel her qualms, which had been increasing as a herd of monstrous stone reptiles lumbered past in single file while the city chanted, in what was evidently a version of her own tongue, something which seemed to be an involved scientific formula in verse form. But she shiv-

102

ered at the city's next remark:

'... *and Dissipation is Desecration and Dishonours All.*
Self-denial is a Seed which grows in the Sunlight of Purified
something or other ... Oh, well – I'll remember – I'll re-
member – just give me time – Time ... It is not much that a
man can save On the sands of life, in the straits of time, Who
swims in sight of the great third wave That never a swimmer
shall cross or climb. Some waif washed up with the strays and
spars That ebb-tide shows to the shore and the stars; Weed
from the water, grass from a grave, A broken blossom, a ruined
rhyme ... Rapid cooling can produce an effect apparently iden-
tical in every respect, and this leads us to assume that, that,
that ... Ah, yes, He who dies serves, but he who serves shall
live forever ... I've got the rest somewhere. Available on Re-
quisition Disc AAA4. Please use appropriate dialect when con-
sulting this programme. Translations are available from most
centres at reasonable swelgarter am floo-oo chardra werty ...'

'The Maxims, mother! The city quotes the Maxims!'

'It mocks them, you mean! Come, we had best return to our
craft.'

'Is the city mad, mama?'

With an effort she reduced the rate of her heart beat and
increased the width of her stride, his hand firmly held.

'Perhaps,' he said, 'the city was not like this when Man lived
here?'

'I must hope that.'

'Perhaps it pines.'

'The notion is ridiculous,' she said sharply. As she had feared,
the place was beginning to have a deteriorating influence upon
her son. 'Hurry.'

The hulls of three great ships, one in silver filigree, one in
milk-jade, one in woven ebony, suddenly surrounded them, then
faltered, then faded.

She considered an idea that she had not passed through Time
at all, but was being subjected by the Elders of Armatuce to a
surprise Test. She had experienced four such tests since she had
become an adult, but none so rigorous, so complex.

She realized that she had lost the road. The purple pathway
was nowhere to be seen; there was not a landmark which had
retained its form since she had entered the city; the little nig-

103

gardly sun had not, apparently, changed position, so offered no clue. Panic found a chink in the armour of her self-control and poked a teasing finger through.

She stopped dead. They stood together beside a river of boiling, jigging brown and yellow gas which bounded with what seemed a desperate gaiety towards a far-off pit which roared and howled and gulped it down. There was a slim bridge across this river. She placed a foot upon the first smooth step. The bridge was a coquette; it wriggled and giggled but allowed the pressure to remain. Slowly she and the boy ascended until they were crossing. The bridge made a salacious sound. She flushed, but marched on; she caught a trace of a smile upon her boy's lips. And she shivered for a second time. In silhouette, throbbing crimson, the city swayed, its buildings undulating as if they celebrated some primitive mass. Were the buildings actually creatures, then? If so, did they enjoy her discomfort? Did she and her son represent the sacrifice in some dreadful post-human ritual? Had the last of the city's inhabitants perished, mad, as she might soon be mad? Never before had she been possessed by such over-coloured terrors. If she found them a touch attractive, nothing of her conscious mind would admit it. The bridge was crossed, a meadow entered, of gilded grass, knee-high and harsh; the sounds of the city died away and peace, of sorts, replaced them. It was as if she had passed through a storm. In relief she hesitated, still untrusting but ready to accept any pause in order to recover her morale, and found that her hand was rising and falling upon her son's shoulder, patting it. She stopped. She was about to offer an appropriate word of comfort when she noted the gleam in his eye, the parted lips. He looked up at her through his little visor.

'Isn't this jolly, though, mama?'

'J –?' Her mouth refused the word.

'What tales we'll have to tell. Who will believe us?'

'We must say nothing, save to the committee,' she warned. 'This is a secret you must bear for the rest of your boyhood, perhaps the rest of your life. And you must make every effort to – to expunge – to dismiss this – this . . .'

'Twa-la! The time twavellers, doubtless. Even now Bwannaht seeks you out. Gweetings! Gweetings! Gweetings! Welcome, welcome, welcome to the fwutah!'

Looking to her right she drew in such a sharp gasp of oxygen that the respirator on her chest missed a motion and shivered; she could scarce credit the mincing young fantastico pressing a path for himself with his over-ornamented dandy-pole through the grass, brushing at his drooping, elaborate eyebrows, which threatened to blind him, primping his thick, lank locks, patting at his pale, painted cheeks. He regarded her with mild, exaggerated eyes, fingering his pole as he paused.

'Can you undahstand me? I twust the twanslatah is doing its stuff. I'm always twisting the wong wing, y'know. I've seahched evewy one of the thiwty-six points of the compass without a hint of success. You haven't seen them, have you? A couple of lawge hunting buttahflies? So big.' He extended his arms. 'No? Then they've pwobably melted again.' He put index finger to tip of nose. 'They'd be yellah, y'know.'

A collection of little bells at his throat, wrists and knees began to tinkle. He looked suddenly skyward, but he was hopeless.

'Are you real?' asked Snuffles.

'As weal as I'll evah be.'

'And you live in this city?'

'Only ghosts, my deah, live in the cities. I am Sweet Ohb Mace. Cuwwently masculine!' His silks swelled, multicoloured balloons in parody of masculature.

'My name is Dafnish Armatuce. Of the Armatuce,' said she in a strangled tone. 'And this is Snuffles, my son.'

'A child!' The dreadful being's head lifted, like a swan's, and he peered. 'Why, the wohld becomes a kindehgahten! Of couwse, the otheh was actually Mistwess Chwistia. But weah! A gweat pwize foh someone!'

'I do not understand you, sir,' she said.

'Ah, then, it is the twanslatah.' He fingered one of his many rings. 'Shoroloh enafnisoo?'

'I meant that I failed to interpret your meaning,' said Dafnish Armatuce wearily.

Another movement of a ring. 'Is that bettah?'

She inclined her head. She was still less than certain that this was not merely another of the city's phantasms, for all that it addressed them and seemed aware that they had travelled through Time, but she decided, nonetheless, to seek the help of

Sweet Orb Mace.

'We are lost,' she informed him.

'In Djeh?'

'That is the city's name?'

'Oah Shenalowgh, pewhaps. You wish to leave the city, at any wate?'

'If possible.'

'I shall be delighted to help.' Sweet Orb Mace waved his hands, made a further adjustment to a ring, and created something which shone sufficient to blind them for a moment. Of course they recognized the black, spare shape.

'Our time craft!' cried Snuffles.

'My povahty of imagination is wenowned, I feah,' said Sweet Orb Mace blithely. 'It's all I could come up with. Not the owiginal, of coahse, just a wepwoduction. But it will sehve us as an aih cah.'

They entered, all three, to find fantasy within. Gone were the instruments and the muted lights, the padded couches, the simple purity of design, the austere dials and indicators. Instead, caged birds lined the walls, shuffling and twittering, their plumage vulgar beyond imagining; there was a carpet which swamped the legs to the calves, glowing a violent lavender, a score of huge clocks with wagging pendulums, a profusion of brass, gold and dark teak.

Noting her expression, Sweet Orb Mace said humbly: 'I saw only the extewiah. I had hoped the inside would sehve foh the shoht time of ouah flight.'

With a sob, she collapsed into the carpet and sat there with her visor resting upon her gauntlets while Snuffles, insensitive to his mother's mood, waggled youthful fingers and tried to get a macaw to reveal its name to him.

'A mattah of moments!' Sweet Orb Mace assured her. He tapped at the clock with his cane and they were swinging upwards into the sky. 'Do not, I pway you, judge the wohld of the End of Time by yoah impwession of me. I am weckoned the most bohwing being on the planet. Soon you shall meet people much moah intewesting and intelligent than me!'

3

A Social Lunch at the End of Time

'Look, Mama! Look at the food!' The boy shuddered in his passion. 'Oh, look! Look!'

They descended from the reproduction time machine. They were in a long broad meadow of blue and white grass. The city lay several miles away, upon the horizon.

'An illusion, my dear.' Her voice softened in awe. 'Perhaps your desires project . . .'

He began to move forward, tugging at her hand, through the patchwork grass, with Sweet Orb Mace, bemused, behind, to where the long table stood alone, spread with dishes, with meats and fruits, pastes and breads. 'Food, mama! I can almost smell it. Oh, mama!'

He whimpered.

'Could it be real?' he entreated.

'Real or false, we cannot eat.' No amount of self-control could stem the saliva gathering upon her palate. She had never seen so much food at one time. 'We cannot remove our helmets, Snuffles.' For a second, her visor clouded at her breath. 'Oh . . .'

In the distance the city danced to a sudden fanfaronade, as if exulting in their wonderment.

'If you wish to begin . . .' murmured their guide, and he gestured at the food with his cane.

Her next word was moaned: 'Temptation . . .' It became a synonym, on her lips, for fulfillment. To eat – to eat and be replete for the first time in her life! To sit back from that table and note that there was still more to eat – more food than the whole of the Armatuce, if they ate absolutely nothing of their rations for a month, could save between them. 'Oh, such wickedness of over-production!'

'Mother?' Snuffles indicated the centre of the table.

'A pie.'

They stared. As the voices of the Sirens entranced the ancient

Navigators, so were they entranced by flans.

'A vewy simple meal, I thought,' said Sweet Orb Mace, un-comfortable. 'You do not eat so much, in yoah age?'

'We would not,' she replied. 'To consume it, even if we pro-duced it, would be disgusting to us.' Her knees were weak; resistance wavered. Of all the terrors she had anticipated in the future, this was one she could not possibly have visualized, so fearsome was it. She tried to avert her eyes. But she was human. She was only one woman, without the moral strength of the Armatuce to call on. The Armatuce and the world of the Armatuce lay a million or more years in the past. Her will drooped at this knowledge. A tear started.

'You cannot pwoduce it? Some disastah?'

'We could. Now, we could. But we do not. It would be the depths of decadence to do so!' She spoke through clenched teeth.

She and the boy remained transfixed, even when others ar-rived and spoke in reference to them.

'Time travellers. Their uniforms proclaim their calling.'

'They could be from space.'

'They are hungry, it seems. Let them eat. You were speaking of your son, maternal Orchid. This other self, what?'

'He lives through her. He tells me that he lives *for* her, Jagged! Where does he borrow these notions? I fear for his – "health", is it?'

'You mean that you disapprove of his behaviour?'

'I suppose so. Jherek "goes too far".'

'I relish the sound of your words, Iron Orchid. I never thought to hear them here.'

'In Djer?'

'In any part of our world. My theories are confirmed. One small change in the accepted manners of a society and the result is hugely rich.'

'I cannot follow you, allusive lord. Neither shall I try . . . The strangers do not eat! They only stare!'

'The twanslatahs,' cautioned Mace. 'They opahwate even now.'

'I fear our visitors find us rude.'

Dafnish Armatuce felt a soft touch upon her shoulder and turned, almost with relief, from the food to look up into the patrician features of a very tall man, clothed in voluminious lemon-coloured lace which rose to his strong chin and framed his face. The grey eyes were friendly, but she would not respond (daughter to father) as her emotions dictated. She drew away. 'You, too, are real?'

'Ah. Call me so.'

'You are not one of the illusions of that city?'

'I suspect that I am at least as real as Sweet Orb Mace. He convinces you?'

She was mute.

'The city is old,' said the newcomer. 'Its whimsicalities proliferate. Yet, once, it had the finest of minds. During those agitated centuries, when beings rushed willy-nilly about the universe, all manner of visitors came to learn from it. It deserves respect, my dear time traveller, if anything deserves it. Its memory is uncertain, of course, and it lacks a good sense of its identity, its function, but it continues to serve what remains of our species. Without it, I suspect that we should be extinct.'

'Perhaps you are,' she said quietly.

His shoulders moved in a lazy shrug and he smiled. 'Oh, perhaps, but there is better evidence supporting more entertaining theories.' His companion came closer, a woman. 'This is my friend the Iron Orchid. We await other friends. For lunch and so on. It is our lunch that you are admiring.'

'The food is real, then? So much?'

'You are obsessed with the question. Are you from one of the religious periods?'

She trusted that the child had not heard and continued hastily. 'The profusion.'

'We thought it simple.'

'Mama!' Tugging, Snuffles whispered, 'The lady's hand.'

The Iron Orchid, long-faced with huge brown eyes, hair that might have been silver filigree, peacock quills sprouting from shoulder blades and waist, had one hand of the conventional, five-fingered sort, but the other (which she flourished) was a white-petalled, murmuring goldimar poppy, having at the centre scarlet lips like welts of blood.

'And I am called here Lord Jagged of Canaria,' said the man in yellow.

'Mama!' An urgent hiss. But no, she would not allow the

109

lapse, though it was with difficulty she redirected her own gaze away from the goldimar. 'Your manners, lad,' she said, and then, to the pair, 'This is my boy, Snuffles.'

The Iron Orchid was rapturous. 'A boy! What a shame you could not have arrived earlier. He would have been a playmate for my own son, Jherek.'

'He is not with you?'

'He wanders Time. The womb, these days, cannot make claims. He is off about his own affairs and will listen to no one, his mother least of all!'

'How old is your son?'

'Two hundred – three hundred – years old? Little more. Your own boy?'

'He is but sixty. My name is Dafnish Armatuce. Of the Armatuce. We . . .'

'And you have travelled through Time to lunch with us.' Smiling, the Orchid bent her head towards the child. Stroking him with the hand that was a goldimar, she cooed. He scarcely flinched.

'We cannot lunch.' Dafnish Armatuce was determined to set an example, if only to herself. 'I thank you, however.'

'You are not hungry?'

'We dare not breathe your atmosphere, let alone taste your food. We wish merely to find our machine and depart.'

'If the atmosphere does not suit you, madam,' said Lord Jagged kindly, and with gentleness, 'it can be adapted.'

'And the food, too. The food, too!' eagerly declared the Iron Orchid, adding, *sotto voce*, 'though I thought it reproduced perfectly. You eat such things? In your own Age?'

'Such things are eaten, yes.'

'The selection is not to your satisfaction?'

'Not at all.' Dafnish Armatuce permitted her curiosity a little rein. 'But how did you gather so much? How long did it take?'

The Iron Orchid was bewildered by the question. 'Gather? How long? It was made a few moments before we arrived.'

'Wustically wavishing!' carolled Sweet Orb Mace. 'A wondahfully wipping wuwal wepast!' He giggled.

'Two or three other time travellers join us soon,' explained Lord Jagged. 'The choice of feast is primarily to please them.'

'Others?'

'They are inclined to accumulate here, you know, at the End of Time. From what Age have you come?'

'The year was 1922'.

'Aha. Then Ming will be ideal.' He hesitated, looking deep into her face. 'You do not find us – sinister?'

'I had not expected to encounter people at all.' The perfection of his manners threw her into confusion. She was bent on defying his charm, yet the concern in his tone, the acuteness of his understanding, threatened to melt resolve. These characteristics were in conflict with the childish decadence of his costume, the corrupt grotesquerie of his surroundings, the idle insouciance of his conversation; she could not judge him, she could not sum him up. 'I had expected, at most, sterility . . .'

He had detected the tension in her. Another touch, upon her arm, and some of that tension dissipated. But she recovered her determination almost at once. Her own hand took her son's. How could such a creature of obvious caprice impress her so strongly of his respect both for her and for himself?

Watching them without curiosity, the Iron Orchid plucked up a plum and bit into it, the fruit and her lips a perfect match. Droplets of juice fell upon the gleaming grass, and clung.

Her eyes lifted; she smiled. 'This must be the first entrant.'

In the sky circled four gauzy, rainbow shapes, dipping and banking.

'Mine weah the fiwst,' said Sweet Orb Mace, aggrieved, 'but they escaped. Or melted.'

'We play flying conceits today,' explained Lord Jagged. 'Aha, it is undoubtably Doctor Volospion. See, he has erected his pavilion.'

The large, be-flagged tent had not been on the far side of the field a moment ago, Dafnish Armatuce was sure; she would have marked its gaudy red, white and purple stripes.

'The entertainment begins.' Lord Jagged drew her attention to the table. 'Will you not trust us, Dafnish Armatuce? You cannot die at the End of Time, or at least cannot remain dead for very long. Try the atmosphere. You can always return to your armour.' He took a backward pace.

Good manners dictated her actions, she knew. But did he seduce her? Again Snuffles eagerly made to remove his helmet, but she restrained him, for she must be the first to take the risk.

111

She raised hesitant hands. A sidelong glance at the dancing city, distant and, she thought, expectant, and then a decision. She twisted.

A gasp as air mingled with air, and she was breathing spice, her balance at risk. Three breaths and she was convinced; from the table drifted the aroma of pie, of apricots and avocados; she failed to restrain a sob, and tingling melancholy swept from toe to tight brown curl. Such profound feeling she had experienced only once before, at the birth of her Snuffles. The lad was even now wrenching his own helmet free – even as he was drawn towards the feast.

She cried 'Caution!' and stretched a hand, but he had seized a fowl and sunk soft, juvenile teeth into the breast. How could she refuse him? Perhaps this would be the only time in his life when he would know the luxury of abundance, and he must become an adult soon enough. She relented for him, but not for herself, yet even her indulgence of the child went hard against instinct.

Chewing, Snuffles presented her with a shining face, a greasy mouth, and eyes containing fires which had no business burning in one of his years. Feral, were they?

The Orchid trilled (artificial in all things, so thought Dafnish Armatuce): 'Children! Their appetites!' (Or was it irony Dafnish Armatuce detected? She dismissed any idea of challenge, placing her hands on her boy's shoulders, restraining her own lust): 'Food is scarce in Armatuce just now.'

'For how long?' Casually polite, the Iron Orchid raised a brow.

'The current shortage has lasted for about a century.'

'You have found no means of ending the shortage?'

'Oh, we have the means. But there is the moral question. Is it *good* for us to end the shortage?'

For a second there came a faint expression of puzzlement upon the Iron Orchid's face, and then, with a polite wave of an ortolan leg, she turned away.

' "Fastness Is Faithlessness",' quoted Dafnish Armatuce. ' "The Lean Alone Learn".' She realized then that these maxims were meaningless to them, but the zeal which touched the missionary touched her, and she continued: 'In Armatuce we believe that it is better to have less than to have enough, for those who have enough always feel the need for too much, whereas we only quell the yearning for sufficient, do you see?' She explained: ' "Greed Kills". "Self-indulgence Is Suicide". We stay hungry so that we shall never be tempted to eat more than we need and thus risk, again, the death of the planet. "Austerity Is Equilibrium".'

'Your world recovers from disaster, then?' said Lord Jagged sympathetically.

'It has recovered, sir.' She was firm. 'Thanks to the ancestors of the Armatuce. Now the Armatuce holds what they achieved in trust. "Stable Is He Who Stoic Shall Be".'

'You fear that without this morality you would reproduce the disaster?'

'We know it,' she said.

'Yet' – he spread his hands – 'you find a world still here when you did not expect it and no evidence that your philosophy has survived.'

She scarcely heard the words, but she recognized the sly, pernicious tone. She squared her shoulders. 'We would return now, if you please. The boy has eaten.'

'You will have nothing?'

'Will you show me to my ship?'

'Your ship will not work.'

'What? You refuse to let me leave?'

As succinctly as possible, Lord Jagged explained the Morphail Effect, concluding, 'Therefore you can never really return to your own Age and, if you left this one, might well be killed or at very least stranded in a less congenial era.'

'You think I lack courage? That I would not take the risk?'

He pursed his lips and let his gaze fall upon the gorging boy. She followed his meaning and put two fingers softly upon her cheek.

'Eat now,' said the tall lord with a tender gesture.

Absently, she touched a morsel of mutton to her tongue.

A shadow moved across the field, cast by a beast, porcine and grey, which with lumbering grace performed a somersault or two in the sky. Overhead there were now several more objects and creatures pirouetting, diving, spiralling – a small red biplane, a monstrous mosquito, a winged black and white cat, a pale green stingray – while below the owners of these entrants

113

jostled, laughed and talked: a motley of races (some Earthly beasts, others extraterrestrial; but mostly humanoid), clothed and decorated in all manner of fanciful array. On the edges of the blue and white field there had sprouted marquees, flagpoles, lines of bunting, crowded together and waving boisterously, so that she could no longer see beyond their confines. She let the mutton melt, took one plum and consumed it, drank an inch of water from a goblet, and her meal was done, though the effort of will involved in resisting a leaf of lettuce only by a fraction succeeded in balancing the guilt experienced at having allowed herself to eat the second half of the fruit. Meanwhile Snuffles' jaws continued to move with dedicated precision.

Several large, fiery wheels went by, a score of feet above her head, drowning with their hissing the loud babble of the crowd.

'Cwumbs!' exclaimed Sweet Orb Mace, with a knowing wink at her, as if they shared a secret. 'Goah Blimey!'

The words were meaningless, but he appeared to be under the impression that she would understand them.

Deliberately, she guided her glance elsewhere. Everyone was applauding.

'Chariots of Fire!' bellowed a deep, proprietorial voice. 'Chariots of Fire! Number Seventy-Eight!'

'We shan't forget, dear Duke of Queens,' sang a lady whose gilded skin clashed sickeningly with her green mouth and glowing, emerald eyes.

'My Lady Charlotina of Below the Lake,' murmured Lord Jagged. 'Would you like to meet her?'

'Can she be of help to me? Can she give me practical advice?' The rhetoric rang false, even in her own ears.

'She is the Patron of Brannart Morphail, our greatest, maddest scientist, who knows more about the Nature of Time than anyone else in history, so he tells us. He will probably want to interview you shortly.'

'Why should one of your folk require a Patron?' she asked with genuine interest.

'We seek traditions wherever we can find them. We are glad to get them. They help us order our lives, I suppose. Doubtless Brannart dug his tradition up from some ancient tape and took a fancy to it. Of late, because of the enthusiasm of the Iron Orchid's son, Jherek, we have all become *obsessed* with morality . . .'

'I see little evidence of that.'

'We are still having difficulty defining what it is,' he told her. 'My Lady Charlotina – our latest time travellers – Mother and Son – Dafnish and Snuffles Armatuce.'

'How charming. How unusual. Tell me, delightful Dafnish, are you claimed yet?'

'Claimed?' Dafnish Armatuce looked back at the departing Jagged.

'We vie with one another to be hosts to new arrivals,' he called. His wave was a little on the airy side. 'You are "claimed", however, as my guests. I will see you anon.'

'Greedy Jagged! Does he restock his menagerie?' My Lady Charlotina of Below the Lake stroked her crochet snood as her eyes swept up from Dafnish's toes and locked with Dafnish's eyes for a moment. 'Your figure? Is it your own, my dear?'

'I fail to understand you.'

'Then it is! Ha! ha!' Mood changed, My Lady Charlotina made a curtsey. 'I will find you some friends. My talent, they say, is as a Catalyst!'

'You are modest, cherubic Charlotina! You have all the talents in the catalogue!' In doublet and hose reminiscent of pre-cataclysm decadence, extravagantly swollen, catechrestically slashed and galooned, bearing buttons the size of cabbages, the shoes with toes a yard or two long and curled to the knees, the cap peaked to jut more than a foot from the face, beruffed and bedecked with thin brass chains, a big-buckled belt somewhere below the waist so as, in whole, to make Sweet Orb Mace seem mother naked, a youth bent a calculated leg before continuing with his catechism of compliment. 'Let me cast myself beneath the cataract of your thousand major virtues, your myriad minor qualities, O mistress of my soul, for though I am considered clever, I am nought but your lowliest catechumen, seeking only to absorb the smallest scraps of your wisdom so that I may, for one so small, be whole!' Whereupon he flung himself to the grass on velvet knees and raised powdered, imploring hands.

'Good afternoon, Doctor Volospion.' She relished the flattery, but paused no longer, saying over her shoulder, 'You smell very well today.'

Unconcerned, Doctor Volospion raised himself to his feet, his cap undulating, his chains jingling, and his rouged lips curved in a friendly smile as he saw Dafnish Armatuce.

'I seek a lover,' he explained, peeling a blade of blue grass from his inner thigh. 'A woman to whom I can give my All. It is late in the season to begin, perhaps, with so many exquisite Romances already under way or even completed (as in Werther's case), but I am having difficulty in finding a suitable recipient.' His expression, as he stared at her, became speculative. 'May I ask your sex, at present?'

'I am a woman, sir, and a mother. An Armatuce, mate to a cousin of the Armatuce, sworn to suffer and to serve together until my son shall be ready to suffer and to serve in my place.'

'You would not like to link your fate with mine, to give yourself body and soul to me until the End of Time (which, of course, is not far off, I hear)?'

'I would not.'

'I came late to the fashion, you see, and now most are already bored with it. I understand. But there is, surely, the fulfillment of abandonment. Is it not delicious to throw oneself upon another's mercy – to make him or her the absolute master of one's fate?' He took a step closer, peering into her immobile countenance, his eye sparkling. 'Ah! Do I tempt you? I see that I do!'

'You do not!'

'Your tone lacks conviction.'

'You are deceived, Doctor Volospion.'

'Could we have our bodies so engineered as to produce another child?'

'My operation is past. I have my child. No more can bloom.'

She turned to search for Snuffles, fearing suddenly for the safety of his person as well as for his mind, for she was now aware that this folk had no scruples, no decency, no proper inhibitions even where that most sacrosanct of subjects was concerned. 'Snuffles!'

'Here, mama!'

The boy was in conversation with a tall, thin individual wearing a crenellated crown as tall as himself.

'To me!'

He came reluctantly, waddling, snatching a piece of pastry from the table as he passed, wheezing, his little protective suit

116

bearing a patina of creams and gravies, his hair sticky with confectionery, his face rich with the traces of his feast.

Someone had begun to build cloud-shapes, interweaving colours and kinds and creating the most unlikely configurations. She seized his sweetened hand, tempted to remonstrate, to read him a lesson, to forbid further food, but she knew the dangers of identifying her own demands upon herself with what she expected from her son. Too often, she had learned, had ancient parents forbidden their children food merely because they could not or would not eat themselves, forbidden children childish pleasures because those pleasures tempted them, too. She would not transfer. Let the boy, at least, enjoy the experience. His training would save him, should they ever return. A lesson would be learned. And if they did not return, well, it would not profit him to retain habits which put him at odds with the expectations of society. And should it seem inevitable that they were permanently marooned, she could decide when he would be mature enough to become an adult, grant him that status herself and so put an end to her own misery.

The crowd seemed to close in on her. Doctor Volospion had already wandered away, but there were others – every one of whom was a living, mocking parody of all she held to be admirable in Man. Her heart beat faster, at last unchecked. She sought for the only being in that whole unnatural, fatuous farrago who might help her escape, but Lord Jagged was gone.

And My Lady Charlotina broke through the throng, Death's Harlequin, grinning and triumphant, drawing another woman with her. 'A contemporary, dear Dafnish. Mutual reminiscence is now possible!'

'I must go . . .' began the time traveller. 'Snuffles wearies. We can sleep in our ship.'

'No, no! The air fête is hardly begun. You shall stay and converse with Miss Ming.'

Miss Ming, at first bored, brightened, giving Dafnish Armatuce a quick glance which was at once questioning and appraising, warm and calculating. Miss Ming was a heavily built young woman whose long fair hair had been carefully brushed but had acquired no more of a lustre than her pale, unwholesome skin. She wore, for this Age, a simple costume, tight dungarees of glowing orange and a shirt and short jacket of pale blue. Now Dafnish Armatuce had her whole attention, was granted Miss Ming's smile of knowing and insincere sympathy.

'Your year?' My Lady Charlotina creased her golden forehead. 'You said . . .'

'1922.'

'Miss Ming is from 2067. Until recently she lived at Doctor Volospion's menagerie. One of the few human survivors, in fact.'

Miss Ming's abrupt, monotonous voice might have seemed surly had it not been for the eagerness with which she imparted meaningless (to Dafnish Armatuce) confidences, coming closer than was necessary and placing intimate fingers upon her shoulder to say: 'Some of Mongrove's diseases escaped and struck down half the inhabitants of Doctor Volospion's menagerie. By the time the discovery was made, resurrection was out of the question. Mongrove refuses to apologize. Doctor Volospion shuns him. I didn't know time travel was discovered in 1922. And,' a girlish pout, 'they told me that I was the first woman to go into Time.'

Surely, Dafnish thought, she sensed aggression here.

'An all-woman team launched the craft.' Miss Ming spoke significantly. 'I was the first.'

And Dafnish Armatuce, her boy hard alongside, chanted at this threat: 'Time travel, Miss Ming, is the creation and the copyright of the Armatuce. We built the first backward-shifting ships two years ago, in 1920. This year, in 1922, I was chosen to go forward.'

Miss Ming pursed lips which became thin and down-turned at the corners, giving her a slight leonine look, but she did not seek conflict. 'Can we both be deluded? I am an historian, after all! I cannot be wrong. Aha! Illumination. A.D.?'

'I regret . . .'

'From what event does your calendar run?'

'From the First Birth.'

'Of Christ?'

'Of a child, following the catastrophe in which all became barren. A method was discovered whereby –'

'There you have the answer! We are not even from the same millennium. Nonetheless,' Miss Ming linked an arm through

118

hers before she could react, and held it tight, 'it needn't stop friendship. How delicate you are. How exquisite. Almost,' insinuatingly, 'a child yourself.'

Dafnish pulled free. 'Snuffles.' She began to dab at his face with her wetted glove. The little boy turned resigned eyes upward and watched the circling machines and beasts. The crowd sighed and swayed, and they were jostled.

'You are married?' implacably continued Miss Ming. 'In your own Age?'

'To a cousin of the Armatuce, yes.' Dafnish's manner became more distant as she tried to move on, but Miss Ming's warm hand slipped again into the crook of her elbow. The fingers pressed into her flesh. She was chilled.

Three white bats swooped by, performing acrobatics in unison, their twenty-foot wings making the air hiss. A trumpet sounded. There was applause.

'I was divorced, before my journey.' Miss Ming paused, perhaps in the hope of some morbid revelation from her new friend, then continued, girl-to-girl: 'His name was Donny Stevens. He was well thought of as a scientist – a popular and powerful family, too – very old – in Iowa. Rich. But he was like all men. You know. They think they're doing you a favour if they can get to your cubicle once a month, and if it's once a week, they're Casanova! No thanks! Someone said – Betty Stern, I think – that he had that quality of aggressive stupidity which so many women find attractive in a man: they think it's strength of character and, once they've committed themselves to that judgement, maintain it against all the evidence. Betty said dozens of the happiest marriages are based on it. (I idolized Betty). Unfortunately, I realized my mistake. If I hadn't, I wouldn't be here, though. I joined an all-woman team – know what I mean? – anyway we got the first big breakthrough and made those dogs look sick when they saw what the bitches could do. And this Age suits me now. Anything goes, if you know what I mean – I mean, really! Wow! What kind of guys do you like, honey?'

She did not want Miss Ming's attentions. Again she cast about for Jagged and, as a rent appeared for a second in the ranks, saw him talking to a small, serious-faced yellow man, clad in discreet denim (the first sensible costume she had observed thus far). Hampered both by reluctant, sleepy son and clinging Ming, she pushed her way through posturing gallants and sparkling frillocks, to home slowly on Jagged, who saw her and smiled, bending to murmur a word or two to his companion. Then, as she closed: 'Li Pao, this is Dafnish Armatuce of the Armatuce. Dafnish, I introduce Li Pao from the 27th century.'

'She won't know what you're talking about!' crowed the unshakeable Miss Ming. 'Her dates go from something she calls the First Birth. 1922. I was baffled myself.'

Lord Jagged's eyes became hooded.

Li Pao bowed a neat bow. 'I gather you find this Age disturbing, Comrade Armatuce?'

Her expression confirmed his assumption.

Li Pao's small mouth moved with soft, sardonic deliberation. 'I, too, found it so, upon arrival. But there is little need to feel afraid, for, as you will discover, the rich are never malevolent, unless their security is threatened, and here there is no such threat. If they seem to waste their days, do not judge them too harshly; they know no better. They are without hungers or frustrations. Nature has long since been conquered by Art. Their resources are limitless, for they feed upon the whole universe (what remains of it). These cities suck power from any available part of the galaxy and transfer it to them so that they may play. Stars die so that on old Earth someone might change the colour of his robe.' There was irony in his tone, but he spoke without censure.

Snuffles cried out as something vast and metallic appeared to drop upon the throng, but it stopped a few feet up, hovered, then drifted away, and the crowd became noisy again.

'The First Birth period?' Lord Jagged made a calculation. 'That would place you in the year 9,478 A.D.. We find the Dawn Age reckoning most convenient here. I understand your dismay. You are reconstituting your entire planet, are you not? From the core, virtually, outward, eh?'

She was grateful for his erudition. Now he and Li Pao seemed allies in this fearful world. She was able to steady her heart and recover something of her self-possession. 'It has been hard work, Lord Jagged. The Armatuce have been fortunate in winning respect for their several sacrifices.'

'Sacrifice!' Li Pao was nostalgic. 'A joy impossible to experience here, where the gift of the self to the common cause would go unremarked. They would not know.'

'Then they are, indeed, unfortunate,' she said. 'There is a price they pay for their pleasure, after all.'

'You find our conceits shallow, then?' Lord Jagged wished to know.

'I do. I grieve. Everywhere is waste and decay – the last stages of the Romantic disease whose symptoms are a wild, mindless seeking after superficial sensation for its own sake, effect piled upon effect, until mind and body disintegrate completely, whose cure is nothing else but death. Here, all is display – your fantasies appear the harmless play of children, but they disguise the emptiness of your lives. You colour corpses and think yourselves creative. But I am not deceived.'

'Well,' he replied equably enough, 'visions vary. To one who cannot conceive of such things, another's terrors and appetites, his day-to-day phantasms, are, indeed, poor conceits, intended merely to display their possessor's originality and to dismay his fellows. But some of us have our joys, even our profundities, you know, and we cherish them.'

She felt a little shame. She had offended him, perhaps, with her candour. She lowered her eyes.

'Yet,' continued Jagged, 'to one of us (one who bothers to contemplate such things at all, and there are few) your way of life might seem singularly dull, denying your humanity. He could claim that you are without any sort of real passion, that you deliberately close your consciousness to the glowing images which thrive on every side, thus making yourself less than half alive. He might not realize that you, or this dour fellow Li Pao here, have other excitements. Li Pao celebrates Logic! A clearly stated formula is, for him, exquisite delight. He feels the same *frisson* from his theorems that I might feel for a well-turned aphorism. I am fulfilled if I give pleasure with a paradox, while he would seek fulfillment if he could order a silly world, build, comfort, complete a pattern and fix it, to banish the very Chaos he has never tasted but which is our familiar environment, and precious to us as air, or as water to the fish. For to us it is not Chaos. It is Life, varied, stimulating, rich with vast dangers and tremendous consolations. Our world sings and shimmers. Its

121

light can blind with a thousand shapes and colours. Its darkness is always populated, never still, until death's own darkness swoops and obliterates all. We inhabit one sphere, but that sphere contains as many worlds as there are individuals on its surface. Are we shallow because we refuse to hold a single point of view?'

Li Pao was appreciative of the argument, but something puzzled him. 'You speak, Lord Jagged, as you sometimes do, as one from an earlier Age than this, for few here think in such terms, though they might speak as you did if they bothered to consider their position at all.'

'Oh, well. I have travelled a little, you know.'

'Are there none here,' asked Dafnish Armatuce, 'who have the will to work, to serve others?'

Lord Jagged laughed. 'We seek to serve our fellows with our wit, our entertainments. But some would serve in what you would call practical ways.' He paused, serious for a second, as if his thoughts had become a little private. He drew breath, continuing: 'Werther de Goethe, perhaps, might have had such a will, had he lived in a different Age. Li Pao's, for instance. Where another sees dreams and beauty, Li Pao sees only disorder. If he could, or dared, he would make our rotting cities stable, clarify and formalize the architecture, populate his tidy buildings with workers, honest and humane, to whom Peace of Mind is a chance of worthy promotion and the prospect of an adequate pension, to whom Adventure is a visit to the sea or a thunderstorm during a picnic – and Passion is Comfort's equal, Prosperity's cohort. But shall I judge his vision dull? No! It is not to him, or to those who think as he, in his own Age, in your own Age, Dafnish Armatuce.' Lord Jagged teased at his fine nose. 'We are all what our society makes of us.'

'When in Rome . . .' murmured Miss Ming piously. Something flapped by and received a cheer.

Jagged was impatient with Miss Ming. 'Indeed.' His cloak billowed in a wind of his own subtle summons, and he looked kindly down on Dafnish Armatuce. 'Explore all attitudes, my dear. Honour them, every one, but be slippery – never let them hold you, else you fail to enjoy the benefits and be saddled only with the liabilities. It's true that canvas against the skin can be as sensual as silk, and milk a sweeter drink than wine, but feel everything, taste everything, for its own sake, and for your own sake, then no one thing shall be judged better or worse than another, no person shall be so judged, and nothing can ensnare you!'

'Your advice is well-meant, sir, I know,' said Dafnish Armatuce, 'and would probably be good advice if I intended to stay in your world. But I do not.'

'You have no choice,' said Miss Ming with satisfaction.

He shrugged. 'I have told you of the Morphail Effect.'

'There are other means of escape.'

Miss Ming, by her superior smirk, felt she had found a flaw in Lord Jagged's argument. 'Cancer?' she demanded. 'Could we love cancer?'

He rose to it willingly enough, replying lightly: 'You are obscure, Miss Ming, for there is no physical disease at the End of Time. But, yes, we could – for what it taught us – the comparisons it offered. Perhaps that is why some of our number seek discomfort – in order to comfort their souls.'

Miss Ming simpered. 'You argue cunningly, Lord Jagged, but I suspect your logic.'

'Is it so dignified, my conversation, as to be termed Logic? I am flattered.' One hand pressed gently against Dafnish Armatuce's back and the other against Li Pao's, rescuing them both. Miss Ming hesitated and then retreated at last.

Eight dragons waltzed the skies above while far away music played; the crowd grew quieter as it watched, and even Dafnish Armatuce admitted, to herself, that it was a delicate beauty they witnessed.

She sighed. 'So this is Utopia, Lord Jagged, for you? You are satisfied?'

'Could I expect more? Many think the days of our universe numbered. Yet, do you find concern amongst us?'

'You sport to forget the inevitable?'

He shook his head. 'We sported thus before we knew. We have not changed our lives at all, most of us.'

'You must sense tension. You cannot live so mindlessly.'

'I do not think we live as you describe. Do you not strive, in your Age, for a world without fear?'

'Of course.'

'There is no fear here, Dafnish Armatuce, even of total

extinction.'

'Which suggests you are far divorced from reality. You speak of the atrophy of natural instinct.'

'I suppose that I do. There are few such instincts to be found among those who are native to the End of Time. You have no philosophers among your own folk who argue that those natural instincts might be the cause of the tragedy once described, I believe, as the Human Condition?'

'Of course. It is part of our creed. But we ensure that the tragedy shall never be played again, for we encourage the virtues of self-sacrifice and consideration of the common good, and we discourage the vices.'

'Which suggests that they continue to exist. Here, they do not; there is no necessity for either vice or virtue.'

'Yet if Hate dies, surely Love dies, too?'

'I think it has been rediscovered, lately. Love.'

'A fad. I spoke with your Doctor Volospion. An affectation, nothing more.' She gasped and shut her eyes, for two great suns had appeared, side by side, glaring scarlet, and drenched the gathering with their light.

Almost at once the suns began to grow smaller, rising away from the Earth. She blinked and recovered her composure, though weariness threatened her thoughts. 'And Love of the sort you describe is no Love at all, for its attendants are Jealousy and Despair, and in Despair lies the most destructive quality of all, Cynicism.'

'You think us cynical, then?'

She looked about her at the chattering press. One of their number, tall, bulky and bearded, festooned in feathers and furs, was being congratulated for what doubtless had been his display. 'I thought so at first.'

'And now?'

She changed the subject. 'I have the impression, Lord Jagged, that you are trying to make this world palatable to me. What if I agree that there is something to be said for your way of life and turn the conversation to a problem rather closer to my heart? My husband, cousin to the Armatuce, and a Grinash on his mother's side, cares for me, as he cares for Snuffles, our son, and eagerly awaits our return, as does the committee which I serve (and which elected me to accomplish my voyage). I would go back to that Age, which you would find grim, no doubt, but which is home, familiar, security for us. You tell me that I cannot, so I must consider my position accordingly. Could I not send a message, at least, or return for a second to assure them of my physical safety?'

'You speak of caring for the common cause,' interrupted Li Pao. 'If you do, you will not make the attempt, for Time disrupts. Morphail warns us. And you risk death. If you tried to go back you might succeed, but you would in all probability flicker for only a moment, unseen, before being flung out again. The time stream would suck you up and deposit you anywhere in your future, in any one of a million less pleasant ages than this, or you could be killed outright (which has happened more than once). The Laws of Time are cruel.'

'I would risk any danger,' she said, 'were it not for –'

'– the child,' softly said Lord Jagged.

'We are used to sacrifice, the Armatuce. But our children are precious. We exist for them.'

Darkness fell and ivory clashed and rattled above her as a great ship, made all of bone, its sections strung loosely together, its wings beating erratically, staggered upon a sea of faintly glowing clouds.

'What a splendid ending,' she heard Lord Jagged say.

4

An Apology and an Explanation from your Auditor

Your auditor, for the most part a mere ear, a humble recorder of that which he is privileged to hear, apologizes if he interrupts the reader's flow with a few words of his own, but it is his aim to speed the narrative on by condensing somewhat the events immediately following Dafnish Armatuce's introduction to the society at the End of Time.

Her reaction was a familiar one (familiar to you who have followed this compilation of legends, gossip, rumours and accredited reminiscence thus far) and to detail it further would risk repetition. Suffice: she was convinced of the Morphail Effect. Time had thrown her (as a shipwrecked English tar of old might have been thrown on the shores of the Caliph's Land) upon the mercies of an alien and self-satisfied culture which considered her an amusing prize. Her protestations? They were not serious. – Her warnings? Irrelevant fancies. – And her sensitivities? Meaningless to those who luxuriated in the inherited riches of an entire race's history; to whom Grief was a charming affectation and Anxiety an archaic word whose meaning had been lost. They were pleased to listen to her insofar as she remained entertaining, but even as their enthusiasms waxed and waned, mayfly swift, so did their favours shift from visitor to visitor.

Ah, if they had known how cruel they were, how they might have explored the sensation – but they were feline, phantasmagorical, and, like careless cats, they played with the poor creatures they trapped until one of them wearied of the game, for even those denizens at the End of Time who claimed to have known pain knew only the play-actor's pain, that grandiose anguish which, at its most profound, resolves itself as hurt pride.

Dafnish Armatuce knew great pain – though she herself would not admit it – particularly where her maternal instincts

126

were involved. Children, like all else, were scarce in Armatuce, and she had worked for half her life to be permitted one. Now her ambition was that her boy be elected to adult status among the Armatuce and take her place so that she might, at last, rest from service, content and proud. For sixty years, since Snuffles' birth, she had looked forward to the day when he would be chosen (she had been certain that he would be) and had known that his voyage through Time would have been a guarantee of early promotion. But here she was, stranded, thwarted of all she had striven for, unable and unwilling to give service to a community which had no needs; thus it is no wonder that she pined and schemed alternately while she remained a guest of Lord Jagged of Canaria, and fought to retain the standards of the Armatuce against every temptation.

However, though she remained rigorously self-disciplined, she indulged the boy, refusing to impose upon him the demands she made of herself. She allowed him a certain amount of decoration in his clothing; she let him eat, within reason, what he wished to eat. And she took him on journeys to see this world, so similar, in much of its topography, to the deserts of their own. Ruined it might be, wasted and tortured, covered with the half-finished abandoned projects of its feckless inhabitants, but it was beautiful, too.

And it was on these trips that she could find a certain peace she had never known before. While Snuffles climbed the remains of mountains, crying out in delight whenever he made a discovery, she would sit upon a rock and stare at the pale, faded sky, the eroded landscape through which dust and the wind sang with quiet melancholy, and she would think the world new and herself its first inhabitant, perhaps its only inhabitant. As an Armatuce, in Armatuce, she had never once spent a full hour alone, and here, at the End of Time, she realized that it was what she had always wanted, that perhaps this was why she had looked forward so much to her commission, that she had secretly hoped for the cold peace of a lifeless planet. Then she would turn brooding eyes upon her son, as he scrambled, ran or climbed, and she would consider her duty and her love and wonder if she had, after all, been prepared to risk his life, as well as her own, in this quest for loneliness. Such thoughts would throw her into a further crisis of conscience and make her more than ever determined to ensure that he should not suffer as a result of her desires.

But if there was a Devil in this dying Eden, then it came in the shape of Miss Ming, who sought out Dafnish Armatuce wherever she went. Lord Jagged was gone from his cage-shaped castle, either to work in his hidden laboratories or else embarked upon a journey. Dafnish did not know, and with him had gone his protection. Miss Ming found excuse after excuse for visiting her, each one increasingly unlikely. And there was no solitude which Miss Ming might not interrupt, in whatever obscure corner of the globe Dafnish flew her little air boat (a gift of Lord Jagged). Miss Ming had observations on every aspect of life; she had gossip concerning every individual in the world; she made criticism of all she met or saw, from Doctor Volospion's new mannikin to the shade of the sky hanging over the Ottawa monuments; but in particular Miss Ming had advice for Dafnish Armatuce, on the care of her skin, her clothes, the upbringing of children (she had had none of her own), her diet, her choice of scenery and of residence.

'I wish,' Miss Ming would say, 'only to help, dear, for you're bound to have difficulty getting used to a world like this. We expatriates must stick together. If we don't, we're in trouble. Don't let it get to you. Don't mope. Don't get morbid.'

And if Dafnish Armatuce would make an excuse, suggesting that Snuffles must be put to bed, perhaps, Miss Ming would exclaim. 'There! You'll do harm to the boy. You must let him grow up, stand on his own feet. You're afraid of experience – you're using him to protect yourself from what this world can offer. While he remains a child, he gives you an excuse to turn away from your own responsibilities as an adult. You're too possessive, Dafnish! Is it doing any good to either of you? He's got to develop his personality, and so have you.'

At last, Dafnish Armatuce turned on the intolerable Ming. She would ask her, direct, to leave. She would say that she found Miss Ming's company unwelcome. She would ask Miss Ming never to return, but Miss Ming knew how to respond to this.

'Menstrual tension,' she would say, sympathetically, undeterred by Dafnish Armatuce's reiteration of the fact that she had never experienced the menstrual cycle. 'You're not yourself

128

today.' Or she would smile a sickly smile and suggest that Dafnish Armatuce get a better night's rest, that she would call tomorrow, in the hope of finding her in an improved mood. Or: 'Something's worrying you about the boy. Let him have his head. Lead your own life.' Or: 'You're frustrated, dear. You need a friend like me, who understands. A woman knows what a woman needs.' And a clammy, white, red-tipped hand would fall upon Dafnish's knee, like a hungry spider.

That Miss Ming wanted her for a lover, Dafnish Armatuce understood quite early, but love-making, even between man and woman, was discouraged in Armatuce; it was thought vulgar, and some would have it that the old sexual drive had been another central cause of the disaster which had nearly succeeded in destroying the whole race. The new methods of creating children, originally developed from necessity, were seen to contain virtues previously unconsidered. Besides, there was plainly no Armatuce blood in Miss Ming, and there was a strong taboo about forming liaisons beyond the clan.

Thus, no matter how lonely she might sometimes feel, Dafnish Armatuce remained unswervingly contemptuous of Miss Ming's advances, which would sometimes bring the accusation from that poor, smitten, unlovely woman that Dafnish Armatuce was 'playing hard to get' and shouldn't 'toy with someone's affections the way you do.'

Scarcely for a day did Miss Ming lift her siege. She tried to dress like Dafnish Armatuce, or impress her with her own coarse taste. She would appear in fanciful frocks or stern tweed; several times she arrived stark naked, and once she had her body engineered so that it was a near-copy of Dafnish's own.

Even Miss Ming's determinedly self-centred consciousness must have understood that the look on Dafnish Armatuce's face, when she witnessed the travesty of her own form, was an expression of revulsion, for the invader did not stay long in that guise.

Harried, horrified and exasperated by Miss Ming's obsessive suit, Dafnish Armatuce began to accept invitations to the various functions arranged by those who were this world's social leaders, for if she could not find peace of mind in the great, silent spaces, then at least she might find some comfort in surrounding herself by a wall of noise, of empty conversation or useless display. To these balls, fêtes and exhibitions she sometimes took her Snuffles, but on other occasions she would trust his security to the sophisticated mechanical servants Lord Jagged had placed at her disposal. Here she would often encounter Miss Ming, but here, at least, there was often someone to rescue her – the Iron Orchid or Sweet Orb Mace or, more rarely and much more welcome, Li Pao. Dafnish Armatuce resented Miss Ming mightily, but since this world placed no premium on privacy, there was no other way to avoid her – and Dafnish resented Miss Ming for that, too: for forcing her into a society with which she had no sympathy, for which she often felt active disgust, and which she suspected might be corrupting the values she was determined to maintain against a day when, in spite of constant confirmation of the impossibility, she might return to Armatuce.

Moreover, it must be said, since she made no effort to adapt herself to the world at the End of Time, she often felt an unwelcome loneliness at the gatherings, for the others found her conversation limited, her descriptions of Armatuce dull, her observations without much wit and her sobriety scarcely worth playing upon; she made a poor topic. Her boy was more attractive, for he was a better novelty; but she balked any effort of theirs to draw him out, to pet him, to (in their terms) improve him. As a result both would find themselves generally ignored (save by the ubiquitous Ming). There was not even food for malicious gossip in her – she was too likeable. She was intelligent and she understood what made her unacceptable to them, that the fault (if fault it were) lay in her, but the treatment she received hardened her, laid her prey to that most destructive of all the demons which threaten the tender, vulnerable human psyche, the Demon of Cynicism. She resisted him, for her son's sake, if not her own, but the struggle was exhausting and took up her time increasingly. Like us all, she desired approval, but, like rather fewer of us, she refused to seek it by relinquishing her own standards. Her son, she knew, had yet to learn this pride, for it was of a kind unattractive in a child, a kind that can only be earned, not imitated. So she did not show active disapproval if he occasionally warmed to some paradox-quoting, clown-costumed fop, or repeated a vulgar rhyme he had overheard, or even criticized her for her dour appearance.

How could she know, then, that all these efforts of hers to maintain a balance between dignity and tolerance would have such tragic results for them both, that her nobility, her fine pride, would be the very instruments of their mutual ruin?

Not that disaster is inherent in these qualities; it required another factor to achieve it, and that factor took the form of the despairing, miserable Miss Ming, a creature without ideals, self-knowledge or common sense (which might well be mutually encouraging characteristics), a creature of Lust which called itself Love and Greed masquerading as Concern, and one who was, incidentally, somewhat typical of her Era. But now we race too fast to our Conclusion. Your auditor stands back, once again no more than an observing listener, and allows the narrative to carry you on.

5

In which Snuffles finds a Playmate

The Duke of Queens, in cloth-of-gold bulked and hung about with lace, pearls in his full black beard, complicated boots upon his large feet, a natural, guttering flambeau in his hand, led his party through his new caverns ('Underground' was the current fad, following the recent discovery of a lost nursery-warren, there since the time of the Tyrant Producers), bellowing cheerfully as he pointed out little grottos, his stalagmites ('Prison-children in the ancient Grautt tongues – a pretty, if unsuitable, name!'), his scuttling troglodytes, his murky rivers full of white reptiles and colourless fish, while flame made shadows which changed shape as the fluttering wind changed and strange echoes distorted their speech.

'They must stretch for miles!' hissed Miss Ming, hesitant between Dafnish and Snuffles and the host she admired. 'Aren't they altogether gloomier than Bishop Castle's, eerier than Guru Guru's?'

'They seem very similar to me,' coldly said Dafnish Armatuce, looking hungrily about her for a branching tunnel down which, with luck, she might escape for a short while.

'Oh, you judge without seeing properly. You close your eyes, as always, to the experience.'

Dafnish Armatuce wondered, momentarily, how much of her self-esteem she might have to relinquish to purchase the good-will of a potential ally, someone willing to rescue her from her remorseless leech, but she dismissed the notion, knowing herself incapable of paying the price.

'Snuffles is enjoying himself – aren't you, dear,' said Miss Ming pointedly.

Snuffles nodded.

'You think they're the best you've seen, don't you.'

Again, he nodded.

'A child's eye!' She became mystical. 'They take for granted

132

what we have to train ourselves to look at. Oh, how I *wish* I was a little girl again!'

Sweet Orb Mace, in loose, navy-blue draperies, waved his torch expansively as he recognized Dafnish Armatuce and her son. His accent had changed completely since their last meeting and he had dropped his lisp. 'Good afternoon, time travellers. The twists and turns of these tunnels, are they not tremendously tantalising? Such a tangle of intricate transits!' The caverns echoed his alliterative Ts so as to seem filled with the ticking of a thousand tiny clocks. A bow; he offered her his arm. Desperate, she took it, uncaring, just then, that Snuffles remained behind with Miss Ming. She needed a respite, for both their sakes. 'And how do you find the grottos?' he enquired.

'Grotesque,' she said.

'Aha!' He brightened. 'You see! You learn! Shall we ogle the gorgeous gulfs together?'

She failed to take his meaning. He paused, waiting for her response. None came. His sigh was politely stifled. The passage widened and became higher. There was a murmur of compliment, but the Duke of Queens silenced it with a modest hand.

'This is a discovery, not an invention. I came upon it while I worked. You'll note it's limestone, and natural limestone was thought extinct.'

Their fingers went to the smooth, damp rock, and it received a reverential stroke.

Sometimes in silhouette, sometimes gleaming and dramatic in the flamelight, the Duke of Queens indicated rock formations which must have lain here since before the Dawn Age: ghastly, smooth, rounded, almost organic in appearance, the limestone dripped with moisture, exuding a musty smell which reminded Dafnish Armatuce, and only Dafnish Armatuce, of a mouldering cadaver, as if this was all that remained of the original Earth, rotting and forgotten. It began to occur to her that it would be long before they were able to leave the caverns; the walls seemed, suddenly, to exert a pressure of their own, and she experienced something of the panic she had felt before, when the crowd had become too dense. She clung to Sweet Orb Mace, who would rather have gone on. She knew that she bored him, but she must have reassurance, some sort of anchor. The party moved: she felt that it pushed her where she did not

133

want to go. She had a strong desire to turn back, to seek the place where they had entered the maze; she did half-turn, but was confronted by the grinning face of Miss Ming. She allowed herself to be carried forward.

Sweet Orb Mace had made an effort to resume the conversation, on different lines. '... would not believe how jealous Brannart Morphail was. But he shall not have it. I was the first to discover it – and you – and while he is welcome to make a reproduction, I shall hold the original. There are few like it.'

'Like it?'

'Your time machine.'

'You have it?'

'I have always had it. It's in my collection.'

'I assumed it lost or destroyed. When I went back to seek it, it had gone, and no one knew where.'

'I must admit to a certain deception, for I knew how desperately Brannart would want it for himself. I hid it. But now it is the pride of my collection and on display.'

'The machine is the property of the Armatuce,' she said gently. 'By rights it should be in my care.'

'But you have no further use for it, surely!'

She did not possess sufficient strength for argument. She allowed him his assumption. From behind her there came an unexpected giggle. She dared to look. Miss Ming was bent low, showing Snuffles a fragment of rock she had picked up. Snuffles beamed and shook with laughter as Miss Ming indicated features in the piece of rock.

'Isn't it the image of Doctor Volospion?'

Snuffles saw that his mother watched. 'Look, mama! Doctor Volospion to the life!'

She failed to note the resemblance. The rock was oddly shaped, certainly, and she supposed that it might, if held at an angle, roughly resemble a human face.

'I hadn't realized Doctor Volospion was so old!' giggled Ming, and Snuffles exploded with laughter.

'Can't you see it, mama?'

Her face softened; she smiled, not at the joke (for there was none, in her view), but in response to his innocent joy. Miss Ming's sense of humour was evidently completely compatible with her son's: the unbearable woman had succeeded in making

134

the boy happy, perhaps for the first time since their arrival. All at once Dafnish Armatuce felt grateful to Miss Ming. The woman had some virtue if she could make a child laugh so thoroughly, so boisterously.

The caverns took up the sound of the laughter so that it grew first louder, then softer, until finally it faded in some deep and far-off gallery.

Now Miss Ming was dancing with the boy, singing some sort of nonsense song, also concerning Doctor Volospion. And Snuffles chuckled and gasped and all but wept with delight, and whispered jokes which made Miss Ming, in turn, scream with laughter. 'Ooh! You *naughty* boy!' She noticed that Mother observed them. 'Your son – he's sharper than you think, Dafnish!'

Infected, Dafnish Armatuce found that she smiled still more. She realized that hers was not only the smile of maternal pleasure but a smile of relief. She felt free of Ming. Having transferred her attentions to the boy, the woman acquired an altogether pleasanter personality. Perhaps because she was so immature, Miss Ming was one of those who only relaxed in the company of children. Whatever the cause of this change, Dafnish Armatuce was profoundly grateful for it. She, too, relaxed.

Stronger light lay ahead as the cavern grew wider. Now they all stood in a vast chamber whose curved roof was a canopy of milky green jade through which sunlight (filtered, delicate, subtly coloured) fell, illuminating rock-carved chairs and benches of the subtlest marble and richest obsidian, while luminous moss and ivy mingled on the walls and floor, revealing little clusters of pale blue and yellow primroses.

'What a *perfect* spot for a fairy feast!' cried Miss Ming, hand in hand with Snuffles. 'We can have fun here, can't we, Prince Snuffles?' Her heavy body was almost graceful as she danced, her green and purple petticoats frothing over sparkling, diamanté stockings. 'I'm the Elf Queen. Ask me what you wish and it shall be granted.'

Buoyed by her exuberance, Snuffles was beside himself with glee. Dafnish Armatuce stood back with a deep sigh, quietly revelling in the sight of her son's flushed, jolly cheeks, his darting eye. It had concerned her that Snuffles had no children with whom he could play. Now he had found someone. If only Miss Ming had earlier discovered his affinity – what was evidently her real affinity – with Snuffles, how much better it might have been for everyone, thought Dafnish.

Her attention was drawn back to Doctor Volospion. In a costume of, for him, unusual simplicity (black and silver) he capered upon one of the tables with the leopard-spotted woman called Mistress Christia, while the rest of the guests, the Duke of Queens amongst them, clapped in time to the music of the jig Doctor Volospion played upon some archaic stringed instrument tucked beneath his goateed chin.

Unusually lighthearted, Dafnish Armatuce was tempted to join them, but she checked the impulse, tolerantly enough, contenting herself with her silent pleasure at the sight of Snuffles and Miss Ming, who, even now, were climbing upon the table. Soon all but Dafnish were dancing.

6

In which Dafnish Armatuce Enjoys a Little Freedom

Having permitted her boy a generous frolic with his new-found friend, Dafnish Armatuce expressed genuine thanks to Miss Ming for devoting so much of her time to the lad's pleasure.

As flushed and happy as Snuffles, looking almost as attractive, Miss Ming declared: 'Nonsense! It was Snuffles who entertained me. He made me feel young again.' She hugged him. 'Thank you for a lovely day, Snuffles.'

'Shall I see you tomorrow, Miss Ming?'

'That's up to mama.'

'I had planned a visit to the Uranian Remains . . .' began Dafnish. 'However, I suppose –'

'Why don't you visit your dull old Remains on your own and let Snuffles and me go out to play together.' Miss Ming became embarrassing again as she made a little-girl face and curtsied. 'If you please, Mrs Armatuce.'

'He'll exhaust you, surely.'

'Not at all. He makes me feel properly, fully alive.'

Dafnish Armatuce tried to disguise the slightly condescending note which crept into her voice, for it now became poignantly plain that the poor creature had never really wanted to grow up at all. Undertanding this, Dafnish could allow herself to be kind. 'Perhaps for an hour or two, then.'

'Wonderful! Would you like that, Snuffles?'

'Oh, yes! Thank you, Miss Ming!'

'You are doing him good, Miss Ming, I think.'

'He's doing *me* good, Dafnish. And it will give *you* a chance to be by yourself and relax for a bit, eh?' Her tone of criticism, of false concern, did not offend Dafnish as much as usual. She inclined her head.

'That's settled, then. I'll pick you up tomorrow, Snuffles. And I'll be thinking of some jolly games we can play, eh?'

'Oh, yes!'

They strolled across the undulating turf to where the air cars waited. Most of the other guests had already gone. Dafnish Armatuce helped her son into their car, which was fashioned in the shape of a huge apple-half, red and green, and, astonished that the woman had made no attempt to return with them to Canaria, bid Miss Ming a friendly farewell.

Snuffles leaned from the car as it rose into the pink and amber sky, waving to Miss Ming until she was out of sight.

'You are happy, Snuffles?' asked Dafnish as he settled himself into his cushions.

'I never had a nicer day, mama. It's funny, isn't it, but I used not to like Miss Ming at all, when she kept hanging around us. I thought she wanted to be your friend, but really she wanted to be mine. Do you think that's so?'

'It seems to be true. I'm glad you enjoyed today, and you shall play with Miss Ming often. But I beg you to remember, my boy, that you are an Armatuce: One day you must become an adult and take my place, and serve.'

His laughter was frankly astonished. 'Oh, mama! You don't really think we'll ever go back to Armatuce, do you? It's impossible. Anyway, it's nicer here. There's a lot more to do. It's more exciting. And there's plenty to eat.'

'I have always seen the attraction this world holds for a boy, Snuffles. However, when you are mature you will recognize it for what it is. I have your good at heart. Your moral development is my responsibility (though I grant you your right to enjoy the delights of childhood while you may), but I feel that you are forgetting . . .'

'I shan't forget, mama.' He dismissed her fears. They were passing over the tops of some blue-black clouds shot through with strands of gleaming grey. He studied them. 'Don't you think Miss Ming a marvellous lady, though?'

'She has an affinity with children, obviously. I should not have suspected that side to her character. I have modified my opinion of her.'

Dafnish did not let Snuffles see her frown as she contemplated her motives in allowing him freedom that would be sheer licence in Armatuce. Events must take their own course, for a while; then she might determine how good or bad were the effects of Miss Ming's company upon her son.

138

The mesa, red sandstone and tall, on which stood golden, cage-shaped Castle Canaria, came into view; the air car lost height, speeding a few feet above the waving, yellow corn which grew here the year round, aiming for the dark entrance at the base of the cliff.

'You must try to remember, Snuffles,' she added, while the car took its old place in the row of oddly assorted companions (none of which Lord Jagged ever seemed to use), 'that Miss Ming regrets becoming an adult. That she wishes she was still, like you, a child. You may find, therefore, a tendency in her to try to make you suppress your maturer thoughts. In my company, I feel, you thought too much as an adult – but in hers you may come to think too much as a child. Do you follow me?'

But Snuffles, played out, had fallen asleep. Tenderly she raised him in her arms and began to walk (she refused to fly) up the ramp towards the main part of the castle.

Through rooms hung in draperies of different shades of soft brown or yellow, through the great Hall of Antiquities, she carried her child, until she came to her own apartments, where mechanical servants received the boy, changed his clothes for night attire and put him to bed. She sat on a chair beside him, watching the servants move gently about the room, and she tenderly stroked his fair curls, so, save for colour, like her own (as was his face), and yearned a trifle for Armatuce and home. It was as she rose to go to her chamber, adjoining his, that she saw a figure standing in the entrance. She knew a second's alarm, then laughed. 'Lord Jagged. You are back!'

He bowed. There was a weariness in his face she had never noted before.

'Was your journey hard?'

'It had its interests. The fabric of Time, those Laws we have always regarded as immutable ...' He hesitated, perhaps realizing that he spoke to himself.

He was dressed in clothes of a pearly grey colour, of stiffer material than he usually preferred. She felt that they suited him better, were more in keeping with the temperament she detected behind the insouciant exterior. Did he stagger as he walked? She put out a hand to help, but he did not notice it.

'You have been travelling in Time? How can that be?'

'Those of us who are indigenous to the End of Time are more

139

fortunate than most. Chronos tolerates us, perhaps because we have no preconceptions of what the past should be. No, I am weary. It is an easier matter to go back to a chosen point from one's own Era. If one goes forward, one can never go all the way back. Oh, I babble. I should not be speaking at all. I would tempt you.'

'Tempt me?'

'To try to return. The dangers are the same, but the checks against those dangers are less rigid. I'll say no more. Forgive me. I will *not* say more.'

She walked beside him, past her own rooms, down the brown and yellow corridor, eager for further information. But he was silent and determined to remain so. At his door he paused, leaning with one hand against the lintel, head bowed. 'Forgive me,' he said again. 'I wish you good night.'

She could not in all humanity detain him, no matter how great her curiosity. But the morning would come: here, at Canaria, the morning would come, for Lord Jagged chose to regulate his hours according to the age-old movements of the Earth and the Sun, and when it did she would demand her right to know if there was any possibility of return to Armatuce.

Thus it was that she slept scarcely at all that night and rose early, with the first vermillion flush of dawn, to note that Snuffles still slept soundly, to hover close by Jagged's door in the hope that he would rise early – though the evidence of last night denied this hope, she knew. Robot servants prowled past her, preparing the great house for the morning, ignoring her as she paced impatiently to the breakfast room with its wide windows and its views of fields, hills and trees, so like a world that had existed before Cataclysm, before Armatuce, and which none of her folk would ever have expected to see again. In most things Lord Jagged's tastes harked to the planet's youth.

The morning grew late. Snuffles appeared, hungry for the Dawn Age food the robots produced at his command, and proceeded to eat the equivalent of an Armatuce's monthly provisions. She had to restrain her impulse to stop him, to warn him that he must look forward to changing his habits, that his holiday could well be over. Dawn Age *kipper* followed antique *kedgeree*, to be succeeded by *sausages* and *cheese*, the whole washed down with primitive tea. She felt unusually hungry, but

140

the time for her daily meal was still hours away. Still Jagged did not come, although she knew it was ever his custom, when at Canaria, to breakfast each morning (he had always eaten solid food, even before the fashion for it). She returned to the passage, saw that his door was open, dared to glance in, saw no one.

'Where is Master?' she enquired of an entering servant.

The machine hesitated. 'Lord Jagged has returned to his work, my lady. To his laboratories. His engines.'

'And where are they?'

'I do not know.'

So Jagged was gone again. Elusive Jagged had disappeared, bearing with him the knowledge which could mean escape to Armatuce.

She found that she was clenching her hands in the folds of the white smock she wore. She relaxed her fingers, took possession of her emotions. Very well, she would wait. And, in the meantime, she had her new freedom.

Dafnish Armatuce returned to the breakfast room and saw that Miss Ming had arrived and was arranging sausages and broccoli on a plate to make some sort of caricature. Snuffles, mouth stuffed, spluttered. Miss Ming snorted through her nose.

'Good morning, good morning!' she trilled as she saw Dafnish. For an instant she stared at bare shoulders and night-dress with her old, heated expression, but it was swiftly banished. 'We're going swimming today, my boyfriend and me!'

'You'll be careful.' She touched her son's cheek. She was warmed by his warmth; she was happy.

'What can happen to him here?' Miss Ming smiled. 'Don't worry. I'll look after him – and he'll look after me – won't you, my little man?'

Snuffles grinned. 'Fear not, princess, you are safe with me.'

She clasped her hands together, piping, 'Oh, sir, you are so *strong*!'

Dafnish Armatuce shook her head, more amused than disturbed by her antics. She found herself thinking of Miss Ming as a child, rather than as an adult; she could no longer condemn her.

They left in the apple-shaped air car, flying south towards the sea. Dafnish watched until they were out of sight before she returned to her apartments. As she changed her clothes she

141

listened obsessively for a hint of Lord Jagged's return. She was tempted to remain at Canaria and wait for him, to beg him to aid her find Armatuce again, if only for a moment, so that she might warn others of their danger and show those nearest to her that she lived. But she resisted the impulse; it would be foolish to waste perhaps the only opportunity she had to seek the silent and remote places and be alone.

Walking down to where the air cars lay, she reflected upon the irony of her situation. Without apparent subtlety Miss Ming had first denied her the freedom she was now granting. Dafnish was impressed by the woman's power. But she lacked the inclination to brood on the matter at this time; instead, she relished her freedom.

She climbed into a boat shaped like a swooping, sand-coloured sphinx. Miss Ming and Snuffles had gone south. She spoke to the boat, a single word: 'North.'

And northward it took her, over the sentient, senile cities, the dusty plains, the ground-down mountains, the decaying forests, the ruins and the crumbling follies, to settle in a green valley through which a silver river ran and whose flanks were spotted with hawthorn and rowan and where a few beasts (what if they were mechanical?) grazed on grass which crunched as they pulled it from the soft earth, the sound all but drowned by the splashing of small waterfalls, sighing as the river made its winding way to a miniature and secluded lake at the far end of the valley.

Here she lay with her back against the turf, spread-eagled and displayed to the grey sky through which the sun's rays weakly filtered. And she sang one of the simple hymns of the Armatuce she had learned as a child and which she thought forgotten by her. And then, unobserved, she allowed herself to weep.

7

In which a Man is Made

Lord Jagged remained away from Canaria for many days, but
Dafnish Armatuce was patient. Every morning Miss Ming,
punctual in arriving, would take Snuffles on some new jaunt,
and she was careful to return at the agreed hour, when a joyful
boy would be reunited with a mother who was perhaps not so
unrelaxed as she had once been; then Miss Ming, with the air of
one who has performed a pleasant duty, would retire, leaving
them to spend the remainder of the afternoon together. If
Dafnish Armatuce thought she detected an unwelcome change
in her son's attitude to certain values she held dear, she told
herself that this was unreasonable fear, that she would be
harming the boy's development if she interfered too much with
his ideas. She hardly listened to his words as he described his
latest escapades with his friend, but the animation in his voice
was music and the sparkle in his eye was sweet to see, and
experience, she told herself, would teach him reverence.

She returned to her private valley time after time, glad that
whoever had created it had forgotten it or had, for some reason,
omitted to dissimilate it. Here, and only here, could she show
the whole Dafnish Armatuce to the world, for here there were
none to judge her, to quiz her as to why she spoke or sang,
laughed or wept. Her favourite maxims she told to trees; her
secret fears were confided to flocks of sheep; and stones were
audience to her hopes or dreams. Long for Armatuce she might,
but she did not despair.

Her confidence repaired, she was able to visit those she chose,
and most frequently she visited Sweet Orb Mace, who
welcomed her, observing to his friends that she was much improved, that she had learned to accept what life at the End of
Time could offer. A few fellow time travellers, also noticing this
improvement, guessed that she had found a lover and that her
lover was none other than haughty Lord Jagged. As a conse-

quence she was often questioned as to her host's whereabouts (for there was always such speculation where Lord Jagged was concerned), but, while she was not aware of the rumours, she kept her own counsel and added no flax to Dame Gossip's wheel. She courted Sweet Orb Mace (another, but less heavily backed contender for the title of Lover) for the simple reason that he possessed her time machine. He allowed her to inspect it, to linger in its cabin when she wished. She reassured him: She could not attempt to use it, her concern for Snuffles' well-being overriding any desire she might have to return to Armatuce. But, privately, she hoped; and should it be foolish to hope against all evidence, then Dafnish Armatuce was foolish.

If she had not found happiness, she had found a certain contentment, during the month which passed, and this gave her greater tolerance for herself, as well as for their society. Two more time travellers arrived in that month, and, perhaps unluckier than she, were snapped up, one for Doctor Volospion's menagerie, which he was patiently restocking, one for My Lady Charlotina's great collection. Dafnish spoke to both, and both agreed that they had little difficulty reaching the Future but that the Past (meaning their own period) had been denied them. She refused to be depressed by the information, consoling herself with the prospect of Jagged's help.

This equilibrium might have been maintained for many more such months had not Miss Ming betrayed (in Dafnish's terms) her trust.

It happened that Dafnish Armatuce, returning from visiting Brannart Morphail, the scientist (a visit cut short by the old misanthrope himself), passed in her air car over an area of parkland still occupied by the remnants of small Gothic palaces and towns which had been constructed, during a recent fad for miniatures, by the Duke of Queens. And there she observed two figures, which she recognized as those of Snuffles and Miss Ming, doubtless playing one of their fanciful games. Noting that it was almost time for Miss Ming to bring Snuffles home, Dafnish decided that she would save Miss Ming the trouble and collect him there and then. So the sphinx car sank to Earth at her command and she crossed a flower-strewn lawn to bend and enter the dim interior of the little chateau into which she had seen them go as she landed.

Having no wish to take them by surprise, she called out, but came upon them almost immediately, to discover Miss Ming dabbing hastily at Snuffles' face. In the poor light it was difficult to see why she dabbed, but Dafnish assumed that the lad had, as usual, been eating some confection of which she might have disapproved.

She chuckled. 'Oh, dear. What have you two been up to while my back was turned?' (This whimsicality more for Miss Ming's sake than her son's). She reached out her hand to the boy, whose guilty glance at Miss Ming seemed more imploring than was necessary, and led him into the sunlight.

She quelled the distaste she felt for the long red robes of velvet and lace in which Miss Ming had clothed him (Miss Ming herself wore tights and doublet) but could not resist a light 'What would they make of you in Armatuce?' and wondered why he kept his face from her.

Turning to Miss Ming, who had a peculiar expression upon her own features, she began, 'I'll take him –' And then her voice died as she saw the smeared rouge, the mascara, the eye shadow, the paint with which Miss Ming had turned the child's face into a parody of a female adult's.

Shocked, she trembled, unable to speak, staring at Miss Ming in accusation and horror.

Miss Ming tried to laugh. 'We were playing Princes and Princesses. There was no harm meant . . . '

The boy began to protest. 'Mama, it was only a game.'

All she could do was gasp, 'Too far. Too far,' as she dragged him to the air car. She pushed him roughly in, climbed in herself and stood confronting the ridiculous woman. She tensed herself to reduce the shaking in her body and she drew a deep breath. 'Miss Ming,' she said carefully, 'you need not call tomorrow.'

'I hardly think,' said Miss Ming. 'I mean, I feel you're over-reacting, aren't you? What's wrong with a little fantasy?'

'This,' indicating the cosmetics on the frightened face, 'is not what children do!'

'Of course they do. They love to dress up and play at being big people.'

'I thought, Miss Ming, you played at children. You are a corrupt, foolish woman. I concede that you are unaware of your folly, but I cannot have my child influenced any longer by it. I admit my own stupidity, also. I have been lazy. I allowed myself to believe that your nonsense could do Snuffles no harm.'

'Harm? You're overstating . . . '

'I am not. I saw you. I saw the guilt. And I saw guilt on my boy's face. There was never guilt there before, in all the years of his life.'

'I've nothing to be ashamed of!' protested Miss Ming as the air car rose over her head. 'You're reacting like some frustrated old maid. What's the matter, isn't Lord Jagged – ?' The rest faded and they were on course again for Canaria.

Metal servants gently bathed the boy as soon as they arrived. Slowly the cosmetics disappeared from his skin, and Dafnish Armatuce looked at him with new eyes. She saw a pale boy, a boy who had become too fat; she saw lines of self-indulgence in his face; she detected signs of greed and arrogance in his defiant gaze. Had all this been put there by Miss Ming? No, she could not blame the silly woman. The fault was her own. Careful not to impose upon him the strictures which she imposed upon herself, she had allowed him to indulge appetites which, per-haps, she secretly wished to indulge. In the name of Love and Tolerance she, not Ming, had betrayed Trust.

'I have been unfair,' she murmured as the robots wrapped him in towels. 'I have not done my duty to you, Snuffles.'

'You'll let me play with Miss Ming tomorrow, mama?'

She strove to see in him that virtue she had always cherished, but it was gone. Had it gone from her, too?

'No,' she said quietly.

The boy became savage. 'Mama! You must! She's my only friend!'

'She is no friend.'

'She loves me. You do not!'

'You are that part of myself I am allowed to love,' she said. 'That is the way of the Armatuce. But perhaps you speak truth, perhaps I do not really love anything.' She sighed and lowered her head. She had, she thought, become too used to crying. Now the tears threatened when they had no right to come.

He wheedled. 'Then you will let me play with Miss Ming?'

'I must restore your character,' she said firmly. 'Miss Ming is banished.'

'No!'

'My duty – '

'Your duty is to yourself, not to me. Let me go free!'

'You *are* myself. The only way in which I could give you freedom is to let you come to adult status . . . '

'Then do so. Give me my life-right.'

'I cannot. It serves the Armatuce. The race. We have to go back. At least we must try.'

'You go. Leave me.'

'That is impossible. If I were to perish, you would have no means of sustenance. Without me, you would die!'

'You are selfish, mama! We can never go back to Armatuce.'

'Oh, Snuffles! Do you feel nothing for that part of you which is your mother?'

He shrugged. 'Why don't you let me play with Miss Ming?'

'Because she will turn you into a copy of her fatuous, silly self.'

'And you would rather I was a copy of a prude like you. Miss Ming is right. You should find yourself a friend and forget me. If I am doomed to remain a child, then at least let me spend my days with whom I choose!'

'You will sleep now, Snuffles. If you wish to continue this debate, we shall do so in the morning.'

He sulked, but the argument, the effort of thinking in this way, had tired him. He allowed the robots to lead him off.

Dafnish Armatuce was also tired. Already she was debating the wisdom of allowing herself to react as she had done. No good was served by insulting the self-justifying Miss Ming; the boy lacked real understanding of the principles involved. She had been guilty of uncontrolled behaviour. She had failed, after all, to maintain her determination, her ideals. In Armatuce there would be no question of her next decision, she would have applied for adult status for her son and, if it had been granted, so settled the matter. But here . . .

And was she justified in judging Miss Ming a worse influence than herself? Perhaps Miss Ming, in this world, prepared Snuffles for survival? But she could not support such an essentially cynical view. Miss Ming was disliked by all, renowned for her stupidity. Lord Jagged would make a better mentor; Sweet Orb Mace, indeed, would make a better mentor than Miss Ming.

All the old confusion swam back into her mind, and she regretted bitterly her misguided tolerance in allowing Miss Ming to influence the boy. But still she felt no conviction; she wondered whether self-interest, loneliness – even jealousy – had dictated her actions. Never before had she known such turmoil of conscience.

That night the sleep of Dafnish Armatuce was again disturbed and there were dreams, vague, prophetic and terrible, from which she woke into a reality scarcely less frightening. Before dawn she fell asleep again, dreaming of her husband and her co-workers in Armatuce. Did they condemn her? It seemed so.

She became aware, as she slept, that there was pressure on her legs. She tried to move them, but something blocked them. She opened her eyes, sought the obstruction, and saw that Miss Ming sat there. She was prim today. She wore black and blue; muted, apologetic colours. Her eyes were downcast. She twisted at a cuff.

'I came to apologize,' said Miss Ming.

'There is no need.' Her head ached; the muscles in her back were knotted. She rubbed her face. 'It was my fault, not yours.'

'I was carried away. It was so delightful, you see, for me. As a girl I had no chums.'

'I understand. But,' more gently, 'you still intrude, Miss Ming.'

'I know you, too, must be very lonely. Perhaps you resent the fact that your son has a friend in me. I don't mean to be rude, but I've thought it over lots. I feel I should speak out. You shouldn't be unkind to Snuffles.'

'I have been. I shall not be in future.'

Miss Ming frowned. 'I thought of a way to help. It would give you more freedom to live your own life. And I'm sure Snuffles would be pleased . . . '

'I know what to do, Miss Ming.'

'You wouldn't punish him! Surely!'

'There is no such thing as punishment in Armatuce. But I must strengthen his character.'

A tear gleamed. Miss Ming let it fall. 'It's all my fault. But we were good friends, Dafnish, just as you and I could be good friends, if you'd only . . . '

'I need no friends. I have Armatuce.'

148

'You need me!' The woman lurched forward, making a clumsy attempt to embrace her. 'You need me!'

The wail was pathetic and Dafnish Armatuce was moved to pity as she pushed Miss Ming by her shoulders until she had resumed her original position on the bed. 'I do not, Miss Ming.'

'The boy stands between us. If only you'd let him grow up normally!'

'Is that what you were trying to achieve?'

'No! We were both misguided. I sought to please *you*, don't you see? You're so proud, such an egotist. And this is what I get. Oh, yes, I was a fool.'

'The customs of the Armatuce are such,' said Dafnish evenly, 'that special procedures must be taken before a child is allowed adult status. There is no waste in Armatuce.'

'But this is *not* Armatuce.' Miss Ming was sobbing violently. 'You could be happy here, with me, if you'd only let me love you. I don't ask much. I don't expect love in return, not yet. But, in time . . . '

'The thought is revolting to me!'

'You suppress your normal emotions, that's all!'

She said gently: 'I am an Armatuce. That means much to me. I should be obliged, Miss Ming, if . . . '

'I'm going!' The woman rose, dabbing at her eyes. 'I could help. Doctor Volospion would help us both. I could . . . '

'Please, Miss Ming.'

Miss Ming looked up imploringly. 'Could I see Snuffles? One last time?'

Dafnish relented. 'To say goodbye to the child? Yes. Perhaps you could help me – '

'Anything!'

'Tell him to remember his destiny. The destiny of an Armatuce.'

'Will he understand?'

'I hope so.'

'I'll help. I *want* to help.'

'Thank you.'

Miss Ming walked unsteadily from the room. Dafnish Armatuce heard her footsteps in the corridor, heard her enter Snuffles' chamber, heard the child's exclamation of pleasure. She drew a deep breath and let it leave her slowly. With considerable effort she got up, washed and dressed, judging, now, that Miss Ming had had a fair allotment of time with the boy.

As she entered the brown and yellow hall, she glanced across to Lord Jagged's door. It was open. She hesitated, and as she did so, Lord Jagged appeared, looking less tired than he had before, but more thoughtful.

'Lord Jagged!'

'Aha, the admirable Dafnish!' His smile was soft, almost melancholy. 'Do you enjoy your stay at Canaria? Is all to your liking?'

'It is perfect, Lord Jagged, but I would go home.'

'You cannot. Are you still unconvinced?'

'When we last met – that night – you said something concerning the fabric of Time. The Laws, hitherto regarded as immutable, were not operating as expected?'

'I was weary. I should not have spoken.'

'But you did. Therefore can I not request a fuller explanation?'

'I would raise hope where none should be permitted.'

'Can I not judge?'

He shrugged, his high, grey collar almost swallowing the lower half of his face. His slim hands fingered his lower lip. 'Very well, but I must ask secrecy from you.'

'You have it. I am an Armatuce.'

'There is little I can tell you, save this: Of late the sturdy, relentless structure of Time, which has always, so far as we know, obeyed certain grim Laws of its own, has begun to show instabilities. Men *have* returned to the past and remained there for much longer periods than was thought possible. By contravening the Laws of Time, they have further weakened them. There are disruptions – distortions – anomalies. I hope to discover the true cause, but every passage through Time threatens the fabric further, producing paradoxes which, previously, Time refused to allow. So far no major disaster has occurred – history remains history – but there is a danger that history itself will be distorted and then – well, we all might suddenly vanish as if we had never been!'

'Is that possible? I have listened to such speculation, but it has always seemed pointless.'

'Who knows if it is possible? But can we take the risk? If, say,

150

you were to return to Armatuce and tell them what the future held, would that not alter the future? You are familiar with these arguments, of course.'

'Of course. But I would tell them nothing of your world. It would be too disturbing.'

'And your boy? Children are not so discreet.'

'He is an Armatuce. He would be silent.'

'No, no. You risk your lives by moving against the current.'

'Our lives are for Armatuce. They serve no purpose here.'

'That is a difficult philosophy for one such as I to comprehend.'

'Let me try!'

'Your boy would go with you?'

'Of course. He would have to.'

'You'd subject him to the same dangers?'

'Here, his soul is endangered. Soon he will be incapable of giving service. His life will be worthless.'

'It is a harsh, materialist assessment of worth, surely?'

'It is the way of the Armatuce.'

'Besides, there is the question of a time vessel.'

'My own is ready. I have access to it.'

'There are only certain opportunities, when the structure wavers . . . '

'I should wait for one. In the machine.'

'Could you not leave the child, at any rate?'

'He would not be able to exist without me. I grant his life-right. He is part of me.'

'Maternal instincts . . . '

'More than that!'

'If you say so.' He shook his head. 'It is not my nature to influence another's decisions, in the normal course of things. Besides, no two consciences are alike, particularly when divorced by a million or two years.' He shook his head. 'The fabric is already unstable.'

'Let me take my son and leave! Now! Now!'

'You fear something more than the strangeness of our world.' He looked shrewdly into her face, 'What is it that you fear, Dafnish Armatuce?'

'I do not know. Myself? Miss Ming? It cannot be. I do not know, Lord Jagged.'

151

'Miss Ming? What harm could that woman do but bore you to distraction? Miss Ming?'

'She – she has been paying court to me. And, in a way, to my child. In my mind she has become the greatest threat upon the face of this planet. It is monstrous to me to permit such notions to flourish, but I do. And because she inspires them, I hate her. And because I hate her, why, I detect something in myself which must resemble her. And if I resemble her, how can I judge her? I, Dafnish Armatuce of the Armatuce, must be at fault.'

'This is complicated reasoning. Perhaps too complicated for sanity.'

'Oh, yes, Lord Jagged, I could be mad. I have considered the possibility. It's a likely one. But mad by whose standards? If I can go back to Armatuce, let Armatuce judge me. It is what I rely upon.'

'I'll agree to debate this further,' he said. 'You are in great pain, are you not, Dafnish Armatuce?'

'In moral agony. I admit it.'

He licked his upper lip, deliberating. 'So strange, to us. I had looked forward to conversations with you.'

'You should have stayed here, then, at Canaria.'

I would have liked that, but there are certain very pressing matters, you know. Some of us serve, Dafnish Armatuce, in our individual ways, to the best of our poor abilities.' His quiet laughter was self-deprecating. 'Shall we breakfast together?'

'Snuffles?'

'Let him join us when it suits him.'

'Miss Ming is with him. They say their farewells.'

'Then give them the time they need.'

She was uncertain of the wisdom of this, but with the hope of escape, she could afford to be more generous to Miss Ming. 'Very well.'

As they sat together in the breakfast room, she said, 'You do not believe that Miss Ming is evil, do you, Lord Jagged?' She watched him eat, having contented herself with the treat of a slice of toast.

'Evil is a word, an idea, which has very little resonance at the End of Time, I'm afraid. Crime does not exist for us.'

'But crime exists here.'

'For you, Dafnish Armatuce, perhaps. But not for us.'

She looked up. She thought she had seen something move past the window, but she was tired; her eyes were faulty. She gave him her attention again. He had finished his breakfast and was rising, wiping his lips. 'There must be victims, you see,' he added.

She could not follow his arguments. He had become elusive once more, almost introspective. His mind considered different, to him more important, problems.

'I must go to the boy,' she said.

All at once she had his full attention. His grey, intelligent eyes penetrated her. 'I have been privileged, Dafnish Armatuce,' he said soberly, 'to entertain you as my guest.'

Did she blush then? She had never blushed before.

He did not accompany her back to the apartments, but made his apologies and entered the bowels of the building, about his own business again. She went swiftly to the room, but it was empty.

'Snuffles!' She called out as she made her way to her own chamber. 'Miss Ming.'

They were gone.

She returned to the breakfast room. They were not there. She ran, panting, to the air-car hangar. She ran through it into the open, standing waist-high in the corn, questing for Miss Ming's own car. The blue sky was deserted. She knew, as she had really known since finding her son's room absented, that she had seen them leaving, seen the car as it flashed past the window.

She calmed herself. Reason told her that Miss Ming was merely taking Snuffles on a last impulsive expedition. It was, of course, what she might have suspected of the silly woman. But the dread would not dissipate. An image of the boy's painted features became almost tangible before her eyes. Her lips twisted, conquering her ability to arrange them, and it seemed that frost ate at the marrow of her bones. Fingers caught in hair, legs shook. Her glance was everywhere and she saw nothing but that painted face.

'Snuffles!'

There was a sound. She wheeled. A robot went by bearing the remains of the breakfast.

'Lord Jagged!'

She was alone.

She began to run through the yellow and brown corridors until she reached the hangar. She climbed into her air car and sat there, unable to give it instructions, unable to decide in which direction she should search first. The miniature palaces of yesterday? Were they not a favourite playground for the pair? She told the car its destination, ordered maximum speed.

But the Gothic village was deserted. She searched every turret, every hall into which she could squeeze her body, and she called their names until her voice cracked. At last she clambered back into her car. She recalled that Miss Ming was still resident at Doctor Volospion's menagerie.

'Doctor Volospion's,' she told the car.

Doctor Volospion's dwelling stood upon several cliffs of white marble and blue basalt, its various wings linked by slender, curving bridges of the same materials. Minarets, domes, conical towers, skyscraper blocks, sloping roofs and windows filled with some reflective but transparent material gave it an appearance of considerable antiquity, though it was actually only a few days old. Dafnish Armatuce had seen it once before, but she had never visited it, and now her difficulty lay in discovering the appropriate entrance.

It took many panic-filled minutes of circling about before she was hailed, from the roof of one of the skyscrapers, by Doctor Volospion himself, resplendent in rippling green silks, his skin coloured to match. 'Dafnish Armatuce! Have you come to accept my tryst? O, rarest of beauties, my heart is cast already – see – at your feet.' And he gestured, twisting a ring. She looked down, kicking the pulsing, bloody thing aside. 'I seek my Snuffles,' she cried. 'And Miss Ming. Are they here?'

'They were. To arrange your surprise. You'll be pleased. You'll be pleased. But have patience – come to me, splendid one.'

'Surprise? What have they done?'

'Oh, I cannot tell you. It would spoil it for you. I was able to help. I once specialized in engineering, you know. Sweet Orb Mace owes much to me.'

'Explain yourself, Doctor Volospion.'

'Perhaps, when the confidences of the bedchamber are exchanged . . . '

'Where did they go?'

154

'Back. To Canaria. It was for you. Miss Ming was overjoyed by what I was able to accomplish. The work of a moment, of course, but the skill is in the swiftness.' With a wave of his hand he changed his costume to roaring red. The light of the flames flooded his face with shadow. But she had left him.

As she fled back to Canaria, she thought she heard Doctor Volospion's laughter; and she knew that her mind could not be her own if she detected mockery in his mirth.

On her right the insubstantial buildings of Djer streamed past, writhing with gloomy colour, muttering to themselves as they strove to recall some forgotten function, some lost experience, re-creating, from a memory partially disintegrated, indistinct outlines of buildings, beasts or men, calling out fragments of song or scientific formulae; almost piteous, this place, which had once served Man proudly, in the spirit with which she served the Armatuce, so that she permitted herself a pang of understanding, for she and the city shared a common grief.

'Ah, how much better it might have been had we stayed there,' she said aloud.

The city cried out to her as if in reply, as if imploringly:

> The world is too much with us; late and soon,
> Getting and spending, we lay waste our powers:
> Little we see in Nature that is ours;
> We have given our hearts away, a sordid boon!

She did not understand the meaning of the words, but she replied: 'You could have helped me, but I was afraid of you. I feared your variety, your wealth.' Then the car had borne her on, and soon Canaria's graceful cage loomed into view, glittering in sparse sunshine, its gold all pale.

With tense impatience she stood stiffly in the car while it docked, until she could leap free, running up the great ramp, through the dwarfing portals, down halls which echoed a magnified voice, calling for her boy.

It was when she had pushed open the heavy doors of Lord Jagged's Hall of Antiquities that she saw three figures standing at the far end, beneath a wall mounted with a hundred examples of heavy Dawn Age furniture. They appeared to be discussing a large piece in dark wood, set with mirrors, brass and mother-of-pearl, full of small drawers and pigeonholes

155

from which imitation doves poked their little heads and crooned. Elsewhere were displayed fabrics, cooking utensils, vehicles, weapons, technical apparatus, entertainment structures, musical instruments, clothing from mankind's first few thousand years of true planetary dominance.

The three she saw were all adults, and she guessed initially that they might, themselves, be exhibits, but as she approached she saw, with lifting heart, that one of them was Lord Jagged and another was Miss Ming. Her anger with Miss Ming turned to annoyance and she experienced growing relief. The third figure she did not recognize. He was typical of those who inhabited the End of Time; a foppish, overdressed, posturing youth, doubtless some acquaintance of Lord Jagged's.

'Miss Ming!'

Three heads turned.

'You took Snuffles. Where is he now?'

'We went to visit Doctor Volospion, dearest Dafnish. We thought you would not notice. You yourself gave me the idea when you told me to remind Snuffles of his destiny. It's my present to you.' She fluttered winsome lashes. 'Because I care so much for you. A tribute of my admiration for the wonderful way you've tried to do your best for your son. Well, Dafnish, I have put your misery at an end. No more sacrifices for you!'

Dafnish Armatuce did not listen, for the tone was as familiar to her as it was distasteful. 'Where is Snuffles now?' she repeated.

The youth, standing behind Miss Ming, laughed, but Lord Jagged was frowning.

Miss Ming's oversweet smile spread across her pallid face. 'I have done you a favour, Dafnish. It's a surprise, dear.' Two clammy hands tried to fold themselves around one of Dafnish's, but she pulled away. Miss Ming had to be content with clinging to an arm. 'I know you'll be pleased. It's what you've looked forward to, what you've worked for. And it means real freedom for us.'

'Freedom? What do you mean? Where is my Snuffles?'

Again the stranger laughed, spreading his arms wide, showing off exotic garments – blue moleskin tabard stitched with silver, shirt of brown velvet with brocaded cuffs, puffed out at the shoulders to a height of at least two feet, hose which curled with snakes of varicoloured light, boots whose feet were the heads of living, glaring dragons, the whole smelling strongly of musk – and pouting in his peacock pride. 'Here, mama!'

She stared.

The youth waltzed forward, the smile languid, the eyes half-closed. 'I am your son! It is my destiny come to fulfilment at last. Miss Ming has made a man of me!'

Miss Ming preened herself, murmuring with false modesty: 'With Doctor Volospion's help. My idea – his execution.'

Dafnish Armatuce swayed on her feet as she stared. The face was longer, more effeminate, the eyes large, darker, luminous, the hair pure blond; but something of Snuffles, something of herself, was still there. There were emeralds in his lobes. His brows had been slimmed and their line exaggerated; the lips, though naturally red, were too full and too bright.

Dafnish Armatuce groaned and her fingers fled to cover her face. A hand touched her shoulder. She shook it off and Lord Jagged apologized.

Miss Ming's voice celebrated the spirit of comfiness: 'It's a shock, of course, at first, until you understand what it means. You don't have to die!'

'Die?' She looked with loathing upon Miss Ming's complacent features.

'He is a man and you are free. Snuffles explained something of your customs to me.'

'Customs! It is more than custom, Miss Ming. How can this be? What of his life-right? He has no soul!'

'Such superstitions,' declared Miss Ming, 'are of little consequence at the End of Time.'

'I have not transferred the life-right! He remains a shadow until that day! But even that is scarcely important at this moment – look what you have made of him! Look!'

'You really are very silly, mother,' said Snuffles, his voice softening in something close to kindness. 'They can do anything here. They can change their shapes to whatever they wish. They can be children, if they want to be, or beasts, or even plants. Whatever fancy dictates. I am the same personality, but I have grown up, at last! Sixty years was too long. I have earned my maturity.'

'You remain an infant!' she spoke through her teeth. 'Like

your fatuous and self-called friend. Miss Ming, he must be restored to his proper body. We leave, as soon as we may, for Armatuce.'

Miss Ming was openly incredulous and condescending. 'Leave? To be killed or stranded?'

Snuffles affected superciliousness. 'Leave?' he echoed. 'For Armatuce? Mother, it's impossible. Besides, I have no intention of returning.' He leaned against the rusted remains of a Nash Rambler and shared (or thought he shared) a conspiratorial wink with Miss Ming and Lord Jagged. 'I shall stay.'

'But' – her lips were dry – 'your life-right . . . '

'Here, I do not need my life-right. Keep it, mother. I do not want your personality, your ridiculous prejudices. Why should I wish to inherit them, when I have seen so much? Here, at the End of Time, I can be myself – an individual, not an Armatuce!'

'His destiny?' Dafnish rounded on Miss Ming. 'You thought I meant *that*?'

'Oh, you . . . ' Miss Ming's blue eyes, bovine and dazed, began to fill.

'I could change him to his original shape,' began Lord Jagged, but Dafnish Armatuce shook her head in misery.

'It is too late, Lord Jagged. What is there left?'

'But this is intolerable for you.' There was a hint of unusual emotion in Lord Jagged's voice. 'This woman is not one of us. She acts without wit or intelligence. There is no resonance in these actions of hers.'

'You would still say evil does not exist here?'

'If vulgar imitation of art is "evil", then perhaps I agree with you.'

Dafnish Armatuce was drained. She could not move. Her shoulder twitched a little in what might have been a shrug. 'Responsibility leaves me,' she said, 'and I feel the loss. Who knows but that I did use it as armour against experience.' She sighed, addressing her son. 'If adult you be, then make an adult's decision. Be an Armatuce, recall your Maxims, consider your Duty.' She was pleading and she could not keep her voice steady. 'Will you return with me to Armatuce? To Serve?'

'To serve fools? That would make a fool of me, would it not? Look about you! This is the way the race is destined to live, mother. Here – ' he spread decorated hands to indicate the world – 'here is my destiny, too!'

'Oh, Snuffles . . . ' Her head fell forward and her body trembled with her silent sobbing. '*Snuffles!*'

'That name's offensive to me, mother. Snuffles is dead. I am now the Margrave of Wolverhampton, who shall wander the world, impressing his magnificence on All! My own choice, the name, with Miss Ming's assistance concerning the details. A fine name, an excellent ambition. Thus I take my place in society, my only duty to delight my friends, my only maxim "Extravagance In Everything!" and I shall give service to myself alone! I shall amaze everyone with my inventions and events. You shall learn to be proud of me, mama!'

She shook her head. 'All my pride is gone.'

Several ancient clocks began to chime at once, and through the din she heard Lord Jagged's voice murmuring in her ear. 'The fabric of Time is particularly weak now. Your chances are at their best.'

She knew that this was mercy, but she sighed. 'If he came, what point? My whole life has been dedicated to preparing for the moment when my son would become an adult, taking my knowledge, my experience, my Duty. Shall I present our Armatuce with – with what he is now?'

The youth had heard some of this and now he raised a contemptuous shoulder to her while Miss Ming said urgently: 'You cannot go! You must not! I did it for you, so that you could be happy. So that we could enjoy a full friendship. There is no obstacle.'

Dafnish's laughter drove the woman back. Fingers in mouth, Miss Ming cracked a nail with her teeth, and the shadow of terror came and went across her face.

Dafnish spoke in an undertone. 'You have killed my son, Miss Ming. You have made of my whole life a travesty. Whether that shell you call "my son" survives or not, whether it should be moulded once more into the original likeness, it is of no importance any longer. I am the Armatuce and the Armatuce is me. You have poisoned at least one branch of that tree which is the Armatuce, whose roots bind the world, but I am not disconsolate; I know other branches will grow. Yet I must protect the roots, lest they be poisoned. I have a responsibility now which supersedes all others. I must return. I must warn my folk

159

never to send another Armatuce to the End of Time. It is evident that our time-travelling experiments threaten our survival, our security. You assure me that – that the boy can live without his life-right, that remaining part of my being which, at my death, I would pass on to him, so that he could live. Very well, I leave him to you and depart.'

Miss Ming wailed: 'You can't! You'll be killed! I love you!'

The youth held some kind of hayfork at arm's length, inspecting its balance and workmanship, apparently unconcerned. Dafnish took a step towards him. 'Snuffles . . . '

'I am not "Snuffles".'

'Then, stranger, I bid you farewell.' She had recovered something of her dignity. Her small body was still tense, her oval face still pale. She controlled herself. She was an Armatuce again.

'You'll be *killed*!' shrieked Miss Ming, but Dafnish ignored her. 'At best Time will fling you back to us. What good will the journey do you?'

'The Armatuce shall be warned. There is a chance of that?' The question was for Lord Jagged.

'A slight one. Only because the Laws of Time have already been transgressed. I have learned something of a great conjunction, of other layers of reality which intersect with ours, which suggests you might return, for a moment, anyway, since the Laws need not be so firmly enforced.'

'Then I go now.'

He raised a warning hand. 'But, Dafnish Armatuce, Miss Ming is right. There is little probability Time will let you survive.'

'I must try. I presume that Sweet Orb Mace, who has my time ship, knows nothing of this disruption, will take no precautions to keep me in your Age?'

'Oh, certainly! Nothing.'

'Then I thank you, Lord Jagged, for your hospitality. I'll require it no longer and you may let Snuffles go to Doctor Volospion's. You are a good man. You would make a worthy Armatuce.'

He bowed. 'You flatter me . . . '

'Flattery is unknown in Armatuce. Farewell.'

She began to walk back the way she had come, past row

upon row, rank upon rank of antiquities, past the collected mementoes of a score of Ages, as if, already, she marched, resolute and noble, through Time itself.

Lord Jagged seemed about to speak, but then he fell silent, his expression unusually immobile, his eyes narrowed as he watched her march. Slowly, he reached a fine hand to his long cheek and his fingers explored his face, just below the eye, as if he sought something there but failed to find it.

Miss Ming blew her nose and bawled:

'Oh, I've ruined everything. She was looking forward to the day you grew up, Snuffles! I *know* she was!'

'Margrave,' he murmured, to correct her. He made as if to take a step in pursuit, but changed his mind. He smoothed the pile of his tabard. 'She'll be back.'

'She'll realize her mistake?' Saucer eyes begged comfort from their owner's creation.

The Margrave of Wolverhampton had found a mirror in a silver frame. He was pleased with what he saw. He spoke absently to his companion.

'Possibly. And if she should reach Armatuce, she'll be better off. You have me for a friend, instead. Shall I call you mother?'

Mavis Ming uttered a wordless yelp. Impatiently the Margrave of Wolverhampton stroked her lank hair. 'She would never know how to enjoy herself. No Armatuce would. I am the first. Why should sacrifices be made pointlessly?'

Lord Jagged turned and confronted him. Lord Jagged was grim. 'She has much, your mother, that is of value. You shall never have that now.'

'My inheritance, you mean?' The Margrave's sneer was not altogether accomplished. 'My life-right? What use is it here? Thanks, old man, but no thanks!' It was one of Miss Ming's expressions. The Margrave acknowledged the origin by grinning at her for approval. She laughed through tears, but then, again, was seized:

'What if she dies!'

'She would have had to give it up, for me, when we returned. She loses nothing.'

'She passes her whole life to you?' said Jagged, revelation dawning. 'Her *whole* life?'

'Yes. In Armatuce but not here. I don't need the life-force.

161

There she would be absorbed into me, then I would change, becoming a man, but incorporating her "soul". What was of use to me in her body would also be used. Nothing is wasted in Armatuce. But this way is much better, for now only a small part of her is in me — the part she infused when I was made — and I become an individual. We both have freedom, though it will take her time to realize it.'

'You are symbiotes?'

'Of sorts, yes.'

'But surely,' said Jagged, 'if she dies before she transfers the life-right to you, you are still dependent on the life-force emanating from her being?'

'I would be, in Armatuce. But here, I'm my own man.'

Miss Ming said accusingly, 'You should have tried to stop her, Lord Jagged.'

'You said yourself she was free, Miss Ming.'

'Not to destroy herself!' A fresh wail.

'But to become your slave?'

'Oh, that's nonsense, Lord Jagged.' Another noisy blowing of the nose. 'Your trouble is, you don't understand real emotions at all.'

His smile as he looked down at her was twisted and strange.

'I loved her,' said Miss Ming defiantly.

8

The Return to Armatuce

Alone in her machine, her helmet once more upon her head, her protective suit once again armouring her body, Dafnish Armatuce quelled pain, at the sight of Snuffles' empty chair, and concentrated upon her instruments. All was ready.

She adjusted her harness, tightening it. She reached for the seven buttons inset on the chair's arm; she pressed a sequence of four. Green light rolled in waves across her vision, subtly altering to blue and then to black. Dials sang out their information, a murmuring rose to a shout: the ship was moving. She was going back through Time.

She watched for the pink light and the red, which would warn her that the ship was malfunctioning or that it was off course: the colours did not falter. She moved steadily towards her goal. Her head ached, but that was to be expected; neuralgia consumed her body (also anticipated); but the peculiar sense of unease was new, and her stare went too frequently to the small chair beneath the main console. To distract her attention, she brought in the vision screen earlier than was absolutely necessary. Outside was a predominantly grey mist, broken occasionally by bright flashes or patches of blackness; sometimes she thought she could distinguish objects for fractions of a second, but they never stayed long enough for her to identify them. The instruments were more interesting. They showed that she moved back through Time at a rate of one minute to the thousand years. The instruments were crude, she knew, but she had already traversed seven thousand years and it would be many more minutes before she came to Armatuce. The machine had automatic devices built into it so that it would return to its original resting place a few moments after it had, so far as the observers in Armatuce were aware, departed. As best she could, she refused to let her thoughts dwell on her return. She would have to lie, and she had never lied before. She would have to admit to having abandoned her boy and she would know disgrace; she would no longer be required to serve. Yet she knew that she *would* serve, if only she were allowed to warn them against further expeditions into the future. She would be content. Yet still her heart remained heavy. It was obvious that she, too, had been corrupted. She would demand isolation, in Armatuce, so that she would not corrupt others.

A shadow darkened the vision screens for a few seconds, then the grey, sparkling mist came back.

She heard herself speaking. 'It was not betrayal. He, too, was betrayed. I must not blame him.'

She had become selfish; she wanted her boy for herself, for comfort. Therefore, she reasoned, she did not deserve him. She must forget . . .

The machine shuddered, but no pink light came. Physical agony made her bite her lip, but the machine maintained its backward course.

It became difficult to breathe. At first she blamed the respirator, but she saw that it functioned perfectly. With considerable effort she made herself breathe more slowly, felt her heartbeat resume its normal rhythm. Why did she persist in experiencing that same panic she had first experienced at the End of Time – the sense of being trapped? No one had known claustrophobia in Armatuce for centuries. How could they? Such phobias had been eliminated.

Ten minutes passed. She was tempted to increase the machine's speed, but such a step would be dangerous. For the sake of the Armatuce, she must not risk her chances of getting home.

She recalled her son's disdainful words, remembered all the others who had told her that the sacrifices of the Armatuce were no longer valid. They had been valid once; they had saved the world, continued the race, passing life to life, building a huge fund of wisdom and knowledge. Like ants, she thought. Well, the ants survived. They and Man were virtually all that had survived the cataclysm. Was it not arrogant to assume that Man had any more to offer than the ant?

Five more minutes went by. The pain was worse, but it was not so sharp. Her sight was a little blurred, but she was able to see that the machine's passage through Time was steady.

Her moods seemed to change rapidly. One moment she was consoled and hopeful; at another she would sink into despair and be forced to fight against such useless emotions as regret and anger. She could not carry such things back to Armatuce! It would be Sin. She strove to recall some suitable Maxim, but none came to her.

The machine lurched, paused, and then it continued. Another six minutes had gone by. The pain suddenly became so intense that she lost consciousness. She had expected nothing else.

She awoke, her ears filled with the protesting whining of the time ship. She opened her eyes to pink, oscillating light. She blinked and peered at the instruments. All were at zero. It meant that she was back.

Hastily, with clumsy fingers, she freed herself of her harness. The vision screen showed the white laboratory, the pale-faced, black-clad figures of her compatriots. They were very still.

She opened the mechanism to raise the hatch, climbed urgently through, crying out: 'Armatuce! Armatuce! Beware of the Future!' She was desperate to warn them in case Time snatched her from her own Age before she could complete her chosen task, her last Service.

'Armatuce! The Future holds Despair! Send no more ships!' She stood half out of the hatch, waving to attract their attention, but they remained absolutely immobile. None saw her, none heard her, none breathed. Yet they were not statues. She recognized her husband among them. They lived, yet they were frozen!

'Armatuce! Beware the Future!'

The machine began to shake. The scene wavered and she thought she detected the faintest light of recognition in her husband's eye.

'We both live!' she cried, anxious to give him hope.

Then the machine lurched and she lost her footing, was swallowed by it. The hatch slammed shut above her head. She crawled to the speaking apparatus. 'Armatuce! Send no more ships!' The pink light flared to red. Heat increased. The machine roared.

Her mouth became so dry that she could hardly speak at all. She whispered, 'Beware the Future . . . ' and then she was burning, shivering, and the red light was fading to pink, then to green, as the machine surged forward again, leaving Armatuce behind.

She screamed. They had not seen her. Time had stopped. She dragged herself back to the chair and flung herself into it. She tried to pull her harness round her, but she lacked the strength. She pressed the four buttons to reverse the machine's impetus, forcing it against that remorseless current.

'Oh, Armatuce . . . '

She knew, then, that she could survive if she allowed the machine to float, as it were, upon the forward flow of Time, but her loyalty to Armatuce was too great. Again she pressed the buttons, bringing a return of the pink light, but she saw the indicators begin to reverse.

She staggered from her chair, each breath like liquid fire, and adjusted every subsidiary control to the reverse position. The machine shrieked at her, as if it pleaded for its own life, but it obeyed. Again the laboratory flashed upon the vision screen. She saw her husband. He was moving sluggishly.

Something seemed to burst in her atrophied womb; tears etched her skin like corrosive acid. Her hair was on fire.

She found the speaking apparatus again. 'Snuffles,' she whispered. 'Armatuce. Future.'

And she looked back to the screen; it was filled with crimson. Then she felt her bones tearing through her flesh, her organs rupturing, and she gave herself up, in peace, to the pain.

9

In which Miss Ming claims a Keepsake

'Adaptability, surely, is the real secret of survival?' The new Margrave of Wolverhampton seemed anxious to impress his unwilling host. Lord Jagged had been silent since Dafnish Armatuce's departure. 'I mean, that's why people like my mother are doomed,' continued the youth. 'They can't bear change. She could have been perfectly content here, if she'd listened to reason. Couldn't she, Lord Jagged?'

Lord Jagged was sprawled in an ancient steel armchair, refusing to give his affirmation to these protestations. Miss Ming had at last dried her eyes, hopefully for the final time. She inspected a 40th-century wall-hanging, feeling the delicate cloth with thumb and forefinger.

'I mean, that whole business about controlling the population. It wasn't necessary in Armatuce. It hadn't been for hundreds of years. There was wealth everywhere, but we weren't allowed to touch it. We never had enough to *eat*!' This last, plaintive, remark caused Lord Jagged to look up. Encouraged, the Margrave became expansive: 'The symbiosis, the ritual passing on of the life-force from one to another. It came about because children couldn't be produced naturally. I was made in a metal tub! She threw in a bit of her – what? – soul? Her "self"? Call it what you like. And there I was – forced to remain, once I'd grown a little, a child for sixty years! Oh, I was content enough, certainly, until I came here and saw what life could be like. If it hadn't been for Miss Ming . . . '

Lord Jagged sighed and closed his eyes.

'Think what you like!' The Margrave's silks rustled as he put a defiant hand to his hip. 'Miss Ming's done me a lot of good, and could have done Mother good, too. Whose fault is it? I was doomed to be linked to her until some complacent, ludicrous committee decided I could become an adult; but my mama would have to die so that I could inherit the precious – and probably non-existent – life-force! I'd have been a copy of her, little more. Great for her ego, eh? Lousy for mine.'

'And now you utter the coarse rhetoric of a Miss Ming!' Lord Jagged rose from his chair, an unusual bitterness in his tone. 'You substitute the Maxims of the Armatuce for the catch-phrases which support a conspiracy of selfishness and greed. There is dignity here, at the End of Time, but you do not ape that, because your mother also had dignity. You are vulgar now, little Snuffles, as no child can ever be vulgar. Do you not sense it? Can you not see how that wretched inhabitant of Doctor Volospion's third-rate menagerie has used you, to further her own stupid, short-sighted ambitions? She lusted for Dafnish Armatuce and thought you stood between her and the object of her desires. So she turned you into this travesty of maturity, with no more wit or originality or intelligence than she, herself, possesses.'

'Oh!' Miss Ming was sneering now. She caught at the young Margrave's arm. 'He's jealous because he wanted her for him-self. He's never kept guests here before. Don't take it out on the lad, Lord Jagged, or on me!'

He began to walk away. She crowed. 'The truth hurts, doesn't it?'

Without looking back, he paused. 'When couched in your terms, Miss Ming, it must always hurt.'

'Aha! You see!' She was triumphant. She embraced her monster. 'Time to go, Snuffles, dear.'

The youth was unresponsive. The ruby lips had turned the colour of ivory, the lustre had gone from the huge eyes. He staggered, clutching at his head. He moaned.

'Snuffles?'

'Marg – I am dizzy. I am hot. My body shakes.'

'A mistake in the engineering? Doctor Volospion can't have . . . We must get you back to him, in case . . . '

'Oh, I feel the flesh fading. My substance . . . ' His face had crumpled in pain. He lurched forward. A dry, retching noise came from a throat which had acquired the wrinkles of extreme old age. He fell to his knees. His skin began to crack. She tried to pull him to his feet.

'Lord Jagged!' cried Miss Ming. 'Help me. He's ill. Oh, why should this happen to me? No one can be ill at the End of Time.

168

Do something with one of your rings. Draw strength from the city.'

Lord Jagged had been watching, but he did not choose to move.

'Mother,' gasped the creature on the floor. 'My life-right . . . '

'He's dying! Help him, Lord Jagged! Save him!'

Lord Jagged seemed to be measuring his steps as he advanced slowly towards them. He stopped and looked without pity at Snuffles as he moved feebly in clothes too large for him. 'They were completely symbiotic, then,' mused Jagged. 'See, Miss Ming – Dafnish Armatuce must be dead – killed somewhere on the megaflow – escaping from this world. Or was she driven from it? Dafnish Armatuce is dead – and that part of her which was her son – a shadow, as she said – dies, too. Snuffles was never an individual, as we understand it.'

'It can't be. He's all I have left! Oh!' She leaned forward in horror, for the body was disintegrating rapidly, becoming fine, brown dust, leaving nothing but an empty suit of moleskin, velvet and brocade. The hose ceased to writhe with light; the dragon shoes scarcely hissed.

She looked up anxiously at the tall man. 'But you can resurrect him, Lord Jagged.'

'I am not sure I could. Besides, I see no reason to do so. There is little there to bring back to life. It is not Dafnish Armatuce. If it were, I would not hesitate. But her body burns somewhere between the end of one moment and the beginning of the next – and this, this is all we have of her now. Dying, she reclaims her son.'

Miss Ming shuddered with frustration. She glared at Lord Jagged, hating him, tensed as if, physically, she might attack him. But she had no courage.

Lord Jagged pursed his lips, then drew a deep breath of the musty air. He left her in his Hall of Antiquities, returning to his mysterious labours.

Later, Miss Ming stood up and unclenched her hand. On her palm lay a little pile of brown dust. She put it in her pocket, for a keepsake.

CONSTANT FIRE

mmanuel Bloom swung himself from the ceiling, an awkward macaw. He no longer wore his paint and motley but was again dressed in his black velvet suit.

Mavis Ming saw that he had entered by means of a hatch. Doubtless, the control cabin of the ship was above.

'My Goddess,' said the Fireclown.

She still sat on the edge of the bed. Her voice was without emotion. 'You traded me for the cup. That's what it was all about. What a fool I am!'

'No, not you. Doctor Volospion proposed the bargain and so enabled me to keep my word to him. He demanded the cup which I kept in my ship. I gave it to him.' He strutted across the cabin and manipulated a dial. Red-gold light began to fill his living quarters. Now everything glowed and each piece of fabric, wood or metal seemed to have a life of its own.

Mavis Ming stood up and edged away from the bed. She drew her kimono about her, over her pendulous breasts, her fat stomach, her wide thighs.

'Listen,' she began. She was breathing rapidly once more. 'You can't really want me, Mr Bloom. I'm fat old Mavis. I'm ugly. I'm stupid. I'm selfish. I should be left on my own. I'm better off on my own. I know I'm always looking for company, but really it's just because I never realized . . . '

He raised a stiff right arm in a gesture of impatience. 'What has any of that to do with my love for you? What does it matter if foolish Volospion thought he was killing two birds with one stone when he was actually freeing two eagles?'

'Look,' she said, 'if . . . '

'I am the Fireclown! I am Bloom, the Fireclown! I have lived the span of Man's existence. I have made Time and Space my toys. I have juggled with chronons and made the Multiverse laugh. I have mocked Reality and Reality has shrivelled to be re-born. My eyes have stared unblinking into the hearts of stars, and I have stood at the very core of the Sun and feasted on freshly created photons. I am Bloom, Eternally Blooming Bloom. Bloom the Phoenix. Bloom, the Destroyer of Darkness. These eyes, these large bulging eyes of mine, do you think they cannot see into souls as easily as they see into suns? Can they not detect an aura of pain that disguises the true centre of a being as smoke hides fire? That is why I choose to make you wise, to enslave you so that you may know true freedom.'

Miss Ming forced herself to speak. 'This is kidnapping and kidnapping is kidnapping whatever you prefer to call it . . . '

He ignored her.

'Of all the beings on that wasteland planet, you were one of the few who still lived. Oh, you lived as a frightened rodent lives, your spirit perverted, your mind enshelled with cynicism, refusing for a moment to look upon Reality for fear that it would detect you and devour you, like a wakened lion. Yet when Reality occasionally impinged and could not be escaped, how did you respond?'

'Look,' she said, 'you've got no right . . . '

'Right? I have every right! I am Bloom! You are my Bride, my Consort, my Queen, my Goddess. There is no woman deserves the honour more!'

'Oh, Christ!' she said. 'Please let me go. Please, I can't give you anything. I can't understand you. I can't love you.' She began to cry. 'I've never loved anyone! No one but myself.'

His voice was gentle. He took a few jerky steps closer to her. 'You lie, Mavis Ming. You do not love yourself.'

'Donny said I did. They all said I did, sooner or later.'

'If you loved yourself,' he told her, 'you would love me.'

Her voice shook. 'That's good . . . '

To Mavis Ming's own ears her words were without resonance of any kind. The collection of platitudes with which she had always responded to pain; the borrowed ironies, the barren tropes with which, instinctively, she had encumbered herself in order to placate a world she had seen as essentially malevolent, all were at once revealed as the meaningless things they were, with the result that an appalling self-consciousness, worse than anything she had suffered in the past, swept over her and every phrase she had ever uttered seemed to ring in her ears for what it had been: a mew of pain, a whimper of frustration, a cry for attention, a groan of hunger.

'Oh . . . '

She became incapable of speech. She could only stare at him, backing around the wall as he came, half-strutting, half-hopping, towards her, his head on one side, an appalling amusement in his unwinking, protruberant eyes, until her escape was blocked by a heavy wardrobe.

She became incapable of movement. She watched as he reached a twitching hand towards her face; the hand was firm and gentle as it touched her and its warmth made her realize how cold, how clammy, her own skin felt. She was close to collapse, only supported by the wall of the ship.

'The Earth is far behind us now,' he said. 'We shall never return. It does not deserve us.' He pointed to the bed. 'Go there. Remove your clothes.'

She gasped at him, trying to make him understand that she could not walk. She did not care, now, what his intentions were, but she was too exhausted to obey him.

'Tired . . . ' she said at last.

He shook his head. 'No. You shall not escape by that route, madam.' He spoke kindly. 'Come.'

The high-pitched ridiculous voice carried greater authority than any she had heard before. She began to walk towards the bed. She stood looking down at the sheets; the light made these, too, seem vibrant with life of their own. She felt his little claw-like hands pull the kimono from her shoulders, undo the tie, removing the garment entirely.

She felt him break the fastening on her bikini top so that her breasts hung even lower on her body. She felt no revulsion, nothing sexual at all, as his fingers pushed the bikini bottom over her hips and down her legs. And yet she was more aware of her nakedness than she had ever been, seeing the fatness, the pale flesh, without any emotion at all, remarking its poor condition as if it did not belong to her.

'Fat . . . ' she murmured.

His voice was distant. 'It is of no importance, this body. Besides, it shall not be fat for very long.

She began to anticipate his rape of her, wondering if, when he

175

began, she would feel anything. He ordered her to lie face down upon the bed. She obeyed. She heard him move away, then. Perhaps he was undressing. She turned to look, but he was still in his tattered velvet suit, taking something from a shelf. He poured sweet-smelling liquid into his palms.

She tried to feel afraid, because she knew that she should feel fear, but fear would not come. She continued to look up at him, over her shoulder, as he returned. Still her body made no response. This was quite unlike her sexual fantasies. What happened now neither excited her imagination nor her body. She wished that she could feel something, even terror. Instead she was possessed by a calmness, a sense of inevitability, unlike anything she had known.

'Now,' she heard him say, 'I shall bring your blood into the light. And with it shall come the devils that inhabit it, to be withered as weeds in the sun. And when I have finished you will know Rebirth, Freedom, Dominion over the Multiverse, and more. For I am the Fireclown and my very touch is fire.'

Was it a mark of her own insanity that she could detect no insanity in his words?

His touch fell upon her flesh. He stroked her buttocks and the pain stole her breath. She did not scream, but she gasped.

He stroked again, just below the first place, and she thought his flames lashed her. Her whole body jerked, trying to escape, but a firm hand held her down again, and again he touched her.

She did not scream, but she groaned as she drew in her breath. Next he stroked her thighs; next behind her knees, and his hands were firm now as she struggled. He held her by the back of the neck; he gripped her by the shoulder, by the loose flesh of her waist, and each time he gripped her she knew fresh pain.

Mavis Ming believed at last that it was Emmanuel Bloom's intention to tear every piece of skin from her body. He held her lips, her ears, her breasts, her vagina, the tender parts of her inner thighs, and every touch was fire.

She screamed, she blubbered for him to stop, she could not believe that he, any more than she, was any longer in control of what was happening. And yet he stroked her with a regularity which denied her even this consolation, until, at length, her whole body burned and she lay still, consumed.

Slowly, the fire faded from this peak of intensity and it seemed to her that, again, her body and her mind were united; this unity was new.

Emmanuel Bloom said nothing. She heard him cross the chamber to replace the bottle. She began to breathe with deep regularity, as if she slept. Her consciousness of her body produced an indefinable emotion in her. She moved her head to look at him and the movement was painful.

'I feel . . . ' Her voice was soft.

He stood with his arms stiffly at his sides. His head was cocked, his expression was tender and expectant.

She could find no word.

'It is your pride,' he said.

He reached to caress her face.

'I love you,' he said.

'I love you.' She began to weep.

He made her rise and look at her body in the oval mirror he revealed. It seemed that her skin was a lattice of long, red bruises; she could see where he had gripped her shoulders and her breasts. The pain was hard to tolerate without making at least a whisper of sound, but she controlled herself.

'Will you do this again?' she asked.

He shook his little head.

She walked back to the bed. Her back, though lacerated, was straight. She had never walked in that way before, with dignity. She sat down. 'Why did you do it?'

'In this manner? Perhaps because I lack patience. It is one of my characteristics. It was quick.' He laughed. 'Why do it to you, at all? Because I love you. Because I wished to reveal to you the woman that you are, the individual that you are. I had to destroy the shell.'

'It won't fade, this feeling?'

'Only the marks will go. It is within you to retain the rest. Will you be my wife?'

She smiled. 'Yes.'

'Well, then, this had been a satisfactory expedition, after all. Better, really, than I expected. Oh, what leaping delights we shall share, what wonders I can show you! No woman could desire more than to be the consort of Bloom, the Good Soldier, the Champion Eternal, the Master of the Multiverse! As you are my mistress, Mavis Ming.' He fell with a peculiar, spastic jerk, on his knees beside her. 'For Eternity. Will you stay? I can return you within an hour or two.'

'I will stay,' she said. 'Yet you gave up so much for me. That cup. It was your honour?'

He looked shamefaced. 'He asked for the cup I kept in my ship. I could not give him the Holy Grail, for it is not mine to give. I gave him something almost as dear to me, however. If Doctor Volospion ever deciphers the inscription on the cup, he will discover that it was awarded, in 1980, to Leonard Bloom, by the Union of Master Bakers, for the best chollah of the Annual Bakery Show, Whitechapel, London. He was a very good baker, my father. I loved him. I had kept his cup in all my journeys back and forth through the Time-streams and it was the most valuable thing I possessed.'

'So you do not have the Grail.' She smiled. 'It was all part of your plan – pretending to own it, pretending to be powerless – you tricked Doctor Volospion completely.'

'And he tricked me. Both are satisfied, for it is unlikely he shall ever know the extent of my trickery and doubtless considers himself a fine fellow! All are satisfied!'

'And now . . . ?' she began.

'And now,' he said, 'I'll leave you. I must set my controls. You shall see all that is left of this Universe and then, through the centre of the brightest star, into the greater vastness of the Multiverse beyond! There we shall find others to inspire and if we find no life at all, upon our wanderings, it is within our power to create it, for I am the Fireclown. I am the Voice of the Sun! Aha! Look! It has come to you, too. This, my love, is Grace. This is our reward!'

The cabin was filled suddenly by brilliant golden light, apparently having as its source a beam which entered through the very shell of the spaceship, falling directly upon the ziggurat at the end of the bed.

A smell, like sweet spring flowers after the rain, filled the cabin, and then a crystal cup, brimming with scarlet liquid, appeared at the top of the ziggurat.

Scarlet rays spread from a hundred points in the crystal, almost blinding her, and, although Mavis Ming could hear nothing, she received an impression of sonorous, delicate music.

178

She could not help herself as she lifted her aching body from the bed to the floor and knelt, staring into the goblet in awe.

From behind her the Fireclown chuckled and he knelt beside her, taking her hand.

'We are married now,' he said, 'before the Holy Grail. Married individually and together. And this is our Trust which shall be taken from us should we ever commit the sin of accidia. Here is proof of all my claims. Here is Hope. And should we ever cease to forget our purpose, should we ever fall into that sin of inertia, should we lose, for more than a moment, our Faith in our high resolve, the Grail will leave us and shall vanish forever from the sight of Man, for I am Bloom, the Last Pure Knight, and you are the Pure Lady, chastised and chaste, who shall share these Mysteries with me.'

She began: 'It is too much. I am not capable . . . ' But then she lifted her head and she smiled, staring into the very heart of the goblet. 'Very well.'

'Look,' he said, as the vision began to fade, 'your wounds have vanished.'

ELRIC AT
THE END OF TIME

For Terry Pratchett

In which Mrs Persson Detects an Above Average Degree of Chaos in the Megaflow

eturning from China to London and the Spring of 1936, Una Persson found an unfamiliar quality of pathos in most of the friends she had last seen, as far as she recalled, during the Blitz on her way back from 1970. Then they had been desperately hearty: it was a comfort to understand that the condition was not permanent. Here, at present, Pierrot ruled and she felt she possessed a better grip on her power. This was, she admitted with shame, her favourite moral climate for it encouraged in her an enormously gratifying sense of spiritual superiority: the advantage of having been born, originally, into a later and probably more sophisticated age. The 1960s. Some women, she reflected, were forced to have children in order to enjoy this pleasure.

But she was uneasy, so she reported to the local Time Centre and the bearded, sullen features of Sergeant Alvarez who welcomed her in white, apologizing for the fact that he had himself only just that morning left the Lower Devonian and had not had time to change.

'It's the megaflow, as you guessed,' he told her, operating toggles to reveal his crazy display systems. 'We've lost control.'

'We never really had it.' She lit a Sherman's and shook her long hair back over the headrest of the swivel chair, opening her military overcoat and loosening her webbing. 'Is it worse than usual?'

'Much.' He sipped cold coffee from his battered silver mug. 'It cuts through every plane we can pick up – a rogue current swerving through the dimensions. Something of a twister.'

'Jerry?'

'He's dormant. We checked. But it's like him, certainly. Most probably another aspect.'

183

'Oh, sod.' Una straightened her shoulders.

'That's what I thought,' said Alvarez. 'Someone's going to have to do a spot of rubato.' He studied a screen. It was Greek to Una. For a moment a pattern formed. Alvarez made a note. 'Yes. It can either be fixed at the nadir or the zenith. It's too late to try anywhere in between. I think it's up to you, Mrs P.'

She got to her feet. 'Where's the zenith?'

'The End of Time.'

'Well,' she said, 'that's something.'

She opened her bag and made sure of her jar of instant coffee. It was the one thing she couldn't get at the End of Time.

'Sorry,' said Alvarez, glad that the expert had been there and that he could remain behind.

'It's just as well,' she said. 'This period's no good for my moral well-being. I'll be off, then.'

'Someone's got to.' Alvarez failed to seem sympathetic.

'It's Chaos out there.'

'You don't have to tell me.'

She entered the make-shift chamber and was on her way to the End of Time.

In which The Eternal Champion Finds
Himself at the End of Time

Elric of Melniboné shook a bone-white fist at the greedy, glaring stars – the eyes of all those men whose souls he had stolen to sustain his own enfeebled body. He looked down. Though it seemed he stood on something solid, there was only more blackness falling away below him. It was as if he hung at the centre of the universe. And here, too, were staring points of yellow light. Was he to be judged?

His half-sentient runesword, Stormbringer, in its scabbard on his left hip, murmured like a nervous dog.

He had been on his way to Imrryr, to his home, to reclaim his kingdom from his cousin Yyrkoon; sailing from the Isle of the Purple Towns where he had guested with Count Smiorgan Bald-head. Magic winds had caught the Filkharian trader as she crossed the unnamed water between the Vilmirian peninsula and the Isle of Melniboné. She had been borne into the Dragon Sea and thence to The Sorcerer's Isle, so-called because that barren place had been the home of Cran Liret, the Thief of Spells, a wizard infamous for his borrowings, who had, at length, been dispatched by those he sought to rival. But much residual magic had been left behind. Certain spells had come into the keeping of the Krettii, a tribe of near-brutes who had migrated to the island from the region of The Silent Land less than fifty years before. Their shaman, one Grrodd Ybene Eenr, had made unthinking use of devices buried by the dying sorcerer as the spells of his peers sucked life and sanity from them. Elric had dealt with more than one clever wizard, but never with so mindless a power. His battle had been long and exhausting and had required the sacrifice of most of the Filkharians as well as the entire tribe of Krettii. His sorcery had become increasingly desperate. Sprite fought sprite, devil fell upon devil, in both physical and astral, all around the region of The Sorcerer's Isle.

Eventually Elric had mounted a massive summoning against the allies of Grrodd Ybene Eenr with the result that the shaman had been at last overwhelmed and his remains scattered in Limbo. But Elric, captured by his own monstrous magickings, had followed his enemy and now he stood in the Void, crying out into appalling silence, hearing his words only in his skull:

'*Arioch! Arioch! Aid me!*'

But his patron Duke of Hell was absent. He could not exist here. He could not, for once, even hear his favourite protégé.

'*Arioch! Repay my loyalty! I have given you blood and souls!*'

He did not breathe. His heart had stopped. All his movements were sluggish.

The eyes looked down at him. They looked up at him. Were they glad? Did they rejoice in his terror?

'*Arioch!*'

He yearned for a reply. He would have wept, but no tears would come. His body was cold; less than dead, yet not alive. A fear was in him greater than any fear he had known before.

'*Oh, Arioch! Aid me!*'

He forced his right hand towards the pulsing pommel of Stormbringer which, alone, still possessed energy. The hilt of the sword was warm to his touch and, as slowly he folded his fingers around it, it seemed to swell in his fist and propel his arm upwards so that he did not draw the sword. Rather the sword forced his limbs into motion.

And now it challenged the void, glowing with black fire, singing its high, gleeful battlesong.

'Our destinies are intertwined, Stormbringer,' said Elric. 'Bring us from this place, or those destinies shall never be fulfilled.'

Stormbringer swung like the needle of a compass and Elric's unfeeling arm was wrenched round to go with it. In eight directions the sword swung, as if to the eight points of Chaos. It was questing – like a hound sniffing a trail. Then a yell sounded from within the strange metal of the blade; a distant cry of delight, it seemed to Elric. The sound one would hear if one stood above a valley listening to children playing far below.

Elric knew that Stormbringer had sensed a plane they might reach. Not necessarily their own, but one which would accept them. And, as a drowning mariner must yearn for the most inhospitable rock rather than no rock at all, Elric yearned for that plane.

'*Stormbringer. Take us there!*'

The sword hesitated. It moaned. It was suspicious.

'*Take us there!*' whispered the albino to his runesword.

The sword struck back and forth, up and down, as if it battled invisible enemies. Elric scarcely kept his grip on it. It seemed that Stormbringer was frightened of the world it had detected and sought to drive it back but the act of seeking had in itself set them both in motion. Already Elric could feel himself being drawn through the darkness, towards something he could see very dimly beyond the myriad eyes, as dawn reveals clouds undetected in the night sky.

Elric thought he saw the shapes of crags, pointed and crazy. He thought he saw water, flat and ice-blue. The stars faded and there was snow beneath his feet, mountains all around him, a huge, blazing sun overhead – and above that another landscape, a desert, as a magic mirror might reflect the contrasting character of he who peered into it – a desert, quite as real as the snowy peaks in which he crouched, sword in hand, waiting for one of these landscapes to fade so that he might establish, to a degree, his bearings. Evidently the two planes had intersected.

But the landscape overhead did not fade. He could look up and see sand, mountains, vegetation, a sky which met his own sky at a point half-way along the curve of the huge sun – and blended with it. He looked about him. Snowy peaks in all directions. Above – desert everywhere. He felt dizzy, found that he was staring downwards, reaching to cup some of the snow in his hand. It was ordinary snow, though it seemed reluctant to melt in contact with his flesh.

'This is a world of Chaos,' he muttered. 'It obeys no natural laws.' His voice seemed loud, amplified by the peaks, perhaps. 'That is why you did not want to come here. This is the world of powerful rivals.'

Stormbringer was silent, as if all its energy were spent. But Elric did not sheath the blade. He began to trudge through the snow towards what seemed to be an abyss. Every so often he glanced upward, but the desert overhead had not faded, sun and sky remained the same. He wondered if he walked around the surface of a miniature world. That if he continued to go forward he might eventually reach the point where the two landscapes met. He wondered if this were not some punishment wished upon him by his untrustworthy allies of Chaos. Perhaps he must choose between death in the snow or death in the desert. He reached the edge of the abyss and looked down.

The walls of the abyss fell for all of five feet before reaching a floor of gold and silver squares which stretched for perhaps another seven feet before they reached the far wall, where the landscape continued – snow and crags – uninterrupted.

'This is undoubtedly where Chaos rules,' said the Prince of Melniboné. He studied the smooth, chequered floor. It reflected parts of the snowy terrain and the desert world above it. It reflected the crimson-eyed albino who peered down at it, his features drawn in bewilderment and tiredness.

'I am at their mercy,' said Elric. 'They play with me. But I shall resist them, even as they destroy me.' And some of his wild, careless spirit came back to him as he prepared to lower himself onto the chequered floor and cross to the opposite bank.

He was half-way over when he heard a grunting sound in the distance and a beast appeared, its paws slithering uncertainly on the smooth surface, its seven savage eyes glaring in all directions as if it sought the instigator of its terrible indignity.

And, at last, all seven eyes focused on Elric and the beast opened a mouth in which row upon row of thin, vicious teeth were arranged, and uttered a growl of unmistakable resentment.

Elric raised his sword. 'Back creature of Chaos. You threaten the Prince of Melniboné!'

The beast was already propelling itself towards him. Elric flung his body to one side, aiming a blow with the sword as he did so, succeeding only in making a thin incision in the monster's heavily muscled hind leg. It shrieked and began to turn.

'Back!'

Elric's voice was the brave, thin squeak of a lemming attacked by a hawk. He drove at the thing's snout with Stormbringer. The sword was heavy. It had spent all its energy and there was no more to give. Elric wondered why he, himself, did not weaken. Possibly the laws of nature were entirely abolished in the Realm of Chaos. He struck and drew blood. The beast paused, more in astonishment than fear.

Then it opened its jaws, pushed its back legs against the snowy bank, and shot towards the albino who tried to dodge it, lost his footing, and fell, sprawling backwards, on the gold and silver surface.

3

In which Una Persson Discovers an Unexpected Snag

The gigantic beetle, rainbow carapace glittering, turned as if into the wind, which blew from the distant mountains, its thick, flashing wings beating rapidly as it bore its single passenger over the queer landscape.

On its back Mrs Persson checked the instruments on her wrist. Ever since Man had begun to travel in time it had become necessary for the League to develop techniques to compensate for the fluctuations and disruptions in the space-time continua; perpetually monitoring the chronoflow and megaflow. She pursed her lips. She had picked up the signal. She made the semi-sentient beetle swing a degree or two SSE and head directly for the mountains. She was in some sort of enclosed (but vast) environment. These mountains, as well as everything surrounding them, lay in the territory most utilized by the gloomy, naturalborn Werther de Goethe, poet and romantic, solitary seeker after truth in a world no longer differentiating between the degrees of reality. He would not remember her, she knew, because, as far as Werther was concerned, they had not met yet. He had not even, if Una were correct, experienced his adventure with Mistress Christia, the Everlasting Concubine. A story on which she had dined out more than once, in duller eras.

The mountains drew closer. From here it was possible to see the entire arrangement (a creation of Werther's very much in character): a desert landscape, a central sun, and, inverted above it, winter mountains. Werther strove to make statements, like so many naïve artists before him, by presenting simple contrasts: The World is Bleak/The World is Cold/Barren am I As I Grow Old/Tomorrow I Die, Entombed in Cold/For Silver My Poor Soul Was Sold — she remembered he was perhaps the worst poet she had encountered in an eternity of meetings with bad poets. He had taught himself to read and write in old, old

190

English so that he might carve those words on one of his many abandoned tombs (half his time was spent in composing obituaries for himself). Like so many others he seemed to equate self-pity with artistic inspiration. In an earlier age he might have discovered his public and become quite rich (self-pity passing for passion in the popular understanding). Sometimes she regretted the passing of Wheldrake, so long ago, so far away, in a universe bearing scarcely any resemblances to those in which she normally operated.

She brought her wavering mind back to the problem. The beetle dipped and circled over the desert, but there was no sight of her quarry.

She was about to abandon the search when she heard a faint roaring overhead and she looked up to see another characteristic motif of Werther's — a gold and silver chessboard on which, upside down, a monstrous dog-like creature was bearing down on a tiny white-haired man dressed in the most abominable taste Una had seen for some time.

She directed the aircar upwards and then, reversing the machine as she entered the opposing gravity, downwards to where the barbarically costumed swordsman was about to be eaten by the beast.

'Shoo!' cried Una commandingly.

The beast raised a bufuddled head.

'Shoo.'

It licked its lips and returned its seven-eyed gaze to the albino, who was now on his knees, using his large sword to steady himself as he climbed to his feet.

The jaws opened wider and wider. The pale man prepared, shakily, to defend himself.

Una directed the aircar at the beast's unkempt head. The great beetle connected with a loud crack. The monster's eyes widened in dismay. It yelped. It sat on its haunches and began to slide away, its claws making an unpleasant noise on the gold and silver tiles.

Una landed the aircar and gestured for the stranger to enter. She noticed with distaste that he was a somewhat unhealthy looking albino with gaunt features, exaggeratedly large and slanting eyes, ears that were virtually pointed, and glaring, half-mad red pupils.

And yet, undoubtedly, it was her quarry and there was nothing for it but to be polite.

'Do, please, get in,' she said. 'I am here to rescue you.'

'*Shaarmraaam torjistoo quellahm vyeearrr*,' said the stranger in an accent that seemed to Una to be vaguely Scottish.

'Damn,' she said, 'that's all we need.' She had been anxious to approach the albino in private, before one of the denizens of the End of Time could arrive and select him for a menagerie, but now she regretted that Werther or perhaps Lord Jagged were not here, for she realized that she needed one of their translation pills, those tiny tablets which could 'engineer' the brain to understand a new language. By a fluke – or perhaps because of her presence here so often – the people at the End of Time currently spoke formal early twentieth-century English.

The albino – who wore a kind of tartan divided kilt, knee-length boots, a blue and white jerkin, a green cloak and a silver breastplate, with a variety of leather belts and metal buckles here and there upon his person – was vehemently refusing her offer of a lift. He raised the sword before him as he backed away, slipped once, reached the bank, scrambled through snow and disappeared behind a rock.

Mrs Persson sighed and put the car into motion again.

4

In which The Prince of Melniboné Encounters Further Terrors

Xiombarg herself, thought Elric as he slid beneath the snows into the cave. Well, he would have no dealings with the Queen of Chaos; not until he was forced to do so.

The cave was large. In the thin light from the gap above his head he could not see far. He wondered whether to return to the surface or risk going deeper into the cave. There was always the hope that he would find another way out. He was attempting to recall some rune that would aid him, but all he knew depended either upon the aid of elementals who did not exist on this plane, or upon the Lords of Chaos themselves – and they were unlikely to come to his assistance in their own Realm. He was marooned here: the single mouse in a world of cats.

Almost unconsciously, he found himself moving downwards, realizing that the cave had become a tunnel. He was feeling hungry but, apart from the monster and the woman in the magical carriage, had seen no sign of life. Even the cavern did not seem entirely natural.

It widened; there was phosphoresent light. He realized that the walls were of transparent crystal and, behind the walls, were all manner of artefacts. He saw crowns, sceptres and chains of precious jewels; cabinets of complicated carving; weapons of strangely turned metal; armour, clothing, things whose use he could not guess – and food. There were sweetmeats, fruits, flans and pies, all out of reach.

Elric groaned. This was torment. Perhaps deliberately planned torment. A thousand voices whispered to him in a beautiful, alien language.

'Bie-meee . . . Bie-meee . . . ' the voices murmured. 'Baa-gen-baa-gen . . . '

They seemed to be promising every delight, if only he could

193

pass through the walls; but they were of transparent quartz, lit from within. He raised Stormbringer, half-tempted to try to break down the barrier, but he knew that even his sword was, at its most powerful, incapable of destroying the magic of Chaos.

He paused, gasping with astonishment at a group of small dogs which looked at him with large brown eyes, tongues lolling, and jumped up at him.

'O, *Nee Tubbens!*' intoned one of the voices.

'Gods!' screamed Elric. 'This torture is too much!' He swung his body this way and that, threatening with his sword, but the voices continued to murmur and promise, displaying their riches but never allowing him to touch.

The albino panted. His crimson eyes glared about him. 'You would drive me insane, eh? Well, Elric of Melniboné has witnessed more frightful threats than this. You will need to do more if you would destroy his mind!'

And he ran through the whispering passages, looking to neither his right nor his left, until, quite suddenly, he had run into blazing daylight and stood staring down into pale infinity – a blue and endless void.

He looked up. And he screamed.

Overhead were the gentle hills and dales of a rural landscape, with rivers, grazing cattle, woods and cottages. He expected to fall, headlong, but he did not. He was on the brink of the abyss. The cliff-face of red sandstone fell immediately below and then was the tranquil void. He looked back:

'*Baa-gen . . . O, Nee Tubbens . . .* '

A bitter smile played about the albino's bloodless lips as, decisively, he sheathed his sword.

'Well, then,' he said. 'Let them do their worst!'

And, laughing, he launched himself over the brink of the cliff.

5

In which Werther de Goethe Makes a Wonderful Discovery

With a gesture of quiet pride, Werther de Goethe indicated his gigantic skull.

'It is very large, Werther,' said Mistress Christia, the Everlasting Concubine, turning a power ring to adjust the shade of her eyes so that they perfectly matched the day.

'It is monstrous,' said Werther modestly. 'It reminds us all of the Inevitable Night.'

'Who was that?' enquired golden-haired Gaf the Horse in Tears, at present studying ancient legendry. 'Sir Lew Grady?'

'I mean Death,' Werther told him, 'which overwhelms us all.'

'Well, not us,' pointed out the Duke of Queens, as usual a trifle literal minded. 'Because we're immortal, as you know.'

Werther offered him a sad, pitying look and sighed briefly. 'Retain your delusions, if you will.'

Mistress Christia stroked the gloomy Werther's long, dark locks. 'There, there,' she said. 'We have compensations, Werther.'

'Without Death,' intoned the Last Romantic, 'there is no point to Life.'

As usual, they could not follow him, but they nodded gravely and politely.

'The skull,' continued Werther, stroking the side of his aircar (which was in the shape of a large flying reptile) to make it circle and head for the left eye-socket, 'is a Symbol not only of our Mortality, but also of our Fruitless Ambitions.'

'Fruit?' Bishop Castle, drowsing at the rear of the vehicle, became interested. His hobby was currently orchards. 'Less? My pine-trees, you know, are proving a problem. The apples are much smaller than I was led to believe.'

'The skull is lovely,' said Mistress Christia with valiant enthusiasm. 'Well, now that we have seen it . . .'

'The outward shell,' Werther told her. 'It is what it hides which is more important. Man's Foolish Yearnings are all encompassed therein. His Greed, his Need for the Impossible, the Heat of his Passions, the Coldness which must Finally Overtake him. Through this eye-socket you will encounter a little invention of my own called The Bargain Basement of the Mind . . . '

He broke off in astonishment.

On the top edge of the eye-socket a tiny figure had emerged.

'What's that?' enquired the Duke of Queens, craning his head back. 'A random thought?'

'It is not mine at all!'

The figure launched itself into the sky and seemed to fly, with flailing limbs, towards the sun.

Werther frowned, watching the tiny man disappear. 'The gravity field is reversed there,' he said absently, 'in order to make the most of the paradox, you understand. There is a snowscape, a desert . . . ' But he was much more interested in the newcomer. 'How do you think he got into my skull?'

'At least he's enjoying himself. He seems to be laughing.' Mistress Christia bent an ear towards the thin sound, which grew fainter and fainter at first, but became louder again. 'He's coming back.'

Werther nodded. 'Yes. The field's no longer reversed.' He touched a power ring.

The laughter stopped and became a yell of rage. The figure hurtled down on them. It had a sword in one white hand and its red eyes blazed.

Hastily, Werther stroked another ring. The stranger tumbled into the bottom of the aircar and lay there panting, cursing and groaning.

'How wonderful!' cried Werther. 'Oh, this is a traveller from some rich, romantic past. Look at him! What else could he be? What a prize!'

The stranger rose to his feet and raised the sword high above his head, defying the amazed and delighted pasengers as he screamed at the top of his voice:

'Heegeegrowinaz!'

'Good afternoon,' said Mistress Christia. She reached in her purse for a translation pill and found one. 'I wonder if you would care to swallow this – it's quite harmless . . . '

The Duke of Queens pointed towards the other socket. A huge, whirring beetle came sailing from it. In its back was someone he recognized with pleasure. 'Mrs Persson!'

Una brought her aircar alongside.

'Is he in your charge?' asked Werther with undisguised disappointment. 'If so, I could offer you . . . '

'I'm afraid he means a lot to me,' she said.

'From your own age?' Mistress Christia also recognized Una. She still offered the translation pill in the palm of her hand. 'He seems a mite suspicious of us.'

'I'd noticed,' said Una. 'It would be useful if he would accept the pill. However, if he will not, one of us . . . '

'I would be happy,' offered the generous Duke of Queens. He tugged at his green and gold beard. 'Werther de Goethe, Mrs Persson.'

'Perhaps I had better,' said Una nodding to Werther. The only problem with translation pills was that they did their job so thoroughly. You could speak the language perfectly, but you could speak no other.

Werther was, for once, positive. 'Let's all take a pill,' he suggested.

Everyone at the End of Time carried translation pills, in case of meeting a visitor from Space or the Past.

Mistress Christia handed hers to Una and found another. They swallowed.

'Creatures of Chaos,' said the newcomer with cool dignity, 'I demand that you release me. You cannot hold a mortal in this way, not unless he has struck a bargain with you. And no bargain was struck which would bring me to the Realm of Chaos.'

'It's actually more orderly than you'd think,' said Werther apologetically. 'Your first experience, you see, was the world of my skull, which was deliberately muddled. I meant to show what Confusion was the Mind of Man . . . '

'May I introduce Mistress Christia, the Everlasting Concubine,' said the Duke of Queens, on his best manners. 'This is Mrs Persson, Bishop Castle, Gaf the Horse in Tears. Werther de Goethe – your unwitting host – and I am the Duke of Queens. We welcome you to our world. Your name, sir . . . ?'

'You must know me, my lord duke,' said Elric. 'For I am Elric of Melniboné, Emperor by Right of Birth, Inheritor of the Ruby Throne, Bearer of the Actorios, Wielder of the Black Sword . . . '

'Indeed!' said Werther de Goethe. In a whispered aside to Mrs Persson: 'What a marvellous scowl! What a noble sneer!'

'You are an important personage in your world, then?' said Mistress Christia, fluttering the eyelashes she had just extended by half an inch. 'Perhaps you would allow me . . . '

'I think he wishes to be returned to his home,' said Mrs Persson hastily.

'Returned?' Werther was astonished. 'But the Morphail Effect! It is impossible.'

'Not in this case, I think,' she said. 'For if he is not returned there is no telling the fluctuations which will take place throughout the dimensions . . . '

They could not follow her, but they accepted her tone.

'Aye,' said Elric darkly, 'return me to my realm, so that I may fulfil my own doom-laden destiny . . . '

Werther looked upon the albino with affectionate delight. 'Aha! A fellow spirit! I, too, have a doom-laden destiny.'

'I doubt it is as doom-laden as mine.' Elric peered moodily back at the skull as the two aircars fled away towards a gentle horizon where exotic trees bloomed.

'Well,' said Werther with an effort, 'perhaps it is not, though I assure you . . . '

'I have looked upon hell-born horror,' said Elric, 'and communicated with the very Gods of the Uttermost Darkness. I have seen things which would turn other men's minds to useless jelly . . . '

'Jelly?' interrupted Bishop Castle. 'Do you, in your turn, have any expertise with, for instance, blackbird trees?'

'Your words are meaningless,' Elric told him, glowering. 'Why do you torment me so, my lords? I did not ask to visit your world. I belong in the world of men, in the Young Kingdoms, where I seek my weird. Why, I have but lately experienced adventures . . . '

'I do think we have one of those bores,' murmured Bishop Castle to the Duke of Queens, 'so common amongst time travellers. They all believe themselves unique.'

But the Duke of Queens refused to be drawn. He had developed a liking for the frowning albino. Gaf the Horse in Tears was also plainly impressed, for he had fashioned his own features into a rough likeness of Elric's. The Prince of Melniboné pretended insouciance, but it was evident to Una that he was frightened. She tried to calm him.

'People here at the End of Time . . . ' she began.

'No soft words, my lady.' A cynical smile played about the albino's lips. 'I know you for that great unholy temptress, Queen of the Swords, Xiombarg herself.'

'I assure you, I am as human as you, sir . . . '

'Human? I, human? I am not human, madam – though I be a mortal, 'tis true. I am of older blood, the blood of the Bright Empire itself, the Blood of R'lin K'ren A'a which Cran Liret mocked, not understanding what it was he laughed at. Aye, though forced to summon aid from Chaos, I made no bargain to become a slave in your realm . . . '

'I assure you – um – your majesty,' said Una, 'that we had not meant to insult you and your presence here was no doing of ours. I am, as it happens, a stranger here myself. I came especially to see you, to help you escape . . . '

'Ha!' said the albino. 'I have heard such words before. You would lure me into some worse trap than this. Tell me, where is Duke Arioch? He, at least, I owe some allegiance to.'

'We have no one of that name,' apologized Mistress Christia. She enquired of Gaf, who knew everyone. 'No time traveller?'

'None,' Gaf studied Elric's eyes and made a small adjustment to his own. He sat back, satisfied.

Elric shuddered and turned away mumbling.

'You are very welcome here,' said Werther. 'I cannot tell you how glad I am to meet one as essentially morbid and self-pitying as myself!'

Elric did not seem flattered.

'What can we do to make you feel at home?' asked Mistress Christia. She had changed her hair to a rather glossy blue in the hope, perhaps, that Elric would find it more attractive. 'Is there anything you need?'

'Need? Aye. Peace of mind. Knowledge of my true destiny. A quiet place where I can be with Cymoril, whom I love.'

'What does this Cymoril look like?' Mistress Christia became just a trifle over-eager.

'She is the most beautiful creature in the universe,' said Elric.

'It isn't very much to go on,' said Mistress Christia. 'If you could imagine a picture, perhaps? There are devices in the old cities which could visualize your thoughts. We could go there. I should be happy to fill in for her, as it were . . . '

'What? You offer me a simulacrum? Do you not think I should detect such witchery at once? Ah, this is loathsome! Slay me, if you will, or continue the torment. I'll listen no longer!'

They were floating now, between high cliffs. On a ledge far below a group of time-travellers pointed up at them. One waved desperately.

'You've offended him, Mistress Christia,' said Werther pettishly. 'You don't understand how sensitive he is.'

'Yes I do.' She was aggrieved. 'I was only being sympathetic.'

'Sympathy!' Elric rubbed at his long, somewhat pointed jaw. 'Ha! What do I want with sympathy?'

'I never heard anyone who wanted it more.' Mistress Christia was kind. 'You're like a little boy, really, aren't you?'

'Compared to the ancient Lords of Chaos, I am a child, aye. But my blood is old and cold, the blood of decaying Melniboné, as well you know.' And with a huge sigh the albino seated himself at the far end of the car and rested his head on his fist. 'Well? What is your pleasure, my lords and ladies of Hell?'

'It is your pleasure we are anxious to achieve,' Werther told him. 'Is there anything at all we can do? Some environment we can manufacture? What are you used to?'

'Used to? I am used to the crack of leathery dragon wings in the sweet, sharp air of the early dawn. I am used to the sound of red battle, the drumming of hooves on bloody earth, the screams of the dying, the yells of the victorious. I am used to warring against demons and monsters, sorcerers and ghouls. I have sailed on magic ships and fought hand to hand with reptilian savages. I have encountered the Jade Man himself. I have fought side by side with the elementals, who are my allies. I have battled black evil . . . '

'Well,' said Werther, 'that's something to go on, at any rate. I'm sure we can . . . '

'Lord Elric won't be staying,' began Una Persson politely. 'You see – these fluctuations in the megaflow – not to mention his own destiny . . . He should not be here, at all, Werther.'

'Nonsense!' Werther flung a black velvet arm about the stiff shoulders of his new friend. 'It is evident that our destinies are one. Lord Elric is as grief-haunted as myself!'

'How can you know what it is to be haunted by grief?' murmured the albino. His face was half-buried in Werther's generous sleeve.

Mrs Persson controlled herself. She rose from Werther's aircar and made for her own. 'Well,' she said, 'I must be off. I hope to see you later, everybody.'

They sang out their farewells.

Una Persson turned her beetle westward, towards Castle Canaria, the home of her old friend Lord Jagged.

She needed help and advice.

6

In which Elric of Melniboné Resists the
Temptations of the Chaos Lords

Elric reflected on the subtle way in which laughing Lords of
Chaos had captured him. Apparently, he was merely a guest
and quite free to wander where he would in their Realm. Actually, he was in their power as much as if they had chained him,
for he could not flee this flying dragon and they had already
demonstrated their enormous magical gifts in subtle ways,
primarily with their shapechanging. Only the one who called
himself Werther de Goethe (plainly a leader in the hierarchy of
Chaos) still had the face and clothing he had worn when first
encountered.

It was evident that this realm obeyed no natural laws, that it
was mutable according to the whims of its powerful inhabitants. They could destroy him with a breath and had, subtly
enough, given him evidence of that fact. How could he possibly
escape such danger? By calling upon the Lords of Law for aid?
But he owed them no loyalty and they, doubtless, regarded him
as their enemy. But if he were to transfer his allegiance to
Law . . .

These thoughts and more continued to engage him, while his
captors chatted easily in the ancient High Speech of Melniboné,
itself a version of the very language of Chaos. It was one of the
other ways in which they revealed themselves for what they
were. He fingered his runesword, wondering if it would be possible to slay such a lord and steal his energy, giving himself
enough power for a little while to hurl himself back to his own
sphere . . .

The one called Lord Werther was leaning over the side of the
beast-vessel. 'Oh, come and see, Elric. Look!'

Reluctantly, the albino moved to where Werther peered and
pointed.

The entire landscape was filled with a monstrous battle.

Creatures of all kinds and all combinations tore at one another with huge teeth and claws. Shapeless things slithered and hopped; giants, naked but for helmets and greaves, slashed at these beasts with great broadswords and axes, but were borne down. Flame and black smoke drifted everywhere. There was a smell. The stink of blood?

'What do you miss most?' asked the female. She pressed a soft body against him. He pretended not to be aware of it. He knew what magic flesh could hide on a she-witch.

'I miss peace,' said Elric almost to himself, 'and I miss war. For in battle I find a kind of peace . . . '

'Very good!' Bishop Castle applauded. 'You are beginning to learn our ways. You will soon become one of our best conversationalists.'

Elric touched the hilt of Stormbringer, hoping to feel it grow warm and vibrant under his hand, but it was still, impotent in the Realm of Chaos. He uttered a heavy sigh.

'You are an adventurer, then, in your own world?' said the Duke of Queens. He was bluff. He had changed his beard to an ordinary sort of black and was wearing a scarlet costume; quilted doublet and tight-fitting hose, with a blue and white ruff, an elaborately feathered hat on his head. 'I, too, am something of a vagabond. As far, of course, as it is possible to be here. A buccaneer, of sorts. That is, my actions are in the main bolder than those of my fellows. More spectacular. Vulgar. Like yourself, sir. I admire your costume.'

Elric knew that this Duke of Hell was referring to the fact that he affected the costume of the southern barbarian, that he did not wear the more restrained colours and more cleverly wrought silks and metals of his own folk. He gave tit for tat at this time. He bowed.

'Thank you, sir. Your own clothes rival mine.'

'Do you think so?' The hell-lord pretended pleasure. If Elric had not known better, the creature would seem to be swelling with pride.

'Look!' cried Werther again. 'Look, Lord Elric – we are attacked.'

Elric whirled.

From below were rising oddly-wrought vessels – something like ships, but with huge round wheels at their sides, like the

203

wheels of water-clocks he had seen once in Pikarayd. Coloured smoke issued from chimneys mounted on their decks which swarmed with huge birds dressed in human clothing. The birds had multi-coloured plumage, curved beaks, and they held swords in their claws, while on their heads were strangely shaped black hats on which were blazed skulls with crossed bones beneath.

'Heave to!' squawked the birds. 'Or we'll put a shot across your bowels!'

'What can they be?' cried Bishop Castle.

'Parrots,' said Werther de Goethe soberly. 'Otherwise known as the hawks of the sea. And they mean us no good.'

Mistress Christia blinked.

'Don't you mean pirates, dear?'

Elric took a firm grip on his sword. Some of the words the Chaos Lords used were absolutely meaningless to him. But whether the attacking creatures were of their own conception, or whether they were true enemies of his captors, Elric prepared to do bloody battle. His spirits improved. At least here was something substantial to fight.

7

In which Mrs Persson Becomes Anxious about the Future of the Universe

Lord Jagged of Canaria was nowhere to be found. His huge castle, of gold and yellow spires, an embellished replica of Kings Cross station, was populated entirely by his quaint robots, whom Jagged found at once more mysterious and more trustworthy than android or human servants, for they could answer only according to a limited programme.

Una suspected that Jagged was, himself, upon some mission, for he, too, was a member of the League of Temporal Adventurers. But she needed aid. Somehow she had to return Elric to his own dimensions without creating further disruptions in the fabric of Time and Space. The Conjunction was not due yet and, if things got any worse, might never come. So many plans depended on the Conjunction of the Million Spheres that she could not risk its failure. But she could not reveal too much either to Elric or his hosts. As a Guild member she was sworn to the utmost and indeed necessary secrecy. Even here at the End of Time there were certain laws which could be disobeyed only at enormous risk. Words alone were dangerous when they described ideas concerning the nature of Time.

She racked her brains. She considered seeking out Jherek Carnelian, but then remembered that he had scarcely begun to understand his own destiny. Besides, there were certain similarities between Jherek and Elric which she could only sense at present. It would be best to go cautiously there.

She decided that she had no choice. She must return to the Time Centre and see if they could detect Lord Jagged for her.

She brought the necessary co-ordinates together in her mind and concentrated. For a moment all memories, all sense of identity left her.

Sergeant Alvarez was beside himself. His screens were no longer completely without form. Instead, peculiar shapes could be seen in the arrangements of lines. Una thought she saw faces, beasts, landscapes. That had never occurred before. The instruments, at least, had remained sane, even as they recorded insanity.

'It's getting worse,' said Alvarez. 'You've hardly any Time left. What there is, I've managed to borrow for you. Did you contact the rogue?'

She nodded. 'Yes. But getting him to return . . . I want you to find Jagged.'

'Jagged? Are you sure?'

'It's our only chance, I think.'

Alvarez sighed and bent a tense back over his controls.

8

In which Elric and Werther Fight Side by Side against Almost Overwhelming Odds

Somewhere, it seemed to Elric, as he parried and thrust at the attacking bird-monsters, rich and rousing music played. It must be a delusion, brought on by battle-madness. Blood and feathers covered the carriage. He saw the one called Christia carried off screaming. Bishop Castle had disappeared. Gaf had gone. Only the three of them, shoulder to shoulder, continued to fight. What was disconcerting to Elric was that Werther and the Duke of Queens bore swords absolutely identical to Stormbringer. Perhaps they were the legendary Brothers of the Black Sword, said to reside in Chaos?

He was forced to admit to himself that he experienced a sense of comradeship with these two, who were braver than most in defending themselves against such dreadful unlikely monsters — perhaps some creation of their own which had turned against them.

Having captured the Lady Christia, the birds began to return to their own craft.

'We must rescue her!' cried Werther as the flying ships began to retreat. 'Quickly! In pursuit!'

'Should we not seek reinforcements?' asked Elric, further impressed by the courage of this Chaos Lord.

'No time!' cried the Duke of Queens. 'After them!'

Werther shouted to his vessel. 'Follow those ships!'

The vessel did not move.

'It has an enchantment on it,' said Werther. 'We are stranded! Ah, and I loved her so much!'

Elric became suspicious again. Werther had shown no signs, previously, of any affection for the female.

'You loved her?'

'From a distance,' Werther explained. 'Duke of Queens, what can we do? Those parrots will ransom her savagely and mishandle her objects of virtue!'

'Dastardly poltroons!' roared the huge duke.

Elric could make little sense of this exchange. It dawned on him, then, that he could still hear the rousing music. He looked below. On some sort of dais in the middle of the bizarre landscape a large group of musicians was assembled. They played on, apparently oblivious of what happened above. This was truly a world dominated by Chaos.

Their ship began slowly to fall towards the band. It lurched. Elric gasped and clung to the side as they struck yielding ground and bumped to a halt.

The Duke of Queens, apparently elated, was already scrambling overboard. 'There! We can follow on those mounts.'

Tethered near the dais was a herd of creatures bearing some slight resemblance to horses but in a variety of dazzling, metallic colours, with horns and bony ridges on their backs. Saddles and bridles of alien workmanship showed that they were domestic beasts, doubtless belonging to the musicians.

'They will want some payment from us, surely,' said Elric, as they hurried towards the horses.

'Ah, true!' Werther reached into a purse at his belt and drew forth a handful of jewels. Casually he flung them towards the musicians and climbed into the saddle of the nearest beast. Elric and the Duke of Queens followed his example. Then Werther, with a whoop, was off in the direction in which the bird-monsters had gone.

The landscape of this world of Chaos changed rapidly as they rode. They galloped through forests of crystalline trees, over fields of glowing flowers, leapt rivers the colour of blood and the consistency of mercury, and their tireless mounts maintained a headlong pace which never faltered. Through clouds of boiling gas which wept, through rain, through snow, through intolerable heat, through shallow lakes in which oddly fashioned fish wriggled and gasped, until at last a range of mountains came in sight.

'There!' panted Werther, pointing with his own rune-sword. 'Their lair. Oh, the fiends! How can we climb such smooth cliffs?'

It was true that the base of the cliffs rose some hundred feet before they became suddenly ragged, like the rotting teeth of the beggars of Nadsokor. They were of dusky, purple obsidian and so smooth as to reflect the faces of the three adventurers who stared at them in despair.

It was Elric who saw the steps put into the side of the cliff.

'These will take us up some of the way, at least.'

'It could be a trap,' said the Duke of Queens. He, too, seemed to be relishing the opportunity to take action. Although a Lord of Chaos there was something about him that made Elric respond to a fellow spirit.

'Let them trap us,' said Elric laconically. 'We have our swords.'

With a wild laugh, Werther de Goethe was the first to swing himself from his saddle and run towards the steps, leaping up them almost as if he had the power of flight. Elric and the Duke of Queens followed more slowly.

Their feet slipping in the narrow spaces not meant for mortals to climb, ever aware of the dizzying drop on their left, the three came at last to the top of the cliff and stood clinging to sharp crags, staring across a plain at a crazy castle rising into the clouds before them.

'Their stronghold,' said Werther.

'What are these creatures?' Elric asked. 'Why do they attack you? Why do they capture the Lady Christia?'

'They nurse an abiding hatred for us,' explained the Duke of Queens, and looked expectantly at Werther, who added:

'This was their world before it became ours.'

'And before it became theirs,' said the Duke of Queens, 'it was the world of the Yargtroon.'

'The Yargtroon?' Elric frowned.

'They dispossessed the bodiless vampire goat-folk of Kia,' explained Werther. 'Who, in turn, destroyed – or thought they destroyed – the Grash-Tu-Xem, a race of Old Ones older than any Old Ones except the Elder Old Ones of Ancient Thriss.'

'Older even than Chaos?' asked Elric.

'Oh, far older,' said Werther.

'It's almost completely collapsed, it's so old,' added the Duke of Queens.

Elric was baffled. 'Thriss?'

'Chaos,' said the duke.

Elric let a thin smile play about his lips. 'You still mock me, my lord. The power of Chaos is the greatest there is, only equalled by the power of Law.'

'Oh, certainly,' agreed the Duke of Queens.

Elric became suspicious again. 'Do you play with me, my lord?'

'Well, naturally, we try to please our guests . . . '

Werther interrupted. 'Yonder doomy edifice holds the one I love. Somewhere within its walls she is incarcerated, while ghouls taunt at her and devils threaten.'

'The bird-monsters . . . ?' began Elric.

'Chimerae,' said the Duke of Queens. 'You saw only one of the shapes they assume.'

Elric understood this. 'Aha!'

'But how can we enter it?' Werther spoke almost to himself.

'We must wait until nightfall,' said Elric, 'and enter under the cover of darkness.'

'Nightfall?' Werther brightened.

Suddenly they were in utter darkness.

Somewhere the Duke of Queens lost his footing and fell with a muffled curse.

9

In which Mrs Persson At Last Makes
Contact with her Old Friend

They stood together beneath the striped awning of the tent
while a short distance away armoured men, mounted on armoured horses, jousted, were injured or died. The two members
wore appropriate costumes for the period. Lord Jagged looked
handsome in his surcoat and mail, but Una Persson merely
looked uncomfortable in her wimple and kirtle.

'I can't leave just now,' he was saying. 'I am laying the
foundations for a very important development.'

'Which will come to nothing unless Elric is returned,' she
said.

A knight with a broken lance thundered past, covering them
in dust.

'Well played Sir Holger!' called Lord Jagged. 'An ancestor of
mine, you know,' he told her.

'You will not be able to recognize the world of the End of
Time when you return, if this is allowed to continue,' she said.

'It's always difficult, isn't it?' But he was listening to her now.

'These disruptions could as easily affect us and leave us
stranded,' she added. 'We would lose any freedom we have
gained.'

He bit into a pomegranate and offered it to her. 'You can
only get these in this area. Did you know? Impossible to find in
England. In the thirteenth century, at any rate. The idea of
freedom is such a nebulous one, isn't it? Most of the time when
angry people are speaking of "freedom" what they are actually
asking for is much simpler – respect. Do those in authority or
those with power ever really respect those who do not have
power?' He paused. 'Or do they mean "power" and not "freedom". Or are they the same . . . ?'

'Really, Jagged, this is no time for self-indulgence.'

He looked about him. 'There's little else to do in the Middle

East in the thirteenth century, I assure you, except eat pomegranates and philosophize . . . '

'You must come back to the End of Time.'

He wiped his handsome chin. 'Your urgency,' he said, 'worries me, Una. These matters should be handled with delicacy – slowly . . . '

'The entire fabric will collapse unless he is returned to his own dimension. He is an important factor in the whole plan.'

'Well, yes, I understand that.'

'He is, in one sense at least, your protégé.'

'I know. But not my responsibility.'

'You must help,' she said.

There was a loud bang and a crash.

A splinter flew into Mrs Persson's eye.

'Oh, zounds!' she said.

10

In which The Castle is Assaulted and The Plot Thickened

A moon had appeared above the spires of the castle which seemed to Elric to have changed its shape since he had first seen it. He meant to ask his companions for an explanation, but at present they were all sworn to silence as they crept nearer. From within the castle burst light, emanating from guttering brands stuck into brackets on the walls. There was laughter, noise of feasting. Hidden behind a rock they peered through one large window and inspected the scene within.

The entire hall was full of men wearing identical costumes. They had black skull caps, loose white blouses and trousers, black shoes. Their eyebrows were black in dead white faces, even paler than Elric's and they had bright red lips.

'Aha,' whispered Werther, 'the parrots are celebrating their victory. Soon they will be too drunk to know what is happening to them.'

'Parrots?' said Elric. 'What is that word?'

'Pierrots, he means,' said the Duke of Queens. 'Don't you, Werther?' There were evidently certain words which did not translate easily into the High Speech of Melniboné.

'Sshh,' said the Last Romantic, 'they will capture us and torture us to death if they detect our presence.'

They worked their way around the castle. It was guarded at intervals by gigantic warriors whom Elric at first mistook for statues, save that, when he looked closely, he could see them breathing very slowly. They were unarmed, but their fists and feet were disproportionately large and could crush any intruder they detected.

'They are sluggish, by the look of them,' said Elric. 'If we are quick, we can run beneath them and enter the castle before they realize it. Let me try first. If I succeed, you follow.'

Werther clapped his new comrade on the back. 'Very well.'

Elric waited until the nearest guard halted and spread his huge feet apart, then he dashed forward, scuttling like an insect between the giant's legs and flinging himself through a dimly lit window. He found himself in some sort of store-room. He had not been seen, though the guard cocked his ear for half a moment before resuming his pace.

Elric looked cautiously out and signalled to his companions. The Duke of Queens waited for the guard to stop again, then he, too, made for the window and joined Elric. He was panting and grinning. 'This is wonderful,' he said.

Elric admired his spirit. There was no doubt that the guard could crush any of them to a pulp, even if (as still nagged at his brain) this was all some sort of complicated illusion.

Another dash, and Werther was with them.

Cautiously, Elric opened the door of the store-room. They looked onto a deserted landing. They crossed the landing and looked over a balustrade. They had expected to see another hall, but instead there was a miniature lake on which floated the most beautiful miniature ship, all mother-of-pearl, brass and ebony, with golden sails and silver masts. Surrounding this ship were mermaids and mermen bearing trays of exotic food (reminding Elric how hungry he still was) which they fed to the ship's only passenger, Mistress Christia.

'She is under an enchantment,' said Elric. 'They beguile her with illusions so that she will not wish to come with us even if we do rescue her. Do you know no counter-spells?'

Werther thought for a moment. Then he shook his head.

'You must be very minor Lords of Chaos,' said Elric, biting his lower lip.

From the lake, Mistress Christia giggled and drew one of the mermaids towards her. 'Come here, my pretty piscine!'

'Mistress Christia!' hissed Werther de Goethe.

'Oh!' The captive widened her eyes (which were now both large and blue). 'At last!'

'You wish to be rescued?' said Elric.

'Rescued? Only by you, most alluring of albinos!'

Elric hardened his features. 'I am not the one who loves you, madam.'

'What? I am loved? By whom? By you, Duke of Queens?'

'Sshh,' said Elric. 'The demons will hear us.'

214

'Oh, of course,' said Mistress Christia gravely, and fell silent for a second. 'I'll get rid of all this, shall I?'

And she touched one of her rings.

Ship, lake and merfolk were gone. She lay on silken cushions, attended by monkeys.

'Sorcery!' said Elric, 'if she has such power, then why – ?'

'It is limited,' explained Werther. 'Merely to such tricks.'

'Quite,' said Mistress Christia.

Elric glared at them. 'You surrounded me with illusions. You make me think I am aiding you, when really . . . '

'No, no!' cried Werther. 'I assure you, Lord Elric, you have our greatest respect – well, mine at least – we are only attempting to – '

There was a roar from the gallery above. Rank upon rank of grinning demons looked down upon them. They were armed to the teeth.

'Hurry!' The Duke of Queens leapt to the cushions and seized Mistress Christia, flinging her over his shoulder. 'We can never defeat so many!'

The demons were already rushing down the circular staircase. Elric, still not certain whether his new friends deceived him or not, made a decision. He called to the Duke of Queens. 'Get her from the castle. We'll keep them from you for a few moments, at least.' He could not help himself. He behaved impulsively.

The Duke of Queens, sword in hand, Mistress Christia over the other shoulder, ran into a narrow passage. Elric and Werther stood together as the demons rushed down on them. Blade met blade. There was an unbearable shrilling of steel mingled with the cacklings and shrieks of the demons as they gnashed their teeth and rolled their eyes and slashed at the pair with swords, knives and axes. But worst of all was the smell. The dreadful smell of burning flesh which filled the air and threatened to choke Elric. It came from the demons. The smell of Hell. He did his best to cover his nostrils as he fought, certain that the smell must overwhelm him before the swords. Above him was a set of metal rungs fixed into the stones, leading high into a kind of chimney. As a pause came he pointed upward to Werther, who understood him. For a moment they managed to drive the demons back. Werther jumped onto Elric's shoulders (again displaying a strange lightness) and reached down to haul the albino after him.

While the demons wailed and cackled below, they began to climb the chimney.

They climbed for nearly fifty feet before they found themselves in a small, round room whose windows looked out over the purple crags and, beyond them, to a scene of bleak rocky pavements pitted with holes, like some vast unlikely cheese.

And there, rolling over this relatively flat landscape, in full daylight (for the sun had risen) was the Duke of Queens in a carriage of brass and wood, studded with jewels, and drawn by two bovine creatures which looked to Elric as if they might be the fabulous oxen of mythology who had drawn the war-chariot of his ancestors to do battle with the emerging nations of mankind.

Mistress Christia was beside the Duke of Queens. They seemed to be waiting for Elric and Werther.

'It's impossible,' said the albino. 'We could not get out of this tower, let alone those crags. I wonder how they managed to move so quickly and so far. And where did the chariot itself come from?'

'Stolen, no doubt, from the demons,' said Werther. 'See, there are wings here.' He indicated a heap of feathers in the corner of the room. 'We can use those.'

'What wizardry is this?' said Elric. 'Man cannot fly on bird wings.'

'With the appropriate spell he can,' said Werther. 'I am not that well versed in the magic arts, of course, but let me see . . . ' He picked up one set of wings. They were soft and glinted with subtle, rainbow colours. He placed them on Elric's back, murmuring his spell:

> Oh, for the wings, for the wings of a dove,
> To carry me to the one I love . . .

'There!' He was very pleased with himself. Elric moved his shoulders and his wings began to flap. 'Excellent! Off you go, Elric. I'll join you in a moment.'

Elric hesitated, then saw the head of the first demon emerging from the hole in the floor. He jumped to the window ledge and leapt into space. The wings sustained him. Against all logic he flew smoothly towards the waiting chariot and behind him came Werther de Goethe. At the windows of the tower the demons crowded, shaking fists and weapons as their prey escaped them.

Elric landed rather awkwardly beside the chariot and was helped aboard by the Duke of Queens. Werther joined them, dropping expertly amongst them. He moved the wings from the albino's back and nodded to the Duke of Queens who yelled at the oxen, cracking his whip as they began to move.

Mistress Christia flung her arms about Elric's neck. 'What courage! What resourcefulness!' she breathed. 'Without you, I should now be ruined!'

Elric sheathed Stormbringer. 'We all three worked together for your rescue, madam.' Gently he removed her arms. Courteously he bowed and leaned against the far side of the chariot as it bumped and hurtled over the peculiar rocky surface.

'Swifter! Swifter!' called the Duke of Queens, casting urgent looks backwards. 'We are followed!'

From the disappearing tower there now poured a host of flying, gibbering things. Once again the creatures had changed shape and had assumed the form of striped, winged cats, all glaring eyes, fangs and extended claws.

The rock became viscous, clogging the wheels of the chariot, as they reached what appeared to be a silvery road, flowing between the high trees of an alien forest already touched by a weird twilight.

The first of the flying cats caught up with them, slashing.

Elric drew Stormbringer and cut back. The beast roared in pain, blood streaming from its severed leg, its wings flapping in Elric's face as it hovered and attempted to snap at the sword.

The chariot rolled faster, through the forest to green fields touched by the moon. The days were short, it seemed, in this part of chaos. A path stretched skyward. The Duke of Queens drove the chariot straight up it, heading for the moon itself.

The moon grew larger and larger and still the demons pursued them, but they could not fly as fast as the chariot which went so swiftly that sorcery must surely speed it. Now they could only be heard in the darkness behind and the silver moon was huge.

'There!' called Werther. 'There is safety!'

On they raced until the moon was reached, the oxen leaping

217

in their traces, galloping over the gleaming surface to where a white palace awaited them.

'Sanctuary,' said the Duke of Queens. And he laughed a wild, full laugh of sheer joy.

The palace was like ivory, carved and wrought by a million hands, every inch covered with delicate designs.

Elric wondered. 'Where is this place?' he asked. 'Does it lie outside the Realm of Chaos?'

Werther seemed non-plussed. 'You mean our world?'

'Aye.'

'It is still part of our world,' said the Duke of Queens.

'Is the palace to your liking?' asked Werther.

'It is lovely.'

'A trifle pale for my own taste,' said the Last Romantic. 'It was Mistress Christia's idea.'

'You built this?' The albino turned to the woman. 'When?'

'Just now.' She seemed surprised.

Elric nodded. 'Aha. It is within the power of Chaos to create whatever whims it pleases.'

The chariot crossed a white drawbridge and entered a white courtyard. In it grew white flowers. They dismounted and entered a huge hall, white as bone, in which red lights glowed. Again Elric began to suspect mockery, but the faces of the Chaos lords showed only pleasure. He realized that he was dizzy with hunger and weariness, as he had been ever since he had been flung into this terrible world where no shape was constant, no idea permanent.

'Are you hungry?' asked Mistress Christia.

He nodded. And suddenly the room was filled by a long table on which all kinds of food were heaped – and everything, meats and fruits and vegetables, was white.

Elric moved to take the seat she indicated and he put some of the food on a silver plate and he touched it to his lips and he tasted it. It was delicious. Forgetting suspicion, he began to eat heartily, trying not to consider the colourless quality of the meal. Werther and the Duke of Queens also took some food, but it seemed they ate only from politeness. Werther glanced up at the faraway roof. 'What a wonderful tomb this would make,' he said. 'Your imagination improves, Mistress Christia.'

'Is this your domain?' asked Elric. 'The moon?'

'Oh no,' she said. 'It was all made for the occasion.'

'Occasion?'

'For your adventure,' she said. Then she fell silent.

Elric became grave. 'Those demons? They were not your enemies. They belong to you!'

'Belong?' said Mistress Christia. She shook her head.

Elric frowned and pushed back his plate. 'I am, however, most certainly your captive.' He stood up and paced the white floor. 'Will you not return me to my own plane?'

'You would come back almost immediately, said Werther de Goethe. 'It is called the Morphail Effect. And if you did not come here, you would yet remain in your own future. It is in the nature of Time.'

'This is nonsense,' said Elric. 'I have left my own realm before and returned – though admittedly memory becomes weak, as with dreams poorly recalled.'

'No man can go back in Time,' said the Duke of Queens. 'Ask Brannart Morphail.'

'He, too, is a Lord of Chaos?'

'If you like. He is a colleague.'

'Could he not return me to my realm? He sounds a clever being.'

'He could not and he would not,' said Mistress Christia. 'Haven't you enjoyed your experiences here so far?'

'Enjoyed?' Elric was astonished. 'Madam, I think . . . Well, what has happened this day is not what we mortals would call "enjoyment"!'

'But you *seemed* to be enjoying yourself,' said the Duke of Queens in some disappointment. 'Didn't he, Werther?'

'You were much more cheerful through the whole episode,' agreed the Last Romantic. 'Particularly when you were fighting the demons.'

'As with many time travellers who suffer from anxieties,' said Mistress Christia, 'you appeared to relax when you had something immediate to capture your attention . . . '

Elric refused to listen. This was clever Chaos talk, meant to deceive him and take his mind from his chief concern.

'If I was any help to you,' he began, 'I am, of course . . . '

'He isn't very grateful,' Mistress Christia pouted.

Elric felt madness creeping nearer again. He calmed himself.

'I thank you for the food, madam. Now, I would sleep.'

'Sleep?' she was disconcerted. 'Oh! Of course. Yes. A bed-room?'

'If you have such a thing.'

'As many as you like.' She moved a stone on one of her rings. The walls seemed to draw back to show bedchamber after bedchamber, in all manner of styles, with beds of every shape and fashion. Elric controlled his temper. He bowed, thanked her, said goodnight to the two lords and made for the nearest bed.

As he closed the door behind him, he thought he heard Werther de Goethe say: 'We must try to think of a better enter-tainment for him when he wakes up.'

11

In which Mrs Persson Witnesses the First
Sign of the Megaflow's Disintegration

In Castle Canaria Lord Jagged unrolled his antique charts. He had had them drawn for him by a baffled astrologer in 1950. They were one of his many affectations. At the moment, however, they were of considerably greater use than Alvarez's electronics.

While he used a wrist computer to check his figures, Una Persson looked out of the window of Castle Canaria and wondered who had invented this particular landscape. A green and orange sun cast sickening light over the herds of grazing beasts who resembled, from this distance at any rate, nothing so much as gigantic human hands. In the middle of the scene was raised some kind of building in the shape of a vast helmet, vaguely Greek in conception. Beyond that was a low, grey moon. She turned away.

'I must admit,' said Lord Jagged, 'that I had not understood the extent . . . '

'Exactly,' she said.

'You must forgive me. A certain amount of amnesia – euphoria, perhaps? – always comes over one in these very remote periods.'

'Quite.'

He looked up from the charts. 'We've a few hours at most.'

Her smile was thin, her nod barely perceptible.

While she made the most of having told him so, Lord Jagged frowned, turned a power ring and produced an already lit pipe which he placed thoughtfully in his mouth, taking it out again almost immediately. 'That wasn't Dunhill Standard Medium.' He laid the pipe aside.

There came a loud buzzing noise from the window. The scene outside was disintegrating as if melting on glass. An eerie golden light spread everywhere, flooding from an apex of deeper gold, as if forming a funnel.

'That's a rupture,' said Lord Jagged. His voice was tense. He put his arm about her shoulders. 'I've never seen anything of the size before.'

Rushing towards them along the funnel of light there came an entire city of turrets and towers and minarets in a wide variety of pastel colours. It was set into a saucer-shaped base which was almost certainly several miles in circumference.

For a moment the city seemed to retreat. The golden light faded. The city remained, some distance away, swaying a little as if on a gentle tide, a couple of thousand feet above the ground, the grey moon below it.

'That's what I call megaflow distortion,' said Una Persson in that inappropriately facetious tone adopted by those who are deeply frightened.

'I recognize the period.' Jagged drew a telescope from his robes. 'Second Candle-maker's Empire, mainly based in Arcturus. This is a village by their standards. After all, Earth was merely a rural park during that time.' He retreated into academe, his own response to fear.

Una craned her head. 'Isn't that some sort of vehicle heading towards the city. From the moon – good heavens, they've spotted it already. Are they going to try to put the whole thing into a menagerie?'

Jagged had the advantage of the telescope. 'I think not.' He handed her the instrument.

Through it she saw a scarlet and black chariot borne by what seemed to be some form of flying fairground horses. In the chariot, armed to the teeth with lances, bows, spears, swords, axes, morningstars, maces and almost every other barbaric hand-weapon, clad in quasi-mythological armour, were Werther de Goethe, the Duke of Queens and Elric of Melniboné.

'They're attacking it!' she said faintly. 'What will happen when the two groups intersect?'

'Three groups,' he pointed out. 'Untangling that in a few hours is going to be even harder.'

'And if we fail?'

He shrugged. 'We might just as well give ourselves up to the biggest chronoquake the universe has ever experienced.'

'You're exaggerating,' she said.

'Why not? Everyone else is.'

12

The Attack on the Citadel of the Skies

'Melniboné! Melnibone!' cried the albino as the chariot circled over the spires and turrets of the city. They saw startled faces below. Strange engines were being dragged through the narrow streets.

'Surrender!' Elric demanded.

'I do not think they can understand us,' said the Duke of Queens. 'What a find, eh? A whole city from the past!'

Werther had been reluctant to embark on an adventure not of his own creation, but Elric, realizing that here at last was a chance of escape, had been anxious to begin. The Duke of Queens had, in an instant, aided the albino by producing costumes, weapons, transport. Within minutes of the city's appearance, they had been on their way.

Exactly why Elric wished to attack the city, Werther could not make out, unless it was some test of the Melnibonéan's to see if his companions were true allies or merely pretending to have befriended him. Werther was learning a great deal from Elric, much more than he had ever learned from Mongrove, whose ideas of angst were only marginally less notional than Werther's own.

A broad, flat blue ray beamed from the city. It singed one wheel of the chariot.

'Ha! They make sorcerous weapons,' said Elric. 'Well, my friends. Let us see you counter with your own power.'

Werther obediently imitated the blue ray and sent it back from his fingers, slicing the tops off several towers. The Duke of Queens typically let loose a different coloured ray from each of his extended ten fingers and bored a hole all the way through the bottom of the city so that fields could be seen below. He was pleased with the effect.

'This is the power of the Gods of Chaos!' cried Elric, a familiar elation filling him as the blood of old Melniboné was fired.

'Surrender!'

'Why do you want them to surrender?' asked the Duke of Queens in some disappointment.

'Their city evidently has the power to fly through the dimensions. If I became its lord I could force it to return to my own plane,' said Elric reasonably.

'The Morphail Effect . . . ' began Werther, but realized he was spoiling the spirit of the game. 'Sorry.'

The blue ray came again, but puttered out and faded before it reached them.

'Their power is gone!' cried Elric. 'Your sorcery defeats them, my lords. Let us land and demand they honour us as their new rulers.'

With a sigh, Werther ordered the chariot to set down in the largest square. Here they waited until a few of the citizens began to arrive, cautious and angry, but evidently in no mood to give any further resistance.

Elric addressed them. 'It was necessary to attack and conquer you, for I must return to my own Realm, there to fulfil my great destiny. If you will take me to Melniboné, I will demand nothing further from you.'

'One of us really ought to take a translation pill,' said Werther. 'These people probably have no idea where they are.'

A meaningless babble came from the citizens. Elric frowned. 'They understand not the High Speech,' he said. 'I will try the Common Tongue.' He spoke in a language neither Werther, the Duke of Queens nor the citizens of this settlement could understand.

He began to show signs of frustration. He drew his sword Stormbringer. 'By the Black Sword, know that I am Elric, last of the royal line of Melniboné! You must obey me. Is there none here who understands the High Speech?'

Then, from the crowd, stepped a being far taller than the others. He was dressed in robes of dark blue and deepest scarlet and his face was haughty, beautiful and full of evil.

'I speak the High Tongue,' he said.

Werther and the Duke of Queens were nonplussed. This was no one they recognized.

Elric gestured. 'You are the ruler of city?'

'Call me that, if you will.'

'Your name?'

'I am known by many names. And you know me, Elric of Melniboné, for I am your lord and your friend.'

'Ah,' said Elric lowering his sword, 'this is the greatest deception of them all. I am a fool.'

'Merely a mortal,' said the newcomer, his voice soft, amused and full of a subtle arrogance. 'Are these the renegades who helped you?'

'Renegades?' said Werther. 'Who are you, sir?'

'You should know me, rogue lords. You aid a mortal and defy your brothers of Chaos.'

'Eh?' said the Duke of Queens. 'I haven't got a brother.'

The stranger ignored him. 'Demigods who thought that by helping this mortal they could threaten the power of the Greater Ones.'

'So you did aid me against your own,' said Elric. 'Oh, my friends!'

'And they shall be punished!'

Werther began: 'We regret any damage to your city. After all, you were not invited . . . '

The Duke of Queens was laughing. 'Who are you? What disguise is this?'

'Know me for your master.' The eyes of the stranger glowed with myriad fires. 'Know me for Arioch, Duke of Hell!'

'Arioch!' Elric became filled with a strange joy. 'Arioch! I called upon thee and was not answered!'

'I was not in this Realm,' said the Duke of Hell. 'I was forced to be absent. And while I was gone, fools thought to displace me.'

'I really cannot follow all this,' said the Duke of Queens. He set aside his mace. 'I must confess I become a trifle bored, sir. If you will excuse me.'

'You will not escape me.' Arioch lifted a languid hand and the Duke of Queens was frozen to the ground, unable to move anything save his eyes.

'You are interfering, sir, with a perfectly – ' Werther too was struck dumb and paralysed.

But Elric refused to quail. 'Lord Arioch, I have given you blood and souls. You owe me . . . '

'I owe you nothing, Elric of Melniboné. Nothing I do not

choose to owe. You are my slave . . . '

'No,' said Elric. 'I serve you. There are old bonds. But you cannot control me, Lord Arioch, for I have a power within me which you fear. It is the power of my very mortality.'

The Duke of Hell shrugged. 'You will remain in the Realm of Chaos forever. Your mortality will avail you little here.'

'You need me in my own Realm, to be your agent. That, too, I know, Lord Arioch.'

The handsome head lowered a fraction as if Arioch considered this. The beautiful lips smiled. 'Aye, Elric. It is true that I need you to do my work. For the moment it is impossible for the Lord of Chaos to interfere directly in the world of mortals, for we should threaten our own existence. The rate of entropy would increase beyond even our control. The day has not yet come when Law and Chaos must decide the issue once and for all. But it will come soon enough for you, Elric.'

'And my sword will be at your service, Lord Arioch.'

'Will it Elric?'

Elric was surprised by this doubting tone. He had always served Chaos, as his ancestors had. 'Why should I turn against you? Law has no attractions for one such as Elric of Melniboné.'

The Duke of Hell was silent.

'And there is the bargain,' added Elric. 'Return me to my own Realm, Lord Arioch, so that I might keep it.'

Arioch sighed. 'I am reluctant.'

'I demand it,' bravely said the albino.

'Oho!' Arioch was amused. 'Well, mortal, I'll reward your courage and I'll punish your insolence. The reward will be that you are returned from whence you came, before you called on Chaos in your battle with that pathetic wizard. The punishment is that you will recall every incident that occurred since then – but only in your dreams. You will be haunted by the puzzle for the rest of your life – and you will never for a moment be able to express what mystifies you.'

Elric smiled. 'I am already haunted by a curse of that kind, my lord.'

'Be that as it may, I have made my decision.

'I accept it,' said the albino, and he sheathed his sword, Stormbringer.

227

'Then come with me,' said Arioch, Duke of Hell. And he drifted forward, took Elric by the arm, and lifted them both high into the sky, floating over distorted scenes, half-formed dream-worlds, the whims of the Lords of Chaos, until they came to a gigantic rock shaped like a skull. And through one of the eye-sockets Lord Arioch bore Elric of Melniboné. And down strange corridors that whispered and displayed all manner of treasures. And up into a landscape, a desert in which grew many strange plants, while overhead could be seen a land of snow and mountains, equally alien. And from his robes Arioch, Duke of Hell, produced a wand and he bade Elric to take hold of the wand, which was hot to the touch and glittered, and he placed his own slender hand at the other end, and he murmured words which Elric could not understand and together they began to fade from the landscape, into the darkness of limbo where many eyes accused them, to an island in a grey and storm-tossed sea; an island littered with destruction and with the dead.

Then Arioch, Duke of Hell, laughed a little and vanished, leaving the Prince of Melniboné sprawled amongst corpses and ruins while heavy rain beat down upon him.

And in the scabbard at Elric's side, Stormbringer stirred and murmured once more.

13

In which There is A Small Celebration at The End Of Time

Werther de Goethe and the Duke of Queens blinked their eyes and found that they could move their heads. They stood in a large, pleasant room full of charts and ancient instruments. Mistress Christia was there, too.

Una Persson was smiling as she watched golden light fade from the sky. The city had disappeared, hardly any the worse for its experience. She had managed to save the two friends without a great deal of fuss, for the citizens had still been bewildered by what had happened to them. Because of the megaflow distortion, the Morphail Effect would not manifest itself. They would never understand where they had been or what had actually happened.

'Who on earth was that fellow who turned up?' asked the Duke of Queens. 'Some friend of yours, Mrs Persson? He's certainly no sportsman.'

'Oh, I wouldn't agree. You could call him the ultimate sportsman,' she said. 'I am acquainted with him, as a matter of fact.'

'It's not Jagged in disguise is it?' said Mistress Christia who did not really know what had gone on. 'This is Jagged's castle – but where is Jagged?'

'You are aware how mysterious he is,' Una answered. 'I happened to be here when I saw that Werther and the Duke were in trouble in the city and was able to be of help.'

Werther scowled (a very good copy of Elric's own scowl). 'Well, it isn't good enough.'

'It was a jolly adventure while it lasted, you must admit,' said the Duke of Queens.

'It wasn't meant to be jolly,' said Werther. 'It was meant to be significant.'

Lord Jagged entered the room. He wore his familiar yellow robes. 'How pleasant,' he said. 'When did all of you arrive?'

'I have been here for some time,' Mrs Persson explained, 'but Werther and the Duke of Queens . . . '

'Just got here,' explained the Duke. 'I hope we're not intruding. Only we had a slight mishap and Mrs Persson was good enough . . . '

'Always delighted,' said the insincere lord. 'Would you care to see my new – ?'

'I'm on my way home,' said the Duke of Queens. 'I just stopped by. Mrs Persson will explain.'

'I, too,' said Werther suspiciously, 'am on my way back.'

'Very well. Goodbye.'

Werther summoned an aircar, a restrained figure of death, in rags with a sickle, who picked the three up in his hand and bore them towards a bleak horizon.

It was only days later, when he went to visit Mongrove to tell him of his adventures and solicit his friend's advice, that Werther realized he was still speaking High Melnibonéan. Some nagging thought remained with him for a long while after that. It concerned Lord Jagged, but he could not quite work out what was involved.

After this incident there were no further disruptions at the End of Time until the beginning of the story concerning Jherek Carnelian and Miss Amelia Underwood.

14

In which Elric of Melniboné Recovers from a Variety of Enchantments and Becomes Determined to Return to the Dreaming City

Elric was awakened by the rain on his face. Wearily he peered around him. To left and right there were only the dismembered corpses of the dead, the Krettii and the Fikharian sailors destroyed during his battle with the half-brute who had somehow gained so much sorcerous power. He shook his milk-white hair and he raised crimson eyes to the grey, boiling sky.

It seemed that Arioch had aided him, after all. The sorcerer was destroyed and he, Elric, remained alive. He recalled the sweet, bantering tones of his patron demon. Familiar tones, yet he could not remember what the words had been.

He dragged himself over the dead and waded through the shallows towards the Filkharian ship which still had some of its crew. They were, by now, anxious to head out into open sea again rather than face any more terrors on Sorcerer's Isle.

He determined to see Cymoril, whom he loved, to regain his throne from Yyrkoon, his cousin . . .

15

In which A Brief Reunion Takes Place at the Time Centre

With the manuscript of Colonel Pyat's rather dangerous volume of memoirs safely back in her briefcase, Una Persson decided it was the right moment to check into the Time Centre. Alvarez should be on duty again and his instruments should be registering any minor imbalances resulting from the episode concerning the gloomy albino.

Alvarez was not alone. Lord Jagged was there, in a disreputable Norfolk jacket and smoking a battered briar. He had evidently been holidaying in Victorian England. He was pleased to see her.

Alvarez ran his gear through all functions. 'Sweet and neat,' he said. 'It hasn't been as good since I don't know when. We've you to thank for that, Mrs P.'

She was modest.

'Certainly not. Jagged was the one. Your disguise was wonderful, Jagged. How did you manage to imitate that character so thoroughly? It convinced Elric. He really thought you were whatever it was – a Chaos Duke?'